LEFT BEHIND

I've sketched Angie countless times, and every time I feel guilty for stripping her naked with my pencil, but that doesn't stop me from doing it again. I've never drawn Margot before, but she's a lot like Angie, physically. They're both tall, and I would start them as a series of oval shapes, their limbs long and graceful as they move toward each other in their dance of apology.

And then there's me, an extra in their drama, sweating in my down coat a few feet away. I'm a pile of bulging circles, half a head shorter than Angie, my thighs like squashed loaves of bread. Angie's always telling me I'm cute, but *cute* is a euphemism for "not sexy."

I turn away so I don't have to see them kiss. I can imagine it just fine on my own.

I fix my blurry gaze on a painting hanging over the side table in the front hall. It's a stroke of gold over indigo blue, the colors so vivid they make me feel light-headed. I take a step closer. The paint is thick, layered onto the canvas as if it had been spread like peanut butter. There are shadows of orange and vermilion beneath the gold, like sunlight sedimented into stone.

Angie and Margot have forgotten about me.

OTHER BOOKS YOU MAY ENJOY

The Arsonist	Stephanie Oakes
The Conspiracy of Us	Maggie Hall
The Dark Days Club	Alison Goodman
Edgeland	Jake Halpern and Peter Kujawinski
Nemesis	Brendan Reichs
Nightfall	Jake Halpern and Peter Kujawinski
Pasadena	Sherri L. Smith
The Sacred Lies of Minnow Bly	Stephanie Oakes
There's Someone Inside Your House	Stephanie Perkins
Wink Poppy Midnight	April Genevieve Tucholke

A LINE IN THE DARK

by Malinda Lo

speak

SPEAK
An imprint of Penguin Random House LLC
375 Hudson Street
New York, New York 10014

First published in the United States of America by Dutton Books,
an imprint of Penguin Random House LLC, 2017
Published by Speak, an imprint of Penguin Random House LLC, 2018

LIBRARY OF CONGRESS CATALOGING-IN-PUBLICATION DATA IS AVAILABLE.

Speak ISBN 9780735227439

Printed in the United States of America

Design by Anna Booth
Text set in Sabon LT Std

This is a work of fiction. Names, characters, places, and incidents either are the product of the author's imagination or are used fictitiously, and any resemblance to actual persons, living or dead, businesses, companies, events, or locales is entirely coincidental.

To Cindy Pon

PROLOGUE

THIS IS WHAT I REMEMBER: THE LEATHER BOX LYING OPEN on the marble kitchen island; inside it a bed of black satin cradling a golden gun. It's small enough to look like a toy.

Across the kitchen, Angie opens the back door, letting in a freezing blast of winter air. She looks upset, and I'm pulled to her almost involuntarily. All I want to do is make sure she's okay, and it doesn't even matter that she probably doesn't understand how much she means to me.

It's purer this way. She can take whatever she wants from me, whenever she wants it, because I'm her best friend.

Margot comes inside behind Angie, grabbing her hand. "Please," she says. Angie doesn't pull away. She doesn't even see me.

The room spins. My tongue is thick from the syrup of too many drinks. I have beached up against the edge of the island, the marble cutting into my stomach, and the box is right in front of me. The gun is engraved with leaves and flowers, and it looks like a charm you might wear on a bracelet next to a miniature dagger and a coil of rope.

I reach for it. The metal is cool, the gun heavier than I expected.

It's pretty. The vines seem to come alive, twining around the grip and the barrel, ending in the small dark muzzle: a silent, open mouth.

Someone says my name.

Ryan, Margot's best friend, lunges toward me from the other side of the island. She's an avenging demon of the ice princess variety, blond and pale with her silver dress glittering over pushed-up breasts while she points her finger at me.

"Liar."

Angie is beside me, her face a mask of shock. "What the hell are you doing?" she demands. "Let's go."

It takes me a second to realize she wants to leave. With me.

She takes my hand, pulls the gun away. Her fingers are so cold it's as if they'd been dipped in a bucket of ice, but they still send an electric jolt all the way through my vodka-induced emotional padding.

Angie puts the gun back in the box. Ryan picks it up, curling her finger around the trigger.

PART ONE

FOURTEEN WEEKS EARLIER

THE AIR CONDITIONER AT THE CREAMERY IS GOING FULL blast but it doesn't make much of a dent in the sticky heat. Every time Angie opens the freezer case to scoop another cone I want to duck my head inside to cool off. She's been opening the case a lot today. It's the first Friday after Labor Day, and the shop is full of students from West Bedford High. When Angie has a break between customers, she glances at me, where I'm sitting on a stool in the corner. There's a little counter back there where I've propped up my history textbook, pretending to study.

"You bored, Jess?" Angie asks. "You don't have to stay, you know. It's so busy I can't really—"

She's called away by another customer's order. She grabs a cone from the upside-down stack near the waffle maker, pulls the ice-cream scoop out of its milky water bath, and leans into the freezer. She's wearing cutoffs. They're not too short when she's standing, but when she bends over, they slide up so that her butt is barely covered. She straightens up with the cone in her left hand while she shapes the ice cream into a perfect ball with the scoop. Her nails are hot pink today; I was with her when she bought the color at the CVS down the street. As she checks the cone to make sure it's good to go, she bites her lower lip—not a lot, just a slight pinch beneath her front teeth. She does this every time she makes a cone. Then she shakes her hair back, and because it's in a ponytail, it bobs as she moves toward the cash register.

When the transaction is finished, she turns back to me. Nobody else is in line right now. "Like I said, you don't have to hang out with me today," she says apologetically. "I'm sure as soon as Brooke lets out we'll get another rush. I can meet you later if you want."

She wasn't supposed to work today. We were supposed to go to the movies tonight. Normally Angie works Saturdays for a full shift, but her boss asked her to fill in on Friday too. I think Angie's more bummed about missing the movie than I am. I don't mind hanging out here with her. I do it all the time on Saturdays.

"I'm fine," I say to Angie. "I'd rather be here than babysitting my sister."

She looks worried. "Are you sure?" She always seems concerned that I'd rather be somewhere else.

"Do you even need to ask? You know Jamie. I'd be doing makeovers all night. No thanks."

She cracks a grin. "Next time she gives you a makeover, call me, okay? I wanna see it."

"Don't hold your breath," I say, shaking my head. Jaime's eleven, and the last time I let her put makeup on me I was washing glitter out of my eyes for days.

She gets a gleam in her eye. "Hey, I know what you need!"

"What?"

She bounces back to the ice-cream case. "We got a new flavor in." She takes one of the small neon-green tasting spoons and scrapes up a bite. She hides the spoon behind herself as she comes back to me. "Close your eyes," she orders. "And open your mouth."

A little shiver hits me deep in my gut. Nervously, I joke, "What if I'm allergic to that? What is it?"

"You're not allergic. It's a surprise." She takes a step toward me. "Now close your eyes."

It feels so vulnerable to close my eyes and open my mouth without knowing what's coming. I trust Angie, but my eyelids tremble as I sense her approaching. My tongue is heavy on my lower lip. I worry that I'm about to drool, and then I smell Angie's jasmine shampoo in a soft cloud of air against my face, and I stop breathing. The spoon grazes my tongue. I shut my mouth, and my lips brush against her fingertip. It startles me so much that I open my eyes and scoot back off the stool, the spoon jerking free from her hand. My face floods with heat while the ice cream melts in my mouth and it's chocolate, rich and sweet, with a grainy chunk of peanut butter embedded inside, and finally, a swirl of caramel with an unexpected salty bite.

Angie's cheeks are a little pink. "Chocolate caramel peanut chunk," she says. Her hand—the one with the finger I accidentally kissed—hangs in midair.

I'm suddenly conscious of the fact that the neon-green spoon is still in my mouth and I pull it out, embarrassed. "It's good," I say, but she immediately makes a face, dismissing what I said.

"You don't like it." She hooks her thumb in the front pocket of her shorts.

"I like it," I insist.

She shakes her head. "I know you, Jess. You don't like it. You want the usual instead?" She turns her back to me and goes to the freezer case, grabbing a paper cup on the way.

I lick my lips and I wonder if I can taste her fingertip. "Sure, okay." I'm grateful that neither of us can look at each other while she bends into the case, scooping out some mint chocolate chip for me. By the time she has carefully packed the scoop into the cup, I've settled back onto my stool, book re-propped in place, pretending like nothing happened.

She hands me my ice cream as the Creamery's front door opens, the bell jingling. It's a group of Pearson Brooke students. They're not in uniforms or anything—Brooke doesn't have uniforms—but they all exude a we-are-the-shit aura by the way they occupy a space. They seem to expand, legs sprawling and backpacks bulging open, requiring twice as much room as anyone else.

Pearson Brooke is a boarding school, so during the summer they don't come to the Creamery. During the summer, the Creamery is full of families with small children who smile warmly at Angie while she makes them kid-size cones or root beer floats, who apologize when they accidentally bump into other customers waiting in line, who stuff dollars into the tip jar. After Labor Day, the Brooke students start returning, and late afternoons in September are especially crowded. Unlike the summer families, Peebs don't apologize, and they generally treat Angie in two ways: she's either invisible or a piece of ass. And they don't tip well.

Some of the West Bed students eye the Peebs as if they're a rival gang encroaching on their territory, but in reality it's the other way around. The Creamery is in East Bedford, and we are the interlopers. Some of us might give them the stink eye, but while we do that we pull our chairs closer together, lean our heads in, lower our voices. We contract. Soon, all of the West Bed people Angie and I know will pack up and disappear, heading back to where we belong, and the Peebs will exhale even more deeply, toss their cell phones carelessly onto the tables, demand free cups of water—with ice—and the bathroom key.

Angie has gone back to work. I eat my free mint chocolate chip as she serves one Peeb after the other. One of the guys checks her out while he waits in line, but he hides it pretty well by simultaneously texting on his phone. Sometimes guys leer at her openly over the counter, as if they believe their googly eyes and panting tongues will turn her on, but she always pretends like she doesn't know what they're doing and asks if they want to add any toppings to their ice cream. They always have enough money for that.

I finish my ice cream and get up to throw the cup and spoon in the trash under the cash register. As I return to my seat, I see one of the Brooke girls in line whisper to her friend in a near parody of secret-passing: one hand cupped over the other girl's ear, a conspiratorial excitement lighting up their eyes. I slide back onto the stool and lean against the wall, opening my history book on my knee so it looks like I'm reading. My gaze is turned down to the text, but I don't see the words. I'm watching the two whispering white girls. I want to know their secret. The one who did the whispering has long dark hair cut in layers like a model's. It catches the light as she moves, pulls the silky length of it over one shoulder, tucks a lock behind her ear. She's pretty; everyone would say so. She's the kind of girl who turns heads. Her friend, the one who heard her secret, is also pretty but in a more average way. She's blond, with her hair drawn back in a tight ponytail, and as the line moves and they approach the cash register, the light sparkles off her earrings. I wonder if they're diamonds.

They're up next. The blonde orders a strawberry cone—one scoop—and then takes her cone with her to find a table, leaving her friend behind. The brunette leans against the counter to give Angie her order. I can't hear it over the background music and people talking, and it looks like Angie can't hear it either because she has to lean in to catch what the brunette says. Her hair hangs down in a rippling sheet between them as she repeats her order, gives Angie a megawatt smile. Angie laughs, warm and throaty, and some instinct within me twitches like a warning. Then Angie steps back and grabs the ice-cream scoop.

The brunette watches Angie working, and I watch the brunette. She's wearing white shorts and a black tank top, and she has a fine silver chain around her neck, the pendant hidden in her cleavage. Angie takes a glass sundae cup down from the wall and fills it with two scoops—one chocolate, one vanilla—and drizzles on hot fudge. As Angie bends down to grab the whipped cream canister, the brunette's gaze flickers behind Angie to me. For a second I meet her gaze, frozen by surprise. The corner of her mouth turns up slightly, and then she looks back at Angie and I look down at my textbook. The words swim. I feel self-conscious, as if someone caught me in the locker room half dressed.

Out of the corner of my eye I see Angie drop a cherry on top of the sundae. I see her hand on the glass, passing it across the counter to the brunette. Their fingers brush. Angie rings up the order, and the brunette casually leans her hip against the counter as she holds out a credit card. For a second she doesn't let go of it, and she and Angie have a tiny game of tug-of-war as the girl says something that makes Angie giggle. As Angie takes the card and turns away to run it, the brunette takes a bag of maple sugar candies from the basket next to the cash register and drops it into her shoulder bag. The candies are marked $4.99, but when Angie returns with the receipt, the girl doesn't say anything about them.

I'm halfway off my stool, about to tell Angie, but the girl has already taken her sundae and left. I watch her saunter toward her friend at a round table in the corner, and whatever I was going to say dies in my throat. I almost admire the girl's nerve. Angie moves on to the next customer, and I subside back onto the stool. Even if I'd said something, I'm sure the girl would've called me a liar.

Angie bends into the freezer case again, oblivious to the theft that just occurred. Her bare legs are creamy under the shop lights. She always describes them as pasty, but they're not pasty; they're smooth and supple. The skin on the backs of her upper thighs looks especially soft, like milk. My face warms up, and I lower my gaze, but I can still see Angie's ankles, the swell of her calves. The vulnerable spot behind her knees where she's ticklish, the snug fit of her cutoffs over her butt. The frayed white edge of the cloth casts a slim shadow over the tops of her thighs, like an invitation to what lies beneath.

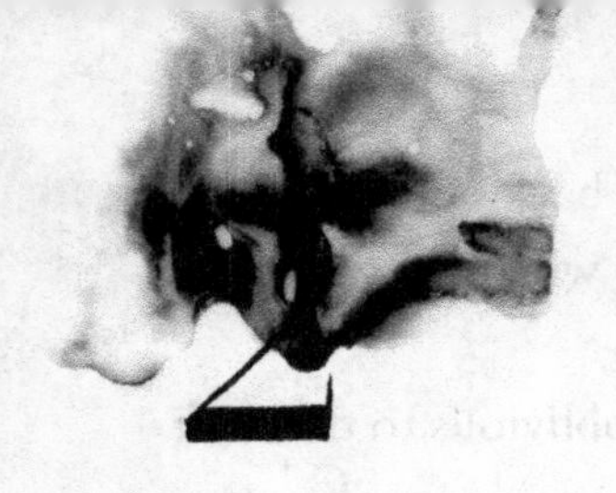

IT'S TEN THIRTY BY THE TIME ANGIE CLOSES UP THE Creamery.

"Oh my God, it's so hot out here," she says as she locks the door behind us. "It was so busy tonight. I hope it's not as busy tomorrow."

"I think it's supposed to be hot again," I say. It has cooled slightly now, but the night air is still warm and humid, and the trash in the Dumpster nearby emits a thick, sweet stink.

"It'll be busy then." She sighs.

Angie's car, her sister's hand-me-down Kia, is parked behind the Creamery right next to the Dumpster. She unlocks the driver's side and leans across to unlock the passenger door for me. I climb in. It's hot and stuffy inside, and Angie turns on the car so that we can unroll the windows.

"What kind of car has power windows but no power locks?" she mutters.

"Your sister's car," I answer. It's not the first time we've had this conversation. I open the glove compartment and take out the front plate for the audio system, handing it to Angie.

"You got it." She snaps the plate into place and the ancient CD player kicks on midway through a Black Eyed Peas song. She flips on the air-conditioning, but it usually takes so long to get going that we'll probably be back at Angie's house before it has any real effect. As she pulls out of the parking space, she says, "I'm not really into this song. Play something else—where's that one CD?"

I dig into the glove compartment again, flipping through Angie's sister's old CDs. "Do you still want to go to a movie?"

"I don't know, I'm kind of tired."

The headlights illuminate the brick walls of the alley behind the Creamery. It looks sort of urban here—there's even a splash of graffiti on the Dumpster—but it's a trick of the dark. East Bedford is the definition of quaint New England town. In the daylight, even the alleys look charming.

"Netflix?" I suggest. I'm wide-awake and staying over at Angie's tonight.

"Yeah, okay," Angie agrees.

I find the KT Tunstall CD that Angie likes and switch out the Black Eyed Peas while she turns onto Washington Street, which connects East Bedford to West Bedford. There isn't much traffic; the town has mostly gone to sleep, even on Friday night. It's not exactly a party destination.

"Hey, what did you think of those Peeb girls?" Angie asks out of the blue.

I know exactly who she means, but I pretend that I don't. "What Peeb girls?"

"The one who got the sundae."

The one. Her attention is focused on the road, but there's something tense about the way she's gripping the steering wheel. "Oh, you mean *that* Peeb girl," I say, and lean toward the open window, hoping to catch a breeze. "Singular."

"I thought she was kinda cute." Angie sounds hesitant. Her face is mostly hidden by the dark, except when the passing streetlights stripe over her profile, revealing and obscuring her again and again. She glances at me, then back at the road. "What did you think?"

I'm sweaty and uncomfortable, and I think about the way the girl looked at me. I hold my hand in front of the air vent, but it's still warm, and the breeze that gusts in through the window is muggy. I finally say, "She seemed different from the other Peebs, I guess."

Now Angie stays quiet. We pass the main entrance to Pearson Brooke Academy on the right. You can't see much of the school from here, but the sign itself is lit up with floodlights. The name of the school is carved into a giant granite block, and there's a shield on the sign too: a coat of arms in the Pearson Brooke colors of purple and gold, with a Latin motto painted on it. I've never been on the campus, but that's going to change this fall when I start the Pearson Brooke Arts Exchange Program. I wonder if that means I'll see that girl again.

"Well, I think she's cute." Angie sounds more confident this time.

A shock runs through me, like static electricity. I don't know what Angie wants me to say.

"Jess."

There's something strange about the tone in her voice. "What?"

"I think she's queer."

I stare at her profile. "You do?"

"Yeah. She—she was flirting with me. I think."

Now I know what the strangeness is. It's hope. "You *want* her to be queer."

"No, I think she really is. Like, I could feel it."

"She's just a preppie straight girl like all the rest of them." There's a mean edge to my voice that I immediately regret.

"What is with you? Did I do something to piss you off?"

The question stings like a rubber-band snap against my skin. "Of course not, it's just—"

"Just what?"

I rub my sweaty palms over my jeans. "I saw her steal some candy."

"What?"

"I saw her steal a pack of the maple candy near the cash register."

"Why would she do that? She had a credit card."

A trickle of sweat runs from my hairline down the side of my face, and I swipe it away in irritation. "I don't know why! I just saw it."

Angie's shoulders are hunched forward now. She doesn't look at me. "You must have made a mistake because that makes no sense. She's a *Peeb*. She has plenty of money."

"Rich people steal all the time."

"Why didn't you tell me when she did it?" She sounds confused.

My frustration is a wedge between us. I glare outside at the passing blur of Ellicott Park, which runs in a comma-shaped band of trees between West Bedford and East Bedford. To get from one town to the other the legitimate way you have to drive around the woods because there's no road that cuts through. On the West Bed side, where Angie and I live, the public high school butts up to the park a few blocks over from my house. West Bed has potholed streets buckled by frost heaves, and small colonials clad in grimy vinyl siding, and intersections where the signs keep getting stolen so people are always getting lost and making awkward U-turns. On the East Bed side is the cute but overpriced village with the Creamery, all the historic homes that people think of when they hear "New England," and Pearson Brooke Academy.

"Jess, why didn't you tell me?"

"I don't know. It seemed weird. And it made no sense." A light blinks in the woods as if it were traveling through the dark trees, and I remember that sometimes people go jogging there at night when it's really hot. I've seen them before, running with headlamps on, like idiots.

Angie lets out a dramatic sigh. "Well, that sucks. I finally meet a girl who might like me and she turns out to be a criminal."

The exaggerated despair in her voice almost makes me smile. "She's not a criminal, just a shoplifter."

"I can't date a shoplifter," she declares.

She's clearly making fun of herself, and instantly the tension between us vanishes. "How were you going to date her in the first place?" I ask, teasing her. "Did you get her number?"

"No. But hey, there's fate, you know? She'll probably come back and ask for mine. Isn't that how it works?"

"In the movies, maybe. For straight people."

"It can happen for non-straight people."

"You wish."

"It better!" Angie slows down and signals before she turns off Washington Street into our neighborhood. "Hey, I know what we should watch tonight."

"What?"

"I'm not going to tell you. You just have to wait."

We spend the rest of the short drive fake-arguing about whether she should tell me, but I like surprises when they come from Angie. One year for my birthday, she framed her favorites of the comics I draw about this girl named Kestrel. It was really cool to see what she liked best, and to hear why. And last summer she took me to Boston Comic Con as a surprise, which is probably the coolest thing anyone has ever done for me.

At Angie's house, her parents have already gone to bed, though the muffled sound of the TV coming from their room suggests that they're still awake. She goes to tell them she's home, and I head upstairs to Angie's room. She has a twin bed and a rollaway that's usually tucked underneath, but her mom has already pulled it out and put sheets and a blanket on it for me. I can't count the number of times I've slept in it. I pull some clothes from my backpack and take them with me into the bathroom to change. My shirt is damp as I peel it off, and my skin feels sticky. I sniff my armpits tentatively, but thankfully I only smell like deodorant. I splash some water on my face and try to stick down the unruly short hairs on the crown of my head, but I just cut my hair so it's hopeless. I leave my bra on under the loose MIT T-shirt I brought to sleep in and pull on my blue plaid boxers.

When I return to Angie's room, she's tugging down a pink tank top. She has taken off her bra, and she's wearing boxers like mine, but hers are purple. She turns as I close the door behind me and smiles. "You ready?"

For a second I can't figure out what she's talking about, and I'm almost overcome with self-consciousness: me and Angie in her bedroom, half undressed. Then I remember the movie. "Yeah," I say. "Of course."

Angie sets up her laptop on the floor, and we both lie on the rug on our stomachs in front of the small screen. There isn't a lot of room; just enough for the two of us to stretch out next to each other. I grab the pillow from the rollaway and prop my arms on it. I like being in Angie's room on Friday nights. I feel at home here in a way I never do at my own house. I start to get a little drowsy, and my eyes slide shut. I can smell Angie's shampoo again, and if I move slightly to the right, a thick brown curl of her hair will brush my shoulder.

"Hey," Angie says, elbowing me in my side. "Wake up. Movie's on." Angie uses her sister's Netflix password because her parents won't pay for Netflix, and besides, we don't want her parents to know what we watch.

It's a romantic comedy, which doesn't surprise me since Angie loves them, but I haven't seen this one. It's set in England and is about this woman who's about to marry this guy, but to her surprise, she falls in love with her wedding florist. A woman. When I realize it's about two women who fall in love with each other, I'm not sleepy anymore. I watch the unfolding of their romance with a pit in my stomach. Like any romantic comedy, the movie throws all sorts of obstacles in their path, but I feel a sense of dread. The odds aren't good that it will end well. The curly-haired girl will probably go back to her man, or the lesbian could get hit by a car. At the end, the two women run toward each other through the traffic on a busy street, and I brace myself for tragedy.

I glance at Angie, who is gazing at the screen with a frightening intensity, as if she could drink in these images all day and night. She licks her lips with the tip of her tongue and then briefly sucks her lower lip between her teeth. It's wet and dark pink, shining in the light of the screen. Her eyes are fixed on the laptop as if it were the most important thing she's ever seen, and when she inhales, her chest swells, causing the material of her tank top to stretch. Her shoulder, right next to me, is bare. The strap of her tank top could slide down at any moment; it's already loose against her skin.

Angie's room isn't as stuffy as her car was, but I am suffocating.

The inch of air between us seems to hum like an electric heater turned all the way up. I force myself to look back at the laptop. I don't even know what's happening in the movie anymore, but I don't ask Angie for a recap. I'm afraid to move. I'm afraid that I will move.

Angie says dreamily, "See, it can totally happen for non-straight people."

I blink. The lesbian didn't get hit by a car. She's snuggling on a park bench with the other girl. I must have missed their happy ending.

3

THE STREETLAMP CLOSEST TO THE TRAILHEAD THAT LEADS into Ellicott Park is busted, but there's enough light from the neighborhood and the half-moon that it's not too hard to see. I can make out the sign next to the trailhead; it originally read NO ALCOHOL ALLOWED, but now it says PORNO & ALCOHOL ALLOWED.

It's almost midnight. I snuck out of my house to meet Angie, who texted me ten minutes ago to say she was on her way. I zip up my hoodie and put my hands in my pockets. The heat wave broke a few days ago, and it's cool out. Not cold, but cool enough to feel like fall is coming. Angie and I don't hang out in the park that often. Everybody does sometimes, because there isn't much else to do around here, but it's been a while since we went.

Finally I see Angie walking briskly down the sidewalk. When she arrives, she asks, "Have you seen anyone else?"

"No. Are we meeting anyone else?" Angie told me everyone is going tonight, even Melissa Weiss, but I figured we'd see them in the park.

"No, let's just go in."

Angie brushes past me and I smell something unfamiliar, slightly floral. "Are you wearing perfume?" I ask.

"Shh! Wait till we're farther in."

Ellicott Park isn't that huge, and at first it's not even that dark. Ambient light from the neighborhood seeps through the foliage, gradually lessening as we move deeper into the woods. The trail is rocky in places, but it's predominantly straight. At first the only noise is our footsteps crunching down the trail, but soon I start to hear dim sounds in the distance: voices, laughter, coughing. About ten minutes into the park we cross the wooden footbridge over the trickle of water known as the Bedford River, and that's when we know it's time to cut through the woods to the left. Angie switches on her phone's flashlight, since we're far enough into the park now that the neighbors won't be able to see it, and uses the light to find the skinny trail that branches off the main path. This isn't an official trail, but enough people have come this way to make it easily passable. It doesn't take long before we find the group of West Bed kids hanging out around the glow of their cell phones.

"Hey," some of them say. I see Jordan Kelly and Courtney Alvarez first, and then I recognize Melissa at the back, hanging out with Lucas Branson. It's all Angie's theater friends.

I sit down on the end of a fallen log next to Jordan, because it's the farthest away from Lucas. Jordan does the light board and set design. Last spring Angie persuaded me to do tech crew with her, and I ended up spending most of my time painting sets with Jordan. He's scribbling on his canvas sneakers, squinting at something I can't make out.

"What are you doing?" I ask.

He sticks his foot out and spotlights it with his phone to show me a pretty decent illustration of a guy holding a sword, slashing at what looks like an orc.

"Cool. But you need a red marker for the blood."

"Blood! That would be awesome. Do you have a red marker?"

"At home I do, but not with me."

"Shit. That would've rocked."

Nearby, Angie has taken a seat next to Courtney on a plaid blanket that I recognize from the theater props closet. Courtney has a joint in her mouth and is trying to light it with a lighter that won't spark. Finally she gets it going, and in the burst of flame that illuminates her face I see that she's painted on extra-thick eyeliner tonight to match her black lipstick. She inhales deeply, then coughs violently. She holds the joint out to Angie, who takes a tentative drag, then offers it to me. I think Angie smokes pot to fit in, because I've only ever seen her take a few hits, and she never gets high. I take the joint from her and the tip of it is soggy from Angie's and Courtney's mouths.

I inhale, and it's harsh. It burns the back of my throat and it feels like I'm sucking in fire. I almost choke coughing out the smoke, and Jordan unhelpfully pounds me on my back a few times.

"Jesus Christ, don't die," Courtney says, grabbing the joint. The sizzle of the paper as she lights up again sounds the way the cells in my lungs feel.

"Here," Jordan says, handing me a bottle. "This'll help."

I sniff it and the alcohol fumes practically burn my nostril hairs off. "Keep it," I say, thrusting it back at him. He laughs at me and drops the bottle on the ground by his feet, goes back to drawing on his shoe. Angie is leaning in to Courtney, whispering something to her I can't hear. My lungs still hurt, but I'm feeling better. I glance around the dark and try to figure out who else is here. I'm not going to talk to Lucas and Melissa, who are giggling together over Lucas's phone. They're probably rating guys on Grindr or something dumb like that. Jordan's not really interested in anything but his own feet. I recognize a few other kids beyond Lucas and Melissa, but they're not my friends. None of these people are really my friends, except for Angie.

I pluck Jordan's bottle from the ground and take a swig. It burns almost worse than the pot, but I manage to swallow it without choking. "Fuck, what is that?" I ask, barely able to talk.

Jordan says, "Just vodka. Really cheap vodka."

"It's disgusting," I say.

"Don't drink it if you don't like it," Jordan says, and takes it away from me.

"I didn't say I didn't like it."

Jordan hands me the vodka again. It's not as bad this time. I can get used to the burn. I hope it kicks in soon. I pull out my phone, but I have no reception in the woods. I scroll through my photos: Angie at the Creamery making a face at the camera; Angie glaring at me over a cup of coffee one morning at her house, full bed head on display; me and Angie at the beach the week before school started, the wind blowing the back of my hair straight up like a goofy black crown. Then there is a series of pictures of my latest Kestrel comic, taken to show Angie: a close-up on Laney, a growl on her face; a long-distance image of Laney and Kestrel running toward the woods; Kestrel standing in front of the trees with the wind blowing her wavy brown hair back, hands fisted at her sides. I really like that one because I feel like it shows Kestrel's courage. I worked a long time on getting her hands just right—not too clenched, not too loose. Fighting fists, not mad ones.

I drink more of Jordan's disgusting vodka and glance up to see what everyone else is up to. Melissa seems to be well on her way to getting stoned. Angie is reading her phone now. Courtney has gone over to some of the other kids, leaving the space on the blanket by Angie empty. I could go over there and sit next to her, but I don't move. I feel self-conscious. I side-eye Jordan, but he's still drawing on his shoe.

My head is fuzzy.

I hear footsteps coming toward us from the unofficial trail. I look over my shoulder and see the bright white beams of two phone flashlights. The beams move in a jerky motion, giving me a seasick feeling. I look away and catch sight of Angie. She has a weird expression on her face, like she's trying to hide her excitement.

The people behind the phones stop. They're here. Their lights shine directly down at the ground, turning the dirt into multiple shades of metallic gray, leaching all the richness out of the fallen leaves. In the ghostly light of everybody's phones, I recognize the newcomers. It's the shoplifting Peeb girl and her friend, the blonde.

Angie scrambles to her feet and says, "Hi."

The shoplifter's name is Margot, and her friend's name is Ryan. There's room for Margot on the plaid blanket beside Angie, but not enough for Ryan. She glances around, hesitates, then pulls off her jean jacket and delicately lays it on the ground between the blanket and where I'm sitting. Everyone gawks openly at Margot and Ryan. Ryan lowers herself onto her jacket, sitting cross-legged, and ignores them all.

Ryan and Margot brought a six-pack with them, and they

distribute the lukewarm beer among the people closest to them. The label is an illustration of the Boston skyline with the words WICKED PISSAH in a ribbon over the buildings. I take one, and the rest are gone in two seconds. Nobody offers them anything in return, and Jordan even pulls his cheap vodka closer to him, as if the Peebs might steal it. Of course, I did see Margot shoplifting.

She's all smiles and flippy hair with Angie, who I can tell is trying super hard to act casual. There's a tension to her posture, though, that spills her secret to anyone who knows her. Angie wants this to go well.

The trees cast wavering shadows in the blue-white light of everyone's phones. I put mine to sleep so my face at least can be in the dark. This feels unreal. There is no world where West Bed kids hang out with Peebs in Ellicott Park.

"Is this where you guys usually meet up?" Ryan asks.

It takes a moment for me to realize she's talking to me. "Um, sometimes," I say. I take a sip of the beer. It's kind of bitter, and I don't really like it, but I keep drinking it because Jordan's vodka is out of reach now. "Um, how did you know we were here?" I ask.

Ryan's face is completely blank. "We were invited," she says coolly.

Before I can ask who invited her, she pulls out her cell phone and starts texting. My face heats up at her dismissal, even though I don't want to talk her anyway. I drink more of the bitter beer and watch as Angie turns toward Margot, engrossed in their low-toned conversation. Courtney and the others are lighting up another joint. Jordan gets up and joins them, leaving me alone on the log next to the furiously texting Ryan. Angie laughs at something Margot says. I usually love the sound of Angie's laugh, but now it grates. I drink the beer faster.

Everything is shivery, the trees and the leaves and even the ground. There are rocks everywhere, poking up through the soles of my sneakers and wedging between my feet as I stumble down the trail. I stub my toe against a sharp outcropping and flail my arms, grabbing at a tree for balance. Something jabs into my palm, and I hiss in pain. Blood trickles down my hand, which throbs.

"Jess."

Angie lied to me. The ground ripples beneath me, an earthquake of rocks and shadows. Something thumps onto the ground.

"Jess, your phone!"

Angie grabs my arm, and I swing wildly.

"Stop it. You dropped your phone." Angie digs her fingers into my arm.

"Ow," I protest.

"You're drunk," she says judgmentally, pressing my phone back into my hand.

"No I'm not," I object, but it sounds like *nome not*. "Leave me alone." *Leeme lone*.

She lied to me.

I keep going, weaving down the narrow unofficial trail by the bouncing light of my phone. The movement makes me feel sick, and I pause to take a gulping breath.

"I'll walk you home," Angie says. "You can't go alone."

She slides an arm around my waist, steadying me, and I want to lean into her except I'm mad at her. I push her away, but she grabs me again.

"I'm fine!" I insist. *You lied you lied you lied*.

Angie's fingers press into the soft fat of my stomach, pulling me closer to her. "I know," she says, "but I'll walk you anyway."

I WAKE UP IN MY BED. MY MOUTH IS DRY. THE SUN SHINES through the mini-blinds, and one beam seems aimed directly at my eyes. I turn over and see a glass of water on my nightstand.

Angie. She walked me home last night. I remember our slow and awkward journey through the park. I kept hoping I would throw up, but I didn't. I don't remember getting back into my house, or coming up the stairs, or even flopping into my bed.

I roll onto my back. There's a lump digging into my hip, and I reach down and pull my phone out of my jeans pocket. A thin crack runs across the upper-right corner of the screen. I don't remember dropping it but at least it still works. The battery's almost dead but there's a text message waiting. It's from Angie.

Call me when u wake up.

It's only 9:14 in the morning, not even that late. I gingerly put a hand to my head, but I feel okay. I sit up slowly. Still okay. I pick up the glass of water and drink some of it, and it feels like all my nerves suddenly switch on. I'm starving. I put the glass down and notice something on my hand. There's a scab there, almost directly in the center of my palm, like stigmata.

Angie lied to me about why she wanted to go to the park.

Suddenly my stomach rumbles, and all the crap I drank lurches up inside me in foul waves. I throw off my blankets and stumble out of my room and down the empty hall to the bathroom. I slam the door shut and fall to the floor in front of the toilet, pushing up the seat. Sweat has broken out all over me, cold and sickening, but nothing comes as I gag over the bowl. There's a light brown stain all around the water line even though my mom cleans the toilets every week, and the sight of that ring forces up the water I just drank. It streams out of me in an acidic, yellow-tinged drip. My chest heaves.

I hug the toilet until the floor stops rocking and then make my way back to my bedroom. I hear noises from down in the kitchen, so I close my bedroom door before anyone can look up the stairs and see me.

My phone is vibrating on my bed. It's Angie, so I answer it. "Hello," I say dully.

"You're alive." She sounds relieved.

"I'm alive," I confirm, and my stomach groans in a desperate echo. "What happened last night? There's like a wound on my hand."

"Oh my God, you were so drunk." Her voice is low and breathy, and I imagine her still lying in bed. I shove that thought away. "You tripped and tried to catch yourself on a tree branch. Are you okay? You should put some Neosporin on it."

I sit down on the edge of my bed. "I'm . . . okay."

"That's good. I was really worried about you."

The concern in her voice makes me feel guilty for being mad at her. "I'm sorry I was such a dumbass," I mumble.

She sighs. "It's okay."

"Thanks for—for getting me home. What are you doing today?"

"I have work. I should get—" She stops mid-sentence, and the line goes silent.

"Angie?"

"Oh my God, she just texted me," she says excitedly.

"Who?"

"Margot Adams!"

I feel queasy again. "What did she say?"

"Just that she liked hanging out last night." Angie breaks into a laugh. "Oh my God, she's so funny!"

"Did you guys plan to meet there last night?" The instant the words are out of my mouth I brace myself as if someone were going to punch me.

"Yeah," Angie says.

A single syllable, but it's so telling. So full of hope and shy happiness.

"You're not mad, are you?" Angie says worriedly. "I didn't really know if she was going to come. She found me online and friended me and we were chatting, and I told her sometimes we hang out in the park on Friday nights, and she thought that was cool. But she didn't say she was going to come."

My phone is getting slippery in my sweaty grip. "Why didn't you tell me?"

I count six beats of my heart, thudding like a fist on the door, before she answers. "Because I didn't want to get my hopes up," she says softly. "I felt like if I said anything, that would be, I don't know, like bad luck. You're not mad at me for not saying anything, are you? I can't stand it if you're mad at me, Jess. Please don't be mad. It made me so much less nervous that you were there too."

My head is starting to throb. "It's okay." I swallow. "I'm not mad."

LAST SPRING, WHEN I TOLD MY PARENTS I GOT INTO THE Pearson Brooke Arts Exchange Program, they initially didn't want me to go. They thought it would take time away from my science classes—even though I consistently get Cs in them. My high school art teacher, Ms. Cooper-Lewis, had to meet with them to explain why I should be allowed to go. She showed them a portfolio of my illustrations—comics, mostly, from my Kestrel series—but my parents didn't understand why my pictures were any good. They thought it was kid stuff. It wasn't until Ms. Cooper-Lewis explained that the Pearson Brooke Arts Exchange Program might help me get into college that they relented.

Today, on the first day of the program, the director ("Call me Kim") takes us on a tour of Pearson Brooke Academy. It has a campus. A real one, with a quad like you see in pictures of colleges: a big green square of grass crisscrossed by brick paths and surrounded by colonial brick buildings that make the place look like a mini Harvard. One of the buildings even has a white cupola with a gold bell in it. West Bedford High was built in the seventies and looks like a blocky, concrete prison, with thin rectangular windows up high to let in light but prevent us from seeing out. West Bed doesn't have a cupola, but it does have a thing that looks like a watchtower that looms over the front entrance of the school.

"The Pearson Brooke Arts Center will be your home when you visit here," Kim says, gesturing to the two-story brick building with tall multipaned windows in front of us. "But before we go inside, I want to show you around the rest of the campus. I'm saving the best for last!" Kim beams, and like a bunch of brownnosers, we smile back nervously.

There are six of us, but I only know one other student, Samantha Green, who's also a junior. She makes weird sculptures out of empty cans and wires that Ms. Cooper-Lewis, our art teacher, apparently thinks are amazing. The other students on the program are sophomores and one freshman. We've been paired up with Peebs who are supposed to be our "Brooke buddies," as if we're still in kindergarten. Mine is a Korean girl named Emily Soon, who seems to alternate between checking out mentally and being annoyed that she's here. She plays the violin. I wonder if they matched us randomly or if Kim or Ms. Cooper-Lewis had some reason for sticking us together. I bet it's because we're both Asian. Ms. Cooper-Lewis is always suggesting that I draw Asian people, which only makes me want to never draw Asian people.

As Kim leads us around the quad, Emily walks next to me but makes sure to avoid looking at me or initiating any conversation. Kim tells us about each of the buildings as we pass them, but I barely pay attention. I'm not going to any English classes or chemistry labs, so it makes no difference to me. All around the campus, big trees dot the landscape, their leaves edging into orange and yellow. Some Peebs lounge on the grass beneath the biggest tree in the quad, laptops and books open. They glance at us as we walk past, a parade of mismatched duos, and I wonder what they think of the arts exchange program—if they even think about it.

We follow Kim down one of the paths that angle diagonally out of the quad, skirting around a building that looks like a courthouse. "This is Jackson Library," Kim says. "There's a wonderful art collection there, and your Brooke buddy can take you inside if you'd like to see it." Behind the library the brick path curves toward a building that's so modern it's jarring after the stuck-in-colonial-New-England look of the rest of the campus. It's got a giant glass atrium-like thing in front and an angled roof that juts into the sky like the wing of a downed airplane.

"This is Cooper Commons," Kim says. "There's a café inside, and you're always welcome to stop in and grab a cup of coffee or tea while you're on campus. Your Brooke buddy has a special meal voucher on their card that they can share with you, so it's all part of the program and you don't have to worry about the cost."

Kim beams again, and I wonder how she can say this stuff without cringing. We don't respond, and maybe our silence flusters her, because she gets a bit pink in the face and says, "All right, let's move on."

Past Cooper Commons is the athletic center, a sprawling building that looks like it was added on to over decades, resulting in a bulky collection of boxes that don't quite match. Pristine practice fields stretch from the athletic center to a line of trees that must be Ellicott Park. I've never seen this side of it before, and I'm kind of surprised that it looks pretty much the same as it does in my neighborhood. Somehow I expected it to be as manicured as the grass, but the oak and pine trees are still trees, as wild as they can be in the tiny strip of woods they're confined to.

Kim takes us down a path that skirts the edge of a hockey field, where two packs of girls dressed in blue and red smocks are chasing after a small neon-orange ball, hockey sticks at the ready. There's a brief commotion as one of the West Bed kids asks to use the bathroom, and Kim announces that she'll take anyone who needs to go. She and a couple of other students head back to the Commons while the rest of us wait by the hockey field. The two teams are all wearing short purple-and-gold skirts, which are the Pearson Brooke colors. Two girls—one in a red smock, one in blue—are fighting over the ball as their teammates try to keep up. Their hockey sticks smack together, the repeated crack of wood against wood ringing through the air. Red's black braid flies up as she gets the better of her opponent, swiping the ball away from her with a swerve to her right. She streaks out behind the ball, driving it toward the goal near us, while Blue runs after her and their teammates shout at them to shoot or block. As the two of them barrel down the field, coming closer to us, I recognize Red. It's Margot.

Blue, who has been sprinting, her brown ponytail flying, catches up to her and tries to steal the ball, but Margot sidesteps. I don't know anything about hockey but it seems like the game suddenly gets serious, because Blue won't give up. She darts closer to Margot, and their sticks tangle, once again battling for control of the ball. Their teammates yell at them, and from across the field an older woman starts jogging toward the melee. She must be their coach, because she's shouting at them to stop and has a whistle around her neck, but she's too far away. Margot and Blue are now in each other's faces, and Margot looks ferocious, more focused on getting in Blue's way than getting the ball. Blue shouts at her, and Margot's lips briefly part over her yellow mouth guard as she smashes her hockey stick against Blue's shins, tripping her. Blue goes flying, face-planting on the grass with a yelp.

The coach, who is gaining on them, blows her whistle and waves her arms frantically. Margot halts, her chest heaving, and it's as if she'd pulled a mask over her face because all of a sudden she looks completely calm. She drops her stick on the ground and readjusts her headband while her teammates crowd around her.

"She just tripped her," I say incredulously.

"Yep," Emily says. She's standing beside me, her eyes on the field and her arms crossed.

"You know her?" I ask.

She shakes her head. "Not anymore."

"What does that mean?"

The coach reaches Blue, who rolls onto her back. Her face is smeared with red from her nose to her chin. The girls swarm around them, blocking her from our view. Margot still stands in the midst of her own group, unmoving.

Emily says, "We used to be friends."

I look at Emily, who glares across the field at Margot. I want to ask what happened, but Kim and the others have returned from their trip to the bathroom.

"Let's continue our tour," Kim calls cheerily. "I want to make sure we have plenty of time at the arts center today."

As Kim leads us down the path, I glance back at the hockey field one more time. Two girls help Blue onto her feet, and the blood on her face has dripped onto the neck of her shirt. The coach approaches Margot, whose teammates fan out behind her like a peacock's tail.

"You two need to knock it off," the coach is saying, her voice carrying toward us on the strength of her irritation.

The way Margot and Blue are looking at each other, it's obvious that there's some history between them that's being played out on the field. Blue wipes the blood off her face with her right hand and smears it on the front of her shirt. Margot's nose wrinkles, as if she smelled something rotten, and she turns away.

IT ALWAYS SEEMS IMPOSSIBLE TO FIND A PARKING SPACE in Boston's Chinatown, and Friday night is probably the worst time ever. Dad inches down the narrow streets while Mom keeps pointing out spots that turn out to be driveways or too short for our long Subaru. Beside me on the backseat, my little sister, Jamie, twists a string bracelet around on her wrist and looks bored.

"Over there!" Mom says.

"No, it's too small," Dad objects.

Mom says in Chinese, "Not that one, the one down the street on your left."

"I have to turn around then," he responds. "There's too much traffic."

The stopping and starting is making me carsick. I roll down the window to take a breath of fresh air, but it smells like a nauseating combination of roast pork and fish bones left to rot in the garbage. It's better than the warm, close air inside the car, though, so I lean toward the open window and try to breathe.

"I wish your brother didn't have to do this dinner on Friday night," Dad says.

"It's the only time he has," Mom says, then adds something I don't fully understand but has something to do with her brother's new girlfriend. Uncle Dennis invited us to meet this new girlfriend tonight at Ocean Garden Restaurant in Chinatown. I didn't want to go because normally I hang out with Angie, but Mom gave me no choice. Of course, my brother, Justin, didn't have to go. He said he had to study, which is bullshit because MIT's fall semester started only two weeks ago and he can't have any tests yet. Ever since he started college last year, he hardly ever comes home anymore. I don't blame him. The minute I get out, I'm not coming back either.

I pull out my phone and send a text to Angie. *Kill me now we're not even at dinner yet and I can't wait to leave*

Finally Dad finds a spot, and as he turns off the car, Mom says in Chinese, "We pay for dinner. He doesn't have the money."

"And we do?" Dad says, but he doesn't give Mom a chance to respond and gets out of the car.

She turns around and smiles at me and Jamie. "Let's go. We're late," she says in English. "Be nice to your uncle Dennis. He wants to impress you."

After Mom climbs out, Jamie says under her breath, "Doesn't that mean *he* should be nice to *us*?"

"Be good," I say, but I grin at Jamie to show I agree with her.

Mom and Dad herd us down the sidewalk, past bakeries with windows fogged by steamed buns and dumplings, past restaurants full of boisterous diners who spill out onto narrow steps, past the Chinese travel agency and the Chinese hair salon and the Vietnamese grocery store. Ocean Garden is crowded too, and as we push our way through the tiny vestibule, I take Jamie's hand so we're not separated.

Ocean Garden isn't huge, but there are mirrors on the two

side walls that make it seem like it expands forever into hundreds of round tables and glass-topped lazy Susans covered with platters of food. Uncle Dennis is at a round table near the far-right corner, standing and waving at my mom. He's wearing a shiny leather jacket over a white button-down shirt and pressed jeans, and when my dad arrives, they shake hands vigorously, patting each other on the opposite shoulder. I'm reminded of awkward photos of politicians pretending that they like each other.

The woman standing slightly behind Uncle Dennis steps forward, and Uncle Dennis puts his arm around her and says in Chinese, "This is my girlfriend, Lin Xiaoli."

She is petite, with a tiny waist and a delicate frame that she shows off in a skintight short-sleeved pink tee over shiny black leggings and high-heeled boots. Her black hair is cut sharply so that tiny pieces frame her face and long strands fall over her shoulders, like an anime character from when I was a kid. Her eyebrows are plucked so thin they look like black pencil marks arching in eternal surprise. She nods and smiles at my parents, who nod and smile awkwardly back at her. They introduce Jamie and me, and she acts super excited to meet us, actually clapping her hands together like a baby.

"Dennis has told me so much about you both! You can call me Sherry," she says with a slight Chinese accent.

"Hi. I . . . I like your nail polish," Jamie says hesitantly.

Xiaoli—or Sherry—laughs and looks at her hands. Her nails are painted sky blue with little birds on them. "Thank you! You're so sweet. I can give you a manicure if your parents let me."

Jamie's eyes light up. "Really? Mom, can I?"

Mom frowns. "Jamie, you just met Auntie Xiaoli. Give her some time to sit down first."

Sherry shakes her head. "Oh, it's no problem. I work at a

salon and I would love to do it." She turns to me with the same overeager smile and says, "And you must be Jessica."

"Hi," I say, shoving my hands into my pockets.

"You're just as pretty as your uncle Dennis said," Sherry coos.

Uncle Dennis has a carefully blank smile on his face, the kind you put on to cover up what you really think. I pull out a chair and slouch into it, saying nothing. Jamie sits next to me.

"I thought maybe you could go down to Xiaoli's salon sometime and she could give you a makeover," Uncle Dennis says.

"Only if you want," Sherry chirps.

I refuse to look at them. I pick up the chopsticks next to my plate and pull them out of their red paper wrapper, then snap them apart. Tiny splinters jut out from the ends, and I rub the sticks together to smooth them out.

"That would be very generous of you," Mom says, and places a hand on my shoulder. "You know I always tell Jessica that if she would grow her hair out and put on some makeup she would be so pretty." Mom brushes her hand over my hair.

I jerk away from her. "I don't want to grow my hair out."

"Some girls take a little longer to blossom," Sherry says soothingly. "And I don't think you need to grow it out either." I glare at her, but she pretends like she doesn't see my dirty look. Instead she turns to Mom as if they've already agreed on a plan of action. "I would suggest giving her a little trim, reshape it, make it more feminine. It's harder with Asian hair because it's so straight, you know? But I do it all the time."

"I'm not getting a makeover," I snap. I push my chair away from my mom, the legs scraping against the floor.

Mom gives me an impatient glance as she takes her own seat.

"Don't be so rude, Jessica. Your auntie Sherry is being helpful. You should be grateful. She's a professional stylist!"

Five minutes ago my mom didn't even know her name. I tug my phone out of my pocket to check if Angie has texted me back. I hear Mom sigh dramatically, and then she switches to Chinese and asks Dennis what he wants to order.

I don't have any messages. I fight the urge to text her again. I should give her some time; she's probably really busy at work. I pocket my phone and stare at the empty white plate in front of me, at its faded red border that shows it has been through the dishwasher thousands of times. I concentrate on it, trying to forget about my silent phone, and I count eighty-eight tiny squares around the border. A lucky Chinese number. I guess they did that on purpose.

I keep checking all throughout dinner, but Angie doesn't respond to my text. Finally I text her again in case my first one didn't go through.

"Put your phone away, Jessica," Mom says.

I finish texting Angie first. *Dinner sucks big time. Mom and uncle's new girlfriend want to give me a makeover. Fuck no.*

Mom gives me a stern look but I ignore it. They've ordered lobster with ginger and scallions, as well as a whole pan-fried sea bass in a tangy sauce. They're going all out, and if Mom and Dad are paying, I wonder who's trying to impress whom. Mom serves Uncle Dennis's girlfriend portions of the fish, spooning the glistening reddish-brown sauce over the white flesh. Uncle Dennis plucks out the white eyeballs and eats them.

The dishes keep coming, far more than we can eat. There's

deep-fried tofu with shrimps embedded in the middle. There's General Tso's chicken because that's the only Chinese food Jamie will eat. There's a platter piled high with roast duck, white fat layered beneath the crispy skin. When the seafood noodles arrive, I make sure to avoid the purple octopus tentacles. I force down a few mouthfuls of stir-fried water spinach because Mom always makes us eat the vegetables. By the time the sweet red bean soup is served, I feel like I've been chained to this table for weeks. There's still no text from Angie, and she hasn't posted anything on her social media sites either. I push the last grains of my white rice around on my plate, spreading them along the border.

"Stop playing with your food," Mom admonishes me.

I let my chopsticks clatter onto the plate. I hold my leg tense, extra alert for the feel of my phone vibrating in my pocket.

Jamie leans against me and whispers, "I'm bored." She stretches out the word *bored* into at least five syllables.

"Me too," I say. "I think we're almost done."

"Can you draw me something?" she asks.

"I don't have anything to draw with."

"Ask Dad," she says.

"You ask him."

"Dad!" she shouts, and everyone at the table turns to look at her. "Can I have something for Jess to draw with?"

He slaps his hand at his jacket pocket and takes out a black ballpoint pen and a receipt. "Here," he says, passing it over to me before returning to his conversation with Uncle Dennis.

"What do you want me to draw?" I ask, pushing my plate aside.

"Something cute," Jamie commands.

On the back of the receipt I draw a little girl who looks like

Jamie, except I give her huge manga-style eyes and put her hair into two Sailor Moon topknots. Jamie giggles. I also give her a big, curved sword and kind of a wicked grin.

"She doesn't look very nice," Jamie whispers.

"She's supposed to be badass," I say. "But also cute." I color her hair in with the pen, adding a few loose strands to make it look like the wind is blowing.

Jamie loves it. She picks it up and says, "Mom, Dad, Uncle Dennis, look! Jess drew this picture of me!"

"Very nice," Dad says.

"So cute!" Sherry squeaks.

Mom says, "Jess is good at drawing." She looks at me while she spins the lazy Susan to get the last of the lobster. "It's good that you can draw for your sister, but remember you need to focus on your schoolwork. Don't spend so much time drawing. Your brother didn't waste his time with drawing, and that's why he got into MIT."

I flip off my bedside lamp, but I'm not sleepy. Angie never texted me back. Sometimes she doesn't respond for a couple hours, but this is really weird. Maybe her phone died. Maybe there was a family emergency. I'm halfway to deciding I should walk over to her house to check on her when I realize how crazy that would be. It's almost midnight and her parents are in bed already.

I wonder how her night went at the Creamery. I wonder if Margot showed up. I imagine Margot smiling at her, getting close to her.

My whole body stiffens as if to reject that thought, to push it out of me as far as it can go.

I turn onto my side, curling into a fetal position. I pull my blankets over my head. It's hot and stuffy, and the blankets magnify the sound of my blood pulsing in my ears: an insistent, pounding *Angie. Angie. Angie.*

THE PEARSON BROOKE ARTS CENTER HAS SEVERAL STUdios with different equipment, including a computer lab especially for art. Kim puts me in Studio B, because it has a row of drafting tables lined up to catch the light coming through a wall of windows. Three workbenches run perpendicular to the windows, and that's where Samantha sets up her wires and cans. Along one of the interior walls is a series of storage units for supplies: tall slots for canvases and frames, wide flat shelves for papers of all sizes and colors, boxes of pencils and pens, neatly labeled bottles and tubes of paint. There must be thousands of dollars of art supplies here, and it's all available for the taking.

At West Bed the art room is one room with two long pockmarked wooden tables. There's a reason that Samantha makes her sculptures from leftover cans and wires, and drawing black-and-white comics only involves pencil and paper. For the first time, I think about branching out, trying one of the Wacom tablets Kim shows me, or maybe learning how to color my panels in Photoshop. Today Kim gives us an assignment: to depict autumn in our chosen medium. I spend some time messing around with a tablet, but it's new to me so it's easier for me to go back to pencil and paper. At Brooke, though, there are really nice mechanical pencils and Bristol board, rather than cheap No. 2 pencils and printer paper.

By the time I get myself set up to draw, I've figured out where I want to go with the assignment. In a series of panels, Kestrel and Laney are going apple picking. I've drawn both of them so many times that it's easy to sketch them out. Kestrel has wavy hair in a ponytail that bounces as she moves. I draw the curves of her body; I put her in jeans and a T-shirt with a bird on it. Laney is shorter, with buzzed hair that sticks up at the crown of her head. She wears baggy shorts, a striped shirt, and high-top sneakers. She carries a heavy bag of apples, munching on one as they move from the first panel to the second, where a farmer stands underneath a tree, the limbs bowed down with fruit. He has wild hair, like Einstein on steroids. I give him ripped overalls and worn boots. I put a sharp axe in his meaty hands.

Kestrel's going to kill him.

I study the farmer again and realize that he must be a mutant. I give him a bulbous blister on his forehead. I turn it into a twisting horn. His eyeballs pop with veins, and I erase his Einstein hair and substitute rough patches like a mangy squirrel's. He lunges toward Kestrel and Laney, axe held high.

Kestrel finds a dead branch on the ground and uses it to knock the farmer's axe out of his hand. Laney picks up the axe, tests the edge on her fingers. Laney's always looking out for Kestrel, but Kestrel does the fighting, so in the next panel Kestrel's holding the axe. I don't draw the moment of the farmer's death; instead I draw a panel showing only Kestrel's eyes, fierce and determined, beads of sweat rising on her forehead. Finally, I draw the mutant farmer with his head cut off by the panel frame, drops of blood splattered on the ground like a Jackson Pollock painting.

It's all still really rough. I wanted to get the flow of the scene down first. I'll have to refine it and then decide if I want to scan it in, maybe try some color. I'd love to see it in fall shades: deep golds and oranges, earthy browns, bright red apples half bitten, the flesh bruised by oxidation. The farmer's blood could splash out of the frame in a bright crimson trail.

Kim comes by to check out what I'm doing. "You draw this character a lot, right?" She adjusts her glasses as she leans closer.

"Yeah."

"What made you think up this story for her?"

"I guess . . . I don't know, fall in New England?"

"Usually apple picking doesn't involve murdering a farmer," Kim observes.

"Yeah, but this is Kestrel's New England."

"How does it differ from ours?"

"Her school is on top of a Doorway to another world, and the magic from that world bleeds through and mutates stuff in our world. Her world, I mean. So the farmer isn't an ordinary farmer. He's a mutant."

Kim looks impressed. "You have a whole backstory and everything?"

"Yeah. I've been drawing Kestrel for almost two years now. She's evolved a lot since I started."

"I'd love to see some of your earlier comics with this character."

"Well, some of the early stuff isn't that good."

"Whatever you're comfortable with sharing is fine." Kim gives me an encouraging smile.

"I guess I can bring some in next time."

After she moves on to Samantha's project, I examine what I've done so far. I need to work on the farmer; his proportions are off, and not in a good way. I pick up my pencil and get back to work, but my phone dings from inside my bag. I pull it out and find a text from Angie.

Can u come over after Brooke? Need 2 talk in person

I text back: *Sure but I have to be home before dinner. What's up?*

She responds: *I'll tell u soon ur the best!!*

ANGIE SPRAWLS ON HER STOMACH ON HER BED, LEANING over the edge to read her history textbook, which is open on the floor. She bounces up onto her knees as I enter her bedroom and says, "Hey! How was Brooke?"

"Fine." I pull out her desk chair—which she never uses—and sit down, spinning around. "I drew a massacre in the woods."

Angie laughs. "I can't wait to see that."

"Kestrel wins."

"She always wins."

"She's the hero."

"Are you going to give Laney more of a story line?"

"I don't know. What do you want Laney to do?"

She shifts, crossing her legs. "I think she needs a love interest, don't you? It would make Kestrel jealous."

"Why would Kestrel be jealous if Laney got a boyfriend?"

Angie gets a mischievous look on her face. "Don't you think Kestrel kind of has a thing for Laney?"

"No, *you* think Kestrel has a thing for Laney." We've been down this road before. I don't know why Angie insists on this; it's not Kestrel who has a thing for Laney, it's the other way around. And anyway, Kestrel is straight.

"Well, she should. It would be awesome!"

There's a fervor to Angie's comments that feels weird. She doesn't often get this intense over my comics. "So what did you want to talk about?" I ask.

Angie seems to rein herself in, squashing down some of her zeal, and her face rearranges itself into a serious expression, eyebrows drawing together slightly. "I just wanted to tell you something in person." She sounds hesitant.

"What?"

"You remember Margot Adams from Pearson Brooke?" Pink blooms on her cheeks.

I tense up. "Yeah. What about her?"

"She and I—" Angie looks super nervous now. "We're seeing each other," she blurts out.

I don't think I heard her right. "What?"

"We're going out, or whatever," Angie says, her eyes not quite meeting mine. "She's been texting me ever since we hung out in the park that night. And she's come by the Creamery a few times."

Angie works at the Creamery on Saturdays and a couple of afternoons during the week. It hasn't been that long since we saw Margot in the park. Margot couldn't possibly have stopped by the Creamery that many times. I've never seen her there, but during the week I don't usually go with Angie.

"We went out last weekend," Angie says.

Last weekend, I had that stupid family dinner in Chinatown. I feel sick.

Angie swings her legs over the edge of the bed and leans toward me. "I like her, Jess. And I think she likes me." She can't suppress her excitement; she trembles with it. Her blush has turned into two irregular splotches, almost feverish in appearance. "Say something," she pleads. "Do you think I'm crazy?"

I should be happy for her; this is what best friends do. They get excited when their best friend meets someone they like. They support them.

I want to leave. I clutch the edge of the desk chair to keep myself there.

The elation on Angie's face shifts into confusion, and then resignation. "I know you don't like her," she says.

It's been five days since their date, and this is the first time she's told me about it.

"I don't—it's not that I don't like her," I manage to say. "I just . . . don't know her."

Angie still looks sad. "That's true. Maybe we should hang out sometime, the three of us."

I try to ignore the burning sensation in my chest. "I don't know," I mumble.

"It'll be fun!" Angie insists. "I'll talk to her about it. I—I want you to be okay with us." She sounds tentative, as if she were asking for my blessing.

"Why wouldn't I be okay with you?" I ask gruffly.

Her face goes blank and she stiffens. "No reason. We're best friends, and sometimes friends just—well, I mean you thought she was a shoplifter."

"She *was* a shoplifter," I snap, and instantly I know I shouldn't have said it. It's as if Margot had entered the room and was standing between us, arms crossed, judging me for my shitty friendship. I can't look at Angie, so I stare at the wall over her bed. There's a Maxfield Parrish print of a color-saturated countryside that she took from her sister Rachel's room; an 8x10 painting of the Virgin Mary her mother framed for her; and all around it are color printouts of comic book art, including an illustration of Kestrel I drew especially for her. We spent a whole day one summer picking out the comics to print at the local copy shop, fifty cents per sheet, which Angie said made the Virgin Mary painting tolerable.

It's been five days since their date. I picture them in my head, sitting at a café together, Margot's hands cupped around a coffee mug, Angie with her head leaning against her hand, her hair brushing against her arm. The image in my mind's eye jumps, and now I imagine them together in a car, and it's dark. Light from a streetlamp cuts across their faces, and Margot is leaning toward Angie, and they kiss. My stomach twists.

"I have to go," I say, standing up on wobbly legs.

"Jess." Angie holds out her hand to me.

I don't touch her. "My parents will be mad if I'm late."

"Don't be upset," she pleads.

"I'm not." I take a few halting steps toward the door.

"You don't like her. You think I'm stupid for liking her."

Now I look at her. Her eyes are bright, as if she were about to cry. "I have never thought you were stupid," I say vehemently. "Why would you think that?"

Her shoulders crumple. "Whatever."

I stare at her. She's sad. I made her sad. I'm such a jerk. I feel like I've tainted our friendship. I know I should walk this back, but all I can do is walk out.

I'M ALMOST LATE TO SCHOOL. I SPRINT DOWN THE HALL-way into first period, sliding into my seat as the bell rings. Angie, who is sitting in front of me, glances back at me briefly. The disappointment in her eyes makes me shrivel inside.

She called me last night, but I didn't pick up. I stared at her name on my phone until the alert disappeared. *Missed Call: Angie.* Every time I hit the home button it flashed up again, and every time I watched it until it vanished.

At lunch, I stop by the vending machines outside the cafeteria to buy a bag of Doritos and a Coke to go with my homemade turkey sandwich and apple. The machine sticks on the soda, and I'm banging the side of it to loosen the can when Courtney shows up. She gives the machine a kick with her combat boots.

"Hey, Jess, you coming to lunch?" she asks.

"I have to do something first," I hedge.

"Angie told me, you know."

The Coke finally rolls out of the machine, and I scoop it up. "Told you what?"

"About the Peeb girl." She smirks. Her black lipstick has worn off in the middle, as if she'd been sucking on a straw.

I brace myself. "What about her?"

She cocks her head, and her dangling black crystal earrings clink. "Don't you think it's a little weird for some Peeb to be into one of us?"

"I don't talk about Angie's business," I tell her curtly.

Courtney's eyes narrow. "I would've thought you'd have an opinion, seeing as how that Peeb basically stole your girlfriend."

My face reddens. My throat clogs up. As I watch the corner of Courtney's mouth creep up, I realize she's about to start laughing at me, frozen in place like a dumbass.

Turning away from her feels like wrenching my feet free of wet concrete. I clutch my Doritos and Coke and brown bag lunch in my arms and walk away from the cafeteria, toward the exit. I'm sweating.

"See you at lunch, Jessica!" Courtney calls, and the curl of laughter on the edge of her words mortifies me. I walk faster.

People are streaming in the opposite direction, and I bump into a guy who mutters, "Hey, jerk!" I don't look at him. I don't look back. I head directly for the main exit, walking faster and faster until I finally reach the heavy front doors and push them open, bursting outside.

I gulp in the air as the doors slam shut behind me. It smells like pavement and gasoline residue and burned french fries from the cafeteria. The school security guard is heading toward the parking lot. I wait till he disappears around the corner of the building, and then I walk off campus.

In Ellicott Park, the overcast sky turns the trees' red and gold leaves into rusty splotches of decay. The main trail is deserted, and the farther I walk the more relief I feel. I cross the bridge, but I don't cut off the trail. I can barely hear the traffic anymore. The loudest sound is my breath, because I'm walking pretty fast and I'm definitely not in shape. But even as sweat drips down my back, I don't slow down. I keep going until I see a big white oak tree, so big its roots have risen up out of the ground like giant knobs of ginger. The tree is at the base of a small rise, and the exposed roots make it easier to climb up the hill. At the top there's an outcropping of reddish-brown boulders, and I carefully edge around them. Beyond the rocks the ground slopes down again, creating a kind of hollow that's protected by trees encircling the top. The sky is a clear shot above: a dome of gray clouds scudding across patches of dusty blue.

I take a deep breath. I wipe the sweat off my forehead with the sleeve of my sweatshirt. I slowly make my way down the slope, almost dropping the Coke when I slip on moss. At the bottom, I set my lunch on the ground and sink down beside it. I crack open the soda, the sound of its fizz unnaturally loud in the quiet of the woods. When I take a drink, my gulps seem to echo.

My phone buzzes as I finish my sandwich. It's from Angie. *Where r u? R u ok?*

I stare at the message for a while. I eat the last few Doritos and crumple up the bag, the plastic crackling loudly in the stillness. I throw the bag across the clearing. It's past lunch now. Angie's probably in study hall, where we usually sit together.

My phone buzzes again. I decide not to answer.

I'm grounded for two weeks. Mom was so furious with me she even got Dad to lecture me about how much worse my life would be if they hadn't sacrificed so much to move to the US, scrimping and saving to buy this house in this school district, and now I disrespect them by cutting class. Even Jamie looked freaked out by how mad they were.

I lie on my bed and try to read the latest *Ms. Marvel*, but the pictures and words swim together into a mess of color and shadow, and eventually I'm staring up at the popcorn ceiling, thinking about Angie. She has sent me six more texts, each one getting increasingly panicked.

R u sick?

Where r u? Teachers have noticed

They're going to call ur parents

R u getting my txts?

What r u doing??? I'm worried about u

R u still mad at me?! Plz tell me

It's satisfying to know that she's thinking of me, concerned about me. I want her to worry about me. I pick up my phone and gaze at her messages. They're evidence that she cares about me.

I don't respond to any of them.

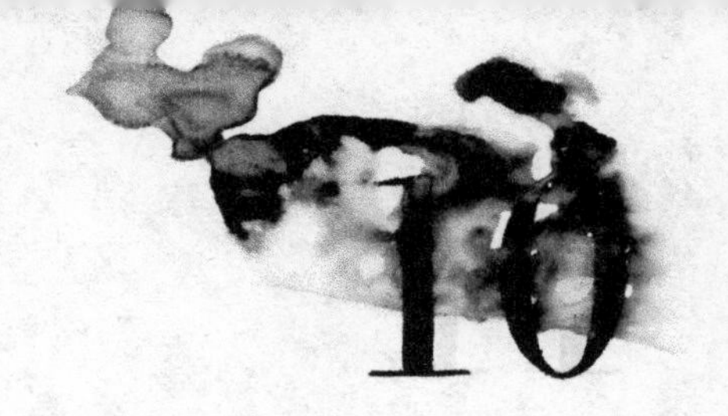

ANGIE HAS STOPPED TEXTING ME. ONLINE SHE POSTS A picture of herself hanging out with Courtney at theater rehearsal. They're both pouting at the camera, wearing matching black lipstick and extra-thick eyeliner. Courtney has commented: *Drama!* It has sixteen likes so far.

ANGIE'S AT HER LOCKER. I'M GOING TO SAY HI TO HER. I'm going to tell her I've been grounded, that my parents took my phone. I hear the blood pulsing in my ears as I walk toward her, and it feels as if I were moving in slow motion underwater, pushing against the tide.

She sees me coming, and her eyes meet mine. She looks sad, and I'm overcome with tenderness toward her. She's sad because of me. She *misses* me.

"Hi," I say.

The furrow on her forehead deepens, while her nose wrinkles slightly. I realize that I miscalculated. She's not sad; she's angry. She closes her locker and turns her back on me, her shoulders stiff as a wall between us. She walks away.

I stare at her in shock, my skin buzzing with heat. Her curly hair bounces in its ponytail as she moves. And then she turns the corner and I'm still standing beside her locker, and everyone else is moving around me as if I'm a rock half submerged in a river, barely even parting the current.

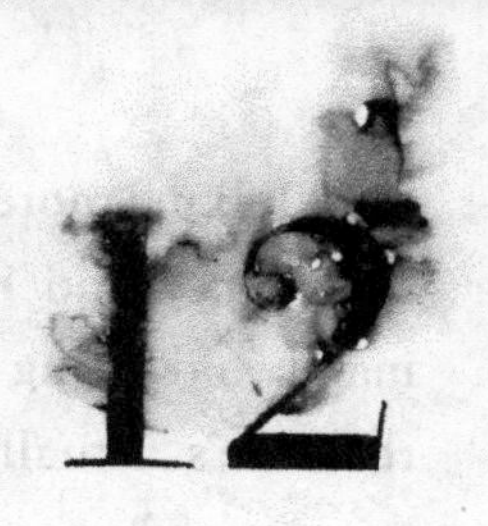

KIM PORES OVER THE KESTREL COMICS I'VE BROUGHT TO show her, spread out on one of the long worktables in Studio B. There are twenty-two black-and-white pages. They chronicle Kestrel's arrival at Blackwood Hall School, where so many strange paranormal things happen that Kestrel begins to suspect something is going on. I've also brought concept sketches for all the main characters.

"This is the Warden," I explain, showing Kim a scarecrow-like guy with a mop of white hair. "He seems really creepy to Kestrel at first, but he's going to be sort of her mentor, or teacher. He's in charge of maintaining the Doorways between the real world and Faerie. The problem is, the Doorways are breaking down, and Blackwood Hall is located right on top of one of the crumbling ones."

"Who's this?" Kim asks, pulling a sketch of a girl in black toward us.

"That's Raven, one of Kestrel's classmates. Her nemesis, really." Raven is tall and beautiful, with long black hair that I love to draw flying through the air.

"Tell me more."

"Laney and Kestrel suspect that Raven is practicing black magic and trying to get into Faerie, but it's going to be revealed that she's actually competing with Kestrel to be the Warden's apprentice."

"What does the Warden's apprentice do?"

"I haven't totally figured that part out yet, but it's basically training to be a new Warden. He's really old and needs to retire, but he hasn't chosen who to train yet."

Kim lays one of the panels featuring Kestrel next to the sketch of Raven. "They're both very striking," Kim says. Kestrel is a little shorter than Raven, but not by much, and she has wavy brown hair as well as a splash of freckles across her face. She's still pretty, just not as femme fatale as Raven. Kim picks up a sketch of Laney and sets it next to Kestrel. "Tell me more about Laney."

"She's Kestrel's best friend. She's normal—I mean, she's not in the running to be an apprentice or anything."

"She's very different from Kestrel and Raven."

"Well, yeah. Not everybody can be the superhero."

"But Kestrel doesn't know she's going to be a superhero, does she?"

"Um . . . what do you mean?"

"Kestrel is just discovering these paranormal events, right?" Kim says. "She doesn't know what they mean—unlike Raven—or what her role in all this is. Not yet."

"I guess, yeah."

"It sounds to me as if you're telling the story of Kestrel discovering her own identity as a superhero."

"Well . . . yeah." I can't decide if Kim thinks I'm stupid. "Kestrel's story has to start somewhere."

Kim smiles tightly, nodding her head. "Yes. And these comics are a wonderful beginning. You've set up some really interesting characters and a fascinating world. But how much do you know about how it ends?"

"I guess I've sort of just been going with it, like I don't have a plan."

"And that's fine. If you were continuing to do this on your own, you'd probably figure things out along the way. But for the program, I want to push you a little." She leans one elbow on the drafting table, bending toward me as if we're best friends. "You're already talented, Jess. You wouldn't be here if you weren't. I want you to put that talent to work a little more consciously. Do you know what I mean?" Her eyebrows draw together as she gazes at me earnestly.

I take a half step back, crossing my arms. "You think I should plan it out before I draw it? I don't really do that. I want it to be natural, you know?"

She straightens up and gives me some room. "Sure, I get that. And I don't want you to feel like your artwork is becoming forced in any way. Just keep in mind that having a vision of the end—knowing what story you want to tell, even if it's only in broad strokes—can help a lot in determining what happens in the middle." She reaches for the character sketches, shuffles to the picture of Laney and pins it down with her finger. "You've obviously given some thought to how the characters should look."

"Well, you have to do that before you can draw them."

She gives me that tight smile again. "Yes. Exactly."

I know what she wants me to say. "Yeah, okay. I get it."

She visibly relaxes, her smile broadening, her shoulders loosening. "I'm not saying you have to do anything in particular. If you want to do this the way you're used to, go ahead. I just want you to consider what kind of story you're telling. If it's an origin story, what would an end point feel like?" She pulls the scene of the mutant farmer toward us. "That will help direct the other scenes in the story. For example, how does this farmer scene fit into the bigger narrative? It might not. But maybe it has some significance you haven't figured out yet."

I spin the mutant farmer panels around. I nod as if I were agreeing with her. "Okay, sure. I'll think about it."

Emily and the other Brooke buddies are waiting in the art lounge outside the studios. Paintings and sculptures are displayed on the white wall across from the floor-to-ceiling windows, and they all have little white cards next to them, like in a museum. We've been invited to stay at Brooke for dinner tonight, courtesy of the arts program. We're supposed to get to know our assigned Peebs better, but judging by the scowl on Emily's face and the slouch in her shoulders, she's not into this.

"Hey," I say when I walk over to her.

"Hey," she replies.

Emily and I stand near each other in awkward silence while everyone else mingles. It's only five o'clock, and dinner at Cooper Commons doesn't start until five thirty. Kim said this was an opportunity to show our works in progress to our Brooke buddies, but I don't want to show my comics to Emily.

"Do you want to wait here or go over to the Commons early?" Emily says abruptly. "The café is open if you want to get some coffee."

"Sure." I try not to sound too eager, but I don't really want to hang around the art lounge saying nothing. "Let's get coffee."

Outside, Emily steps off the brick path to cut across the grassy quad. The sun is low in the west, stretching our shadows across the green, our legs like stilts. Emily and I trudge toward Cooper Commons in silence. Strangely, it feels less awkward to be walking together, even if we're not talking. At the corner of the quad we take the path that leads around the library. A pack of girls is coming toward us, all dressed in athletic gear, and Emily and I move over to the right side of the path so we can edge past them. They've almost passed us when one of the last few girls stops right in front of me and says, "Hey! Hey, I know you."

I look up, startled, into Margot's face. She has a sheen of sweat on her forehead, and her Brooke jersey is damp around the collar. She's carrying a gym bag over one shoulder, and a few strands of dark hair have worked loose from her ponytail and are plastered to her neck.

Ahead of me and behind Margot, Emily stops and turns back. There's a weird expression on her face, somewhere between impatience and worry.

"Aren't you Angie's friend?" Margot asks. There's something accusatory about her tone that rubs me the wrong way.

"Yeah," I say curtly.

Margot's eyes are unusual; the irises are surrounded by a golden-brown circle that shades into an outer ring of brownish-green. "What are you doing here?" She sounds genuinely confused. "Do you go here now?"

Her entitled tone is grating, and the intensity of her gaze rattles me. "I'm in the arts exchange program," I explain, and somehow it comes out sounding defensive.

Margot's confusion clears. "Oh." She shrugs her gym bag into better position on her shoulder. The simple gesture has a bluntly athletic grace to it, and I'm suddenly aware that I can smell her: metallic sweat over crushed grass and a hint of powdery deodorant. I back away.

One of the girls she was with comes running toward us. "Margot, what are you doing? We have to go." It's Ryan. She glances at me, at Margot, and then back at me. "You were in Ellicott Park that night. What are you doing here?"

"She's in that art program for the local high school," Margot says.

"Oh." Ryan's gaze flickers past Margot, and I know that she sees Emily because Emily visibly stiffens. "What are you lurking around for?" Ryan asks Emily.

"Fuck off," Emily snaps.

I flinch at the unexpected loathing in Emily's voice. Ryan acts shocked but I can tell that she's actually pleased by Emily's reaction. As Margot turns to look at Emily, Ryan says, "You're the one who should fuck off. You're not supposed to hang around us."

"Are you actually hoping for a restraining order?" Margot taunts.

Emily's expression is cold as winter. "You go ahead and try that," she says, then glances at me briefly. "Come on. Let's go."

"Oh my God, you two are *together*?" Margot says, her voice rising in disbelief.

"We're not *together*," Emily objects, and two pink spots burn into being on her cheeks.

The cutting rejection of Emily's words stings. It also has the ring of something painfully familiar, as if she'd made that declaration before. Emily's eyes flicker to me for a second, and I think I see a note of apology in them, but that hint is gone as soon as I recognize it.

"Stop being so self-hating," Ryan says. "You really need to face your feelings, Emily. It's not healthy for you to deny these things." The sugar-sweet tone of her voice is blatantly false, and Emily's face reddens further.

"Stop following me around," Margot says coolly. Then she looks at me with her sharp hazel eyes and adds, "I'd steer clear of her if I were you. She's a little stalkery."

I don't respond. I feel like I stumbled into somebody else's fight and I just want out.

"I'm not the stalker, Margot, and we all know it," Emily says. All her previous coolness has vanished, and she quivers with anger, her hands fisted at her sides as if to prevent them from smashing into Margot's face.

Margot flips her off and saunters away, Ryan in tow.

"I'm sorry," Emily says brusquely. She's booking it down the path toward the Commons, and I'm not sure if I want to keep up with her.

"Whatever," I say, and let myself fall back.

We're nearly at the Commons when she unexpectedly turns around and says, "Really, I'm sorry. I normally wouldn't care if people thought we were together, but Ryan and Margot are—they're different."

"Whatever," I say again, more forcefully, but Emily doesn't stop.

She says earnestly, "Listen, I don't care if you're gay or whatever, but I'm straight. Ryan and Margot like to act like I'm some big secret homo with a crush on Margot, and it's just not true."

I feel the blood rush to my head. "I don't give a shit. Are we getting coffee or not?"

All the fight seems to go out of her like a balloon popping. Her shoulders sag. "Yeah, sure."

Cooper Commons is an old building—one of those brick colonial types—that has been sheathed in a glass shell. Entering through the main glass doors puts us in an atrium in front of the facade of the original Cooper Hall. There are round wooden tables scattered across the atrium's stone floor, and an actual coffee cart covered by a large purple-and-orange umbrella is parked by the closed doors to the old building. Emily leads the way to the coffee cart, where a middle-aged woman is working.

"Hi, sweetie, what can I getcha?" the woman asks Emily.

"I'll have a soy chai latte," Emily replies. She looks at me hesitantly. "What do you want?"

"Just a coffee. Small."

"I can get you anything," Emily says. "We have credit from the arts program." She takes out a plastic card and waves it at me. "Get a macchiato if you want. It's on Brooke."

I shake my head slightly. "Coffee is fine."

Emily pays with the card and when our drinks show up, I take mine over to the cream and sugar station and liberally dump in cream and sugar. I don't really like coffee. By the time I get my coffee into drinkable shape, Emily has taken a seat at a table by the outer glass wall. There are a few students sitting at other tables, studying, but the space is largely empty. I take a sip of my coffee. I've put in so much cream it's only lukewarm now.

Emily peels off the top of her drink, which gives off a spicy, Christmas-y smell. "How's your coffee?" she asks.

"Fine. How's your—yours?"

"It's a little sweet. They're always a little sweet." She frowns at her drink and says, "I know this is awkward, but I should tell you what that was about."

"It's none of my business."

She bites her top lip nervously, then tucks her hair behind her right ear. "Well, I might as well tell you before you find out some other way. Margot and Ryan and I used to be friends. When I first came to Brooke last year, when I was a sophomore transfer, they were the first girls to make friends with me. I was stupid enough to think they liked me, but what they wanted was somebody to do their dirty work for them. I was new and I'd just come from a pretty crappy situation back at home, so I did what they wanted."

Emily sounds disgusted with herself. I take a sip of my lukewarm coffee. "What did you do?"

Emily fixes her drink with a gaze so intense I'm surprised the paper cup doesn't catch on fire. "Just gossip, saying shit online," she answers. "Trolling other people they didn't like. I shouldn't have done it, but it happened to me at my old school, and I didn't want it to happen to me again. But then they wanted me to do something so mean I—" She stops, takes a shaky breath. "I wouldn't do it. And that pissed them off so they started a rumor about me, saying that I was obsessed with Margot, following her around and taking pictures of her. And then Margot came out, and everybody at school thought she was so *brave*"—Emily's tone hardens sarcastically—"and that I was such a sick jerk for stalking her."

Finally Emily raises her gaze to me, and she looks like she's about to throw up.

"The only thing I could do was say it wasn't true, but nobody believed me," Emily continues. "I even had a boyfriend at the end of last semester but still nobody believed me. He ended up breaking up with me because he couldn't deal with it anymore. I was hoping that over the summer everybody would forget about it, but I don't think Margot and Ryan forget about anything. And if they don't forget, nobody does."

She takes a quick sip of her drink and almost chokes on it. Behind us the glass doors open and a group of students comes in, heading toward the entrance to the brick building. Emily quickly turns her chair so that her back faces the newcomers, but I catch the damp shine in her eyes as she blinks away rising tears.

I reach out hesitantly, my hand hovering in the air behind Emily's shoulder, but I drop it before I touch her. "I'm sorry," I say.

Her shoulders are curved defensively. "Don't be," Emily says in a low voice. "I just wanted you to know because when we go into the Commons for dinner, nobody's going to want to sit with us. I'm sorry you got stuck with me."

AFTER SCHOOL, I HEAD TO ELLICOTT PARK. I KEEP AN EYE out for the giant white oak at the bottom of the little hill, and when I step off the trail, I run my fingers over the rough bark, scraping off white flakes of lichen. At the top of the hill I pick my way around the outcropping of boulders, and then I gingerly descend the other side, trying to avoid slipping on the mossy patches. I skid the last few feet, my arms windmilling to catch my balance, and then I'm at the bottom of the hollow.

I shrug off my backpack and sit down, leaning against the rock. I take out my sketchbook and pencil, flipping it open to a blank page, and outline four panels of equal size. Since talking to Kim, I've been thinking about the mutant farmer. He's probably not that significant, but the woods where he dies are, and I feel like I have to get a better grasp on the setting. In the first panel, I sketch the forest floor. I only have a black pencil with me, so it's all about shadows, attempting to capture the way the mottled leaves create a soft layer over the darker earth. I draw an axe half buried in a pile of leaves, its honed edge a sharp, straight line.

In the next panel I sketch a boulder, white pine trees clustering above it. I turn to study the rock I'm leaning against, the pattern of dark gray and reddish-brown specks against a pale, reddish-gray background. At the place where the rock meets the ground, the earth is a soft black seam. I run my finger against it: It's damp, clumping on my fingertip like potting soil. I wipe my finger off on the rock and return to my sketch. I add an outstretched hand lying on the ground next to the boulder, the forearm, clothed in a black sleeve, disappearing into the panel frame. The fingers of the hand are curled up. Black soil smudges the fingertips, and the nails are broken.

I check my phone; it's after three already. I have to get home soon. Now that my pencil has stopped scratching against the paper, I hear the sounds of the park more clearly. It's quiet, but not silent. Birds twitter nearby, and the wind sweeps in one long sigh through the dry leaves. A gull screams overhead, and I look up to see it crossing the circle of sky above, white wings outstretched. The hollow where I'm sitting is surrounded by oak and pine trees, so that it feels like I'm at the bottom of a deep well. I set down the sketchpad and pencil and push my backpack over to create a lumpy pillow. I lie down and gaze up at the sky, where white clouds are slowly moving across the blue. The gull returns, swooping around, and disappears again.

I hear a series of thumps that sound like something pattering onto the leaf-strewn ground. Acorns, maybe. A single louder engine rumbles over the muted hum of traffic in a long, slow acceleration, then fades. I hear girls' voices in the distance. I can't make out the words but their tone has an excited edge. One of them laughs, and then her laughter cuts off abruptly, as if she or someone else clapped a hand over her mouth. The girls are coming closer. They aren't approaching from the trail but the opposite direction, the East Bedford side—from Pearson Brooke. I don't move. Their voices sound familiar.

I hear their footsteps now, quickening, irregular. They're close enough that I can understand what they're saying. There are two of them.

"It's almost three fifteen."

"We're almost there."

"Good, because we don't have much time for this."

"Come on, I promise it's good."

They're so close I'm afraid they'll see me. I feel hidden down here, at the bottom of this well created by trees and rocks, but I'm not hidden. All it takes is for someone to walk up to the edge of the hollow and look down, and I'll be exposed clear as day. I train my eyes on the trees across from the boulder. Some of their roots are exposed where the ground was torn away at some point in the recent past, like a mini mudslide. I can't see the girls, but they have to be just past those trees. I hold myself still as a stone, as if that might hide me from view.

"Here it is!"

I see a flash of color. One of the girls is wearing red. I hold my breath.

There's a slow, rough scraping noise as something is dragged across the ground. I hear the rasp of a metal buckle unfastening, the unmistakable rustle of paper sliding against paper, unfolding.

"Look! I told you."

The paper flexes, the sound ricocheting through the park.

"'My darling,'" one of the girls says, and breaks into giggles. "My *darling*?"

"Shut up, it's so sweet. He can't exactly write my name."

The giggler coughs, turns serious. "'My darling,'" she says

again. "'I have been thinking about you constantly. I wake up and think of you. I make my coffee and think of you. I drive to school and think of you.'" More giggles. "Wow. He really *thinks* of you!"

Something about the girl's voice clicks in my mind. It's Margot.

"Shh, don't read it out loud if you're going to make fun of it," says the other girl. She has to be Ryan.

"Oh, relax," Margot says, then falls silent.

The crackle of paper is as loud as lightning. Every muscle in my body is tense with the effort to will myself invisible. I stare anxiously at the spot in the trees where I saw the flash of red, but there's no movement now.

Finally Margot says, "Aw . . . he's really sweet."

"I told you!"

"But you know you can't do this."

"Don't be such a prude!"

A moment of silence, and then the sound of papers shuffling again. "You have to be careful," Margot says.

"Why do you think we're communicating this way?"

"He doesn't text you?"

"Never."

The buckle is fastened again, and something is shoved along the ground.

"Well, I'm glad he makes you so happy. Just be careful."

"You already said that, *Mom*."

Laughter. "Okay. Come on, we have to get to practice."

I hold my breath as they move, listening to their footsteps retreat back in the direction they came from. When I can't hear them anymore, I get up. My left arm has fallen asleep and I rub the tingling life back into it as I walk over to the edge of the hollow. I pick my way up the small hillside. Small bits of rock and gravel clatter down the slope in the wake of my passage. At the top of the slope, several pine trees cluster around a fallen log. It has lodged against one trunk, causing it to lean slightly to the right. I step over the log and look back. I can't see down into the hollow from here. The woods seem to end in a steep drop a couple of feet beyond the fallen log.

I glance around. This area is exactly like every other part of Ellicott Park: trees, rocks, more trees. There aren't a lot of hiding places; there's only one. I lean over to look into the shadowy recess beneath the juncture where the log pushes against the tree. The ground is damp here, and some of the leaves that cover the forest floor have been scraped aside, revealing chocolate-brown earth. The impression of a running shoe is clear, the ridges standing up fresh and new.

I kneel down near the mud and peer into the small, dark space. Something has been shoved in there. I reach in and feel something smooth, like leather. I wrap my fingers around it and tug. As I pull, I hear the scrape of an object against the underside of the log—exactly the same sound I heard when the girls were here.

It's a leather messenger bag with metal buckles. The leather is water stained, discolored in patches so that it looks almost like the forest floor itself. I unbuckle the bag and open the flap. Inside is a small collection of envelopes. The paper is thick and creamy, only slightly mottled by the moisture that must collect inside the bag. I open one envelope and remove a note that's handwritten in small, precise printing.

There are seven of them, all addressed to "My Darling," all signed with simply, "Yours."

I read every one.

ANGIE POSTS A SELFIE WITH THE CAPTION, "TGIF!" SHE'S wearing dark eye makeup, which she normally doesn't; it makes her look older. Her hair is pulled over one shoulder in a loose braid, and she's wearing a sleeveless pink eyelet shirt over tight black jeans. The picture was only posted ten minutes ago but it already has a bunch of likes and comments, all praising her look. Normally I'd like it too, but I don't do that anymore. I scroll through the people who liked or commented on her picture, and I know all of them except for one: gogo43, who wrote, "hottt." I click on the link to gogo43's profile, but it's locked. The tiny profile picture shows the back of a girl's bare shoulder and a sweep of dark hair.

My fingers tighten on my phone, and the crack that runs across the upper-right corner of the glass shoots off a tributary. I force my grip to loosen, but I keep staring at gogo43's shoulder as blood rushes to my head. It throbs in my ears in a thick pulse.

It's been two weeks since Angie stopped texting me.

I walk over to her house just before seven o'clock. It's already dark, and half the streetlights are burned out on my block. I pass

West Bed High, where the parking lot is almost full. Behind the school a dim glow emanates from the football field. Scattered cheers float on the cool night air.

Angie's house is a couple of blocks past the high school. Lights shine in the front windows, and a TV flickers through the lace curtains. Angie's room is the right-hand window on the second floor. Her lights are on too, and the mini-blinds are half closed.

I stand across the street in the shadow between two streetlights, staring at her window.

I could call her. I imagine hearing her answer the phone, her voice in my ear. I imagine the tentative welcome in her *hello?*, a hopeful lift as she says my name. I slide my hand into my pocket and feel my phone, but I don't take it out.

There is movement behind her mini-blinds. Angie comes to the window and spreads the blinds open with her fingers, peeking out as if she could feel me watching. I freeze, afraid that she'll see me, but after a couple of seconds she retreats. I let out my breath. I move to the right so that I'm halfway behind an SUV parked on the side of the road, but I still have a good view of her window.

I run my finger along the crack on my phone's screen over and over, lightly tracing the glass edges. Talking to Angie feels impossible, like placing a telephone call to yesterday. I remove my sweaty hand from my pocket and wipe it on my jeans. I keep watching her window.

Two blocks away a sustained cheer rises from the school. Maybe we scored a touchdown. I haven't been to a football game since last year, with Angie and her friends. It was cold that night, and Angie and I huddled together, our jackets draped over the two of us in a poor semblance of a blanket. I remember her shivering against me like a rabbit, all breath and softness.

A Mini comes down the street, slows down, and pulls to a stop outside Angie's house. The bumper has a sticker on it that reads BROOKE PRIDE in rainbow letters. I shrink farther behind the SUV, peering around the end of the vehicle. The streetlight angles into the Mini so that it outlines the driver's silhouette. Her hair is loose and long. A phone glows on in her hand, briefly illuminating her face. It's Margot. A moment later Angie appears at her window again, waving down at the car. She's wearing the pink top that was in her photo.

My mouth has gone dry. My thighs are quivering from my uncomfortable half-squatting position, but if I stand up I'm sure they'll see me. I want to watch Angie emerge from her house, but my quads burn too much. I sink down so that I'm kneeling on the cold sidewalk, my view completely blocked by the SUV. I hear Angie's front door close, and a few moments later I hear the Mini's passenger door open.

"Hi," Angie says brightly, her voice carrying across the street.

"Hi back," says Margot, more faintly.

The door to the Mini closes with a perky-sounding crunch. The engine revs slightly, and then I listen to the car pull away from the curb and head down the street. I stand up in time to see the Mini's red taillights turn right at the end of the block.

ANGIE HAS THEATER REHEARSAL ON MONDAYS AND Wednesdays after school. On Tuesdays she usually studies in the library with her other friends. I used to study with them too, but now I linger in the hallway until I see Angie enter the library, and then I leave. Thursdays are uncertain. Sometimes she has GSA meetings, sometimes drama club, sometimes the library. I can usually tell by the direction she heads from her locker.

Today I don't see her. I've gotten my backpack and jacket from my locker, but Angie is nowhere in sight. I feel twitchy when I don't know where she is, my brain constantly rotating through options. She could be hanging out with Courtney in the drama department. She could be talking to a teacher. She could have already left, and if that's the case it means I won't see her until tomorrow morning first period, when I slide into my seat behind her and say nothing, again.

I close my locker. I head for the exit, passing the trophy cases and the framed photos of all of West Bed's sports teams. Outside, the main drive is thronged with cars. There are parents picking up their kids; students inching their way out of the parking lot;

yellow school buses idling. Angie is sitting on a bench, looking at her phone.

I cut across the patchy brown grass in front of the school, keeping Angie in my peripheral vision. There's another bench over here, sort of behind her, so she won't see me if she doesn't turn around. I sit down. She's still staring at her phone. When she looks up a minute later, I follow her gaze toward the cars inching down the drive. I see it instantly: the blue Mini.

Every time I see it I feel a hot, ugly twist inside me. I keep expecting it to fade, but it only seems to intensify. It eats at me as Margot sticks her arm out the Mini's driver's side window and waves. Angie gets up, waving back. She moves toward the car, and just before she reaches it she turns her head and sees me.

When our eyes meet, I am pinned in place by her gaze. She is disgusted with me.

THE CREAMERY HAS A PRIME SPOT IN THE MIDDLE OF EAST Bedford's central square, where Washington and Essex Streets intersect at an angle. The Creamery's at the apex of that angle, with big glass windows that overlook the little cobblestoned triangle with the statue of George Washington. I usually walk down Essex Street to the Creamery, but today I take Milk, a side street that perpendiculars onto Washington about half a block away from the square. Coming down Milk gives me a good view into the ice-cream shop, but it also means that whoever's inside has a good view of me. I keep to the wall of the café on the corner of Milk Street, pulling the hood of my sweatshirt farther over my face, and take out my phone so that it looks like I'm doing something.

Angie's working today. Inside the empty Creamery, she is standing behind the counter. Peak ice-cream season is over by now. Last year I loved hanging out with Angie on late fall Saturdays at the Creamery. We usually had the place to ourselves and would make mini batches of milk shakes using the specialty flavors. Sometimes families would come in with their kids, but today it looks like Angie's alone.

She's not, though. I peeked down the alley behind the Creamery before I walked down Milk Street, and I saw Margot's Mini parked next to Angie's car.

Soon enough, I see Margot too. She leans over the counter toward Angie, who hangs back. Even from where I'm standing, I can tell that Angie's smiling. There's something flirty about her posture. She's holding back, but not because she doesn't want Margot to come closer; she's reeling her in.

Margot takes the lure. She reaches over the counter for Angie's hands. Angie laughs, backing away. Margot bends over the counter and captures Angie's hand in hers, and now Margot's the one in the lead. Angie leans toward her. They are in full view of the street, but they seem oblivious to that fact.

I have stopped breathing. Something hot and acidic boils up in my belly.

Margot kisses her. It's a sweet kiss, a public kiss. It's the first time I've seen Angie kiss a girl, and suddenly she seems like a stranger. When she first came out to me, it was an abstract idea, entirely theoretical. This is concrete, as real as a punch in my face.

I turn away, feeling sick and sweaty and angry and envious all at once. I force myself to put one foot in front of the other, walking faster and faster down Milk Street until I'm practically running, gasping, my skin burning, and the only thing I can see is the way Margot reaches out and slides her hand around Angie's neck as she kisses her: the sense of possession in her movements, as if Angie were hers alone.

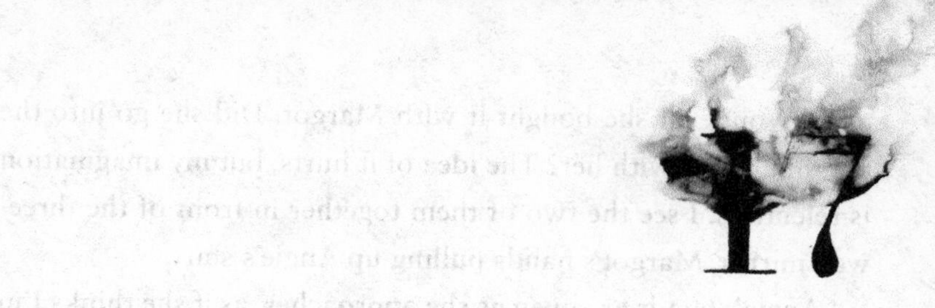

AFTER THE ARTS PROGRAM, THE BUS DROPS US OFF AT West Bed High. I go inside to get my math homework out of my locker. The hallways are empty now, and my footsteps echo on the recently mopped linoleum. A burst of music peals through the air from the theater wing, and then is silenced as a door slams. I reach my locker and spin the combination, grabbing my homework and stuffing it into my backpack. Footsteps are coming down the hallway. I glance in the direction of the sound.

It's Angie.

Nervousness bubbles in my stomach. I close my locker and swing my backpack onto my shoulder, turning to leave.

"Jess, wait."

The resigned tone of her voice makes me pause in unexpected hope. It's been over three weeks since she stopped texting me. I think I've been waiting for this moment. I've imagined it before. She'll apologize. She'll tell me she's breaking up with Margot. She'll say she misses me.

I turn back. Her wavy hair is loose and wild around her face. She's wearing skinny jeans and a green Henley I don't recognize, and I wonder if she bought it with Margot. Did she go into the dressing room with her? The idea of it hurts, but my imagination is relentless. I see the two of them together in front of the three-way mirror, Margot's hands pulling up Angie's shirt.

Angie's hands are open as she approaches, as if she thinks I'm a wild animal that needs to be gentled. "I know you're following me around," she says quietly.

The hallway seems to close in on me, all the air vacuumed out.

She comes closer. She is only a few feet away from me. There's a wrinkle in her forehead, a soft downward tug to her lips. "If you want to talk to me, let's talk. That's why you're following me, isn't it?"

I open my mouth. I close it. The green Henley skims her breasts, the six small buttons half undone, revealing the smooth, pale skin of her chest, the shadow leading to her cleavage. I see the faint pattern of a lace bra through the close-fitting fabric. Angie never used to wear lace bras.

She takes another step toward me. I feel completely exposed beneath the bright fluorescent lights, as if I were in an interrogation room. She says, "I want to talk to you too. I don't like whatever is happening between us. You're my best friend—we should be able to talk about this."

It's been a long time since I've looked into Angie's eyes. She's wearing purplish-gray eyeshadow and mascara. It looks like the same eye makeup she wore in that photo from Friday night. It's jarring to see it on her in person. She looks older, more confident.

"Jess," she says again.

My name sounds like a sigh on her lips. It makes me shiver.

"Are you going to say anything?" she asks.

I hear impatience in her voice and my own heartbeat quickens as if to push me forward, but all my words are trapped in my throat.

She shakes her head. She starts to turn around, to leave me.

"Wait," I burst out. "Wait, I—I do want to talk."

She turns back, eyebrows raised. "Really?"

"I'm—" *I'm sorry.*

"You're what?"

"I know this girl at Brooke, Emily?"

She looks confused. "Yeah, so?"

"She knows Margot, and she told me that Margot is—that she's not very nice."

Now she's disappointed. "That's what you want to talk about?"

"Margot spread a lot of lies about Emily. She's not who she seems. She made Emily do all sorts of shitty stuff and then when Emily stopped, she started spreading lies about her. You're not seeing the real Margot." My words tumble out of me faster and faster, but even as I say them I know they're the wrong ones. Angie stiffens defensively, her face darkening.

"Quit it," she says angrily. "Just quit it. I know you don't like Margot, but you don't know her!" Her voice rises. "You need to get over this. Even if you don't like her, *I* like her, and you're my best friend—or you *were* my best friend—and you should want me to be happy. Don't you want that?"

"Yes, but—"

"There's no *but*. You're either my friend who supports me, or you're not. So quit it with this BS and quit it with the stalking and get over it."

Her eyes are hard and bright. I've never seen her this angry, and I want to take back everything I said, but it's too late now. "I'm—"

"When you're ready to be normal about this, let me know." She gives me one last disappointed look, then shakes her head, and leaves.

I CAN'T SLEEP. I KEEP LOOKING AT MY ALARM CLOCK TO watch the glowing red numbers tick slowly toward two a.m.

At 2:06, I throw off the covers and get out of bed. The room is chilly because my parents turn the heat down to practically freezing at night, so I put on a sweatshirt. I turn on my desk lamp and pull out my sketchbook. I flip through the pages to the panels I've been working on most recently. Kestrel is facing off with Raven, and Kestrel's going to demand the truth from her: Is Raven really trying to open the Doorway to Faerie? They're standing nose to nose, and I've given Kestrel a fierce expression to contrast with Raven's smirk. I've also drawn two small panels that are close-ups on Kestrel's and Raven's faces. Now I start on a wide-angle shot, with Kestrel and Raven small figures in the lower right part of the rectangle. They're standing in a field next to the woods where Kestrel killed the mutant farmer. I work on the trees for a while, and then I sketch Laney into the shadows between the trees. She's watching the two of them, and I insert a small box in the bigger image that shows a close-up on Laney's face.

She's jealous. She suspects that Kestrel and Raven are secretly in love. I haven't decided if that's true yet, but as I draw Laney's eyes, a new idea takes shape. It's startling. I flip back through the sketchbook to see whether it would work, because it's not what I originally intended. It means redoing the scene I'm working on and probably throwing away a bunch of stuff. I hate throwing stuff out, but the idea is so intriguing I want to try it immediately.

I open to a new blank page and rough out a two-page spread. Kestrel and Raven will be in the library together. I sketch the bones of a room with tall Gothic ceilings, where bookshelves line the walls. I place Kestrel and Raven in front of one of the arched windows. Raven is holding a book bound in black that's titled *Magick*, and Kestrel approaches her, an expression of concern on her face. I outline two other panels, one focusing on Kestrel's face and the other on Raven's. I'll add in dialogue bubbles later. Finally, on the right-hand page I draw a short, wide panel in which I'll depict the library from the outside. It's nighttime, so the windows will be lit up, and Kestrel and Raven will appear as black silhouettes. In the lower-left corner of this panel, Laney stands on the lawn, gazing up at the window. From her perspective, Kestrel and Raven are leaning toward each other in the window as if they're about to kiss. I draw Laney's mouth as a hard, distrustful slash. I draw her hands curled into fists.

I SQUAT DOWN IN FRONT OF THE HIDING PLACE AND reach my gloved hand into the shadowed recess. Emily makes a face and says, "Ugh, I would not stick my hand in there. What if there's a snake or something?"

"There aren't any snakes here," I say.

She rubs her hands on her arms and says, "Because it's too cold!"

It is cold in the woods, but I like the crisp dryness of the air. It smells like winter. "It's not that cold. You're just a wimp." I wrap my fingers around the strap of the leather bag and tug. It's stuck for a second, but then it comes free, scraping across the ground.

"Hey, I'm from California," she objects. "Winter is not my natural habitat."

I unbuckle the bag and pull out the stash of letters. There are a couple of new ones. Emily reaches for them but I hold back. "Wait a sec," I say. "You have to read them in order."

She gives me an impatient look but says, "Fine. Which is the first?"

I find the first one and hand it over, and while she reads it,

I unfold the new letters. One is like the others, written to "My Darling" and signed "Yours," but the second letter is on scalloped stationery and has different handwriting. It's clearly a girl's cursive, angled to the right with rounded loops.

Dear J,

I can't believe I'm going to be away from you for a week and a half! Thanksgiving is going to suck. You have to promise me that as soon as we both get back here that we can meet right away. Can we go to that place in Maine you keep talking about? I bet it'll be empty because nobody goes to Maine in December if they can help it. We can be all cozy in the snow and stay in bed all day (wink) and it'll be amazing.

I know you have to leave early for Thanksgiving but don't forget, you can text me on that app and I'll get it and nobody will know. I can't go a whole ten days without hearing from you. You are the best thing about my life right now, and ever. I'm going to miss you so much. Nobody makes me feel like you do. I'm going to wear the underwear you bought me to Thanksgiving dinner and nobody will know, but I'll feel your hands on me all night.

XXX, Your Darling

Emily has a look of fascinated disgust on her face. "Oh my God," she says. "I thought you were exaggerating, but this is real."

"I told you. Look at this one." I hand her the newest letter. "I think the guy who writes the letters must come here to get notes from her too, but he takes them away with him. He must not have picked this one up yet."

Emily skims the newest one and grimaces when she gets to the end. "This is gross."

"Any idea who's writing them?" I ask.

Emily's forehead wrinkles as she flips through the letters. "I don't know. They're clearly both at Brooke, but . . ." She fixes me with a suspicious look. "How did you say you found them?"

I take a seat on the log and drum my fingers against the side. Damp bits of bark fall off. "I overheard some girls talking in the woods about them. They were Peebs."

Emily sits back on her heels, her eyebrows rising. "Peebs? That's what you call us?"

I raise my eyebrows back in a challenge. "Like you don't know. Don't you call us Bedwetters?"

Emily exhales sharply. "So why are you showing these to me?"

"You don't recognize the handwriting? The girl's handwriting?"

She frowns but looks at the girl's letter again. "No. Should I?"

"I thought you might want to know what Ryan's been up to."

Her gaze snaps up to me, startled, and then back down to the girl's letter. "Ryan?"

I watch the way her eyes narrow, her mouth flattening as she reads. She shakes her head slightly. She lets out her breath in a little *hmph*. When she looks up at me, she's trying to contain her excitement.

"Ryan," she says again, but this time her tone says, *I should have known*.

"Yep."

She carefully lays the letters on top of the log beside me, placing Ryan's note on top. Then she takes out her cell phone, stands up, and begins to take photos.

IT'S BEEN THIRTY-FOUR DAYS SINCE ANGIE LAST TEXTED me. I sketch a picture of Angie and me standing in the hallway at school. The lockers march in a receding line into the distance, creating a tunnel effect behind the two of us in the foreground. We face each other, but I am not looking at her.

I don't draw myself that often. I could make myself taller and thinner, cuter or better dressed, but that has always felt like cheating. I get a kind of bitter satisfaction out of exaggerating the roundness of my face, the pooch of my belly under my flat breasts, the puddling of my too-long jeans around my ankles. The hardest part is getting the expression on my face right. I'm embarrassed, eyes downcast, cheeks shaded to suggest a blush, mouth in a slight grimace.

I draw Angie looking at me with a wary expression, one eyebrow slightly arched up, lips drawn together in a flat line. It's easy to make her look good. I dress her in tight jeans, the Henley with six buttons. Her arms are crossed beneath the curve of her breasts. I give her really great hair and tuck some of it behind one ear.

I sketch a dialogue bubble, connect it to me, and letter in the words I couldn't say out loud: *I'm sorry for being a shithead. Can we be friends again?*

In the next panel I draw a close-up on Angie's face. I take my time with her eyes, her nose, her mouth. I don't need a photo for reference; I've been drawing her since we first met in art class in sixth grade. I know every line of her body by heart. I add a dialogue bubble above her head, and inside it I place only an ellipsis.

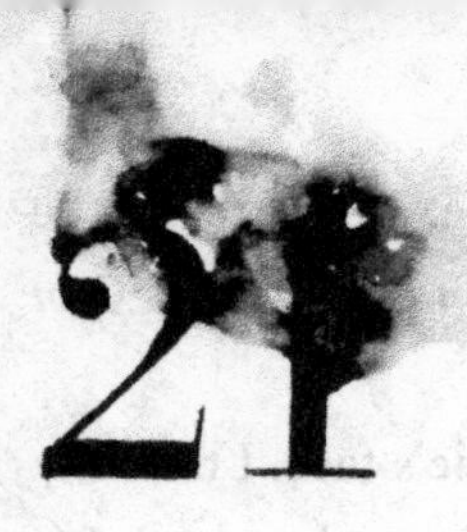

SATURDAY MORNING, I'M WORKING ON MY KESTREL COMIC when I hear a knock on my bedroom door.

"Jess?"

The sound of Angie's voice is so startling I almost knock over my chair in my haste to get up. I open the door and she is standing on the other side, still wearing her down coat. Her cheeks are flushed, and she flashes me a brief, nervous smile.

"Jamie let me in," she says.

I slid the comic I drew of us into her locker yesterday morning, but she didn't say a thing to me all day at school. I had already started to think about what my next move should be—another comic? send her flowers?—and now I'm caught completely off guard.

She asks, "Can I come in?"

"Oh. Yeah." I step back.

She comes into my bedroom and shuts the door behind her. She pulls off her coat and tosses it on the end of my bed. She sweeps her gaze around my room, skates over me—frozen in place beside the door—and sees the papers strewn over my desk.

"What are you working on?" she asks.

"Kestrel. My project for the arts exchange program."

She takes a couple of steps toward my desk, then gives me a quick sidelong glance. "Is it okay if I look?"

Her hesitance surprises me. "Sure, yeah," I say.

She touches the paper, gently moving one sheet aside. I feel as if her fingertips were on my skin rather than the comics. I can't believe she's in my room, acting like nothing is wrong between us.

"What's going on in this scene?" she asks. "Who's this girl Kestrel is with?"

"That's Raven." I join her at my desk and flip through the loose pages until I find the start of the story arc. "Here. This is how it begins." Her arm brushes mine as she takes the first page. Between us is an electric field of unspoken words. I'm listening extra hard, trying to hear what she's not saying. I pass her the next page and the next, and then Angie sits down in my chair to continue reading. I am standing above her, looking down at the back of her head, her reddish-brown hair tumbling over her shoulders. She's wearing a blue sweater that has a thread coming loose near the shoulder. She tucks her hair behind her ear, and a strand of it catches in the clasp of her earring, a seashell as pink as the flesh of her earlobe.

She gasps. "I can't believe Kestrel did that!" She glances up at me, something between horror and glee in her eyes. "Why did she do that?"

"Because she—" I shake my head. "I can't tell you, it's a spoiler."

"Come on," she says dramatically. "I have to know. I've been reading your comics the longest. I deserve to know."

She bounces in my chair with eagerness. She is all sweetness and smiles, and it unnerves me because it erases everything from the last five weeks. I back away to sit on the edge of my bed, to put some space between us. When I put that picture in her locker, I wanted her to know I was sorry for how I treated her, but I don't know if I wanted her to pretend like nothing happened.

She leans forward, and her hair tumbles over her shoulder, brushing against her upper arm. "You can tell me," she says conspiratorially. "I won't tell anyone."

The tone of her voice makes me ache, as if she were rubbing out a knot in my neck. It feels so good, but at the same time, she put the knot there. She ties me up inside, and only she can undo me.

I tell her about my most recent plans for Kestrel; how it affects her friendship with Laney; how it changes the way the Warden sees Kestrel and Raven. Angie listens, rapt, and then I take out my sketchbook and flip to a series of thumbnail-size panels I've drawn to rough out the story. We both sit down on the rug, leaning over the sketchbook together. Her hair smells like peaches; she must have changed her shampoo. I feel the warmth of her body beside me as she comes closer so she can see better, her arm against mine, her knee brushing my thigh. The charge between us seems to amplify; my blood is buzzing with her nearness. After so long apart, I'm overwhelmed by how it feels to be together—like sinking into water so hot it burns at first, but when you're finally submerged, you never want to climb out.

By the time she has to leave, I'm high on her, her smile, the sound of her voice, the scent of her hair. She tells me she has to go to work and asks, "Are you going to come by later? It's probably going to be pretty dead."

"Sure," I agree. "I'll stop by."

Her smile reaches her eyes, and I think I see relief too. "Yay!" she says. "It was so good to catch up."

She puts on her coat, but before she opens the door she pulls me into an unexpected hug. Her coat is still hanging open, so it's as if I'm enveloped in a down blanket. Her breasts press against me, and her whole body shudders as she takes in a deep, shaking breath. My hands, trapped beneath her coat, slide around her waist, across her lower back. My fingertips run over her spine, the vertebrae like pebbles beneath the knit of her sweater. She fits in my arms perfectly. Beneath the smell of her shampoo is the deeper, hidden scent of her skin. I don't know when I learned to recognize that fragrance as distinctly Angie's, but it is instantly familiar to me. It makes my knees weak.

"I don't want to go so long without talking to you ever again," she whispers. Her breath tickles my ear, and tiny sparks travel all the way down my spine. "Don't do that again."

I want to clutch her closer to me, and I have to force myself not to. "I won't," I whisper back.

"Promise," she orders.

I feel a molten twist in my belly. "I promise."

I'm still buzzed on her. I lie awake staring at the faint glow of light through the mini-blinds, thinking about Angie. The feel of her against me is burned into my body, and it makes me twitch beneath my blankets.

I have a rule. I don't think about Angie when I get off. I have the internet. I don't need to mess up my mental relationship with my best friend by thinking about her naked.

It's hard to avoid it tonight, though.

I push off my blankets. My skin is flushed and damp. I pick up my phone. I look at the shitty Tumblr porn, scrolling past the dicks and the weird stuff, searching for something that looks sort of real, or at least not obviously fake. I pause on a girl with curly brown hair and rhythmically rocking breasts. I can't see her face, just her hair as it slides over her nipples. It's easy to imagine Angie's face on this girl's body, but it feels disrespectful. More disrespectful than simply imagining her, her hair, her breasts, her freckled shoulders, her mouth, her kiss.

I drop the phone. It's a stupid rule.

AT MIDNIGHT, THE HOUSE IS SO QUIET THE ONLY SOUND I hear is the scratch of my pencil across the paper. Tomorrow is the last meeting of the arts program before Thanksgiving, and I want to get this batch of comics completed to show Kim.

Over a series of several pages, I've roughed out Kestrel and Laney hiking into the woods. It's winter, and the trees are skeletons against a slate-colored sky. Laney and Kestrel are tiny in the first panel, but in the next one I zoom in to focus on Kestrel, a determined expression on her face, the black book peeking out from her backpack. Laney, following close behind her, looks frightened. They approach a hollow in the woods that's like a scooped-out bowl rimmed with evergreens and bare oaks. Kestrel, standing on the edge of the hollow, opens the black book while Laney holds an empty horn cup. According to the rules of magic in Kestrel's world, every spell has kickback, sort of like the recoil of a gun. In order to contain that kickback, an inanimate object must be nearby to receive it. The horn cup, which Laney took from the Warden's magical stockroom, is their kickback vessel.

Kestrel believes that the crumbling Doorway to Faerie is manifesting in this hollow in the woods, and she has decided to test her theory with a truth spell. I've been trying to figure out how to depict the Doorway for a while now. It can't look exactly like a doorway because that would be stupid, and I want it to look magical somehow. I've tried a bunch of different options, but the one I like best involves inverting the colors. That means the trees become white, the sky becomes black, and in the center of the hollow an egg-shaped black hole opens up, defined by jagged white lightning-like strikes. The cool part of this is that I can sketch it out the normal way, with black pencil, and when I scan it into the computer at Brooke, I can invert the colors digitally.

On the next page I outline two panels of roughly equal size on the top half of the paper, and one wide one on the bottom half. The first square panel shows Kestrel casting the spell, one hand raised and the other holding her book. I draw a dialogue bubble from Kestrel's head, where I write in the words of the spell. The second square panel shows Laney realizing that the spell isn't the one they originally planned on; this one edges close to black magic. Horrified, Laney tries to stop her, but Kestrel is already consumed by the magical aura of spell casting, and Laney is unable to touch her. I draw Laney's shocked expression and above her head, I outline her dialogue bubble. *Kestrel, what are you doing?* Laney demands. *That spell is too dangerous!*

I glance at the clock. It's almost two thirty, and I have to get up by six. I should stop but I want to at least rough out the last scene. In the bottom rectangular panel I draw a distant shot of the hollow with Kestrel and Laney on its edge, magic swirling from Kestrel's book to join with the bolts of light from the Doorway that's manifesting before them. The point of view in this panel is in the lower left, where a girl with long black hair stands watching Kestrel and Laney. It's Raven, and I spend a long time on her expression, trying to get it right. I want her to look both stunned and fascinated by what Kestrel's doing. I block out a rectangle over Raven's head, and I pencil in her thoughts: *She's using the Black Book. She has more power than I thought. I have to stop her.*

A FEW FLAKES OF SNOW SPIRAL FROM THE GRAY SKY AS Angie and I walk down Washington Street. The shops put up their Christmas decorations right after Halloween this year, but now that Thanksgiving has passed, East Bedford has become an explosion of holly and red ribbons and Christmas trees and mini white lights. Normally we wouldn't go shopping here—it's expensive—but Angie wants to get something special for Margot.

Angie opens the door to a boutique where a stuffed reindeer draped in Christmas sweaters sits in the front window. Inside I'm assaulted by a blast of hot air from the vent over the door. I unzip my coat as Angie starts to browse. The shop is a combination of kitschy New England junk—stuffed lobsters, lighthouse figurines—and piles of expensive cashmere sweaters. I wander to the back of the store and discover a display of Christmas ornaments: more lobsters; tiny fake jugs of maple syrup hanging on gold threads; Pearson Brooke shields on purple ribbons.

It's only a few minutes before Angie joins me and says, "I don't think there's anything in here for Margot."

"What do you want to get her?"

"I don't know," Angie says anxiously. "Something good. It's our first Christmas. I want to get her something that says, you know, I'm an awesome girlfriend." Angie's phone chirps and she pulls it out of her pocket. "Oh, it's Margot. Hang on."

She leaves me by the Christmas ornaments and retreats behind a rack of stuffed lobsters. Whenever Margot texts, Angie has to respond right away. If she doesn't, Margot tends to freak out. Angie says it shows that Margot cares about her.

The miniature maple syrup ornament costs $9.99. I spin it around and watch it bang gently against the Pearson Brooke shield while I listen to Angie's phone chime another couple of times. Last week at Brooke I saw Margot outside the arts building. She acted like she was happy to run into me and asked if Angie liked any particular bath products.

"Lush?" she questioned. "Or that shop down by the Creamery—Milk and Honey?"

"She's allergic to perfumes," I lied.

Margot looked confused. "But she wears perfume."

"She can only wear that one kind. Don't get her soap."

Margot's eyes narrowed on me as I gave her a bland, fake smile. "Yeah, okay," she said caustically. "Thanks for the advice."

Finally Angie returns. She looks excited but hesitant. "Margot wants to meet up for coffee in an hour. Do you want to come?"

"Uh . . . I have to get home and watch Jamie."

Her face falls. "Come on, I know you don't have to be home till later."

"Jamie just texted me. Mom's going out."

She looks irritated with me. "I know it's because you don't want to hang out with Margot. You would barely come shopping today because I'm shopping for her present."

"What are you talking about?" I flap my coat to get a breeze in the overheated shop. "That's not true."

She gives me a stony glance. "You know what I'm talking about. You don't like her, but you won't try to get to know her either."

"She's *your* girlfriend," I snap. This is the first time I've said that out loud. The words stick in my throat and I can't continue.

"That's right," Angie says, as if she'd won an argument. "And you're my *best* friend. Is it so weird that I want you guys to get along?"

A woman in a Santa sweater is eyeing us from behind the counter to the right of the Christmas ornaments. I shift so that she can't see my face. "I just have to get home soon," I say.

"Why don't you give her a chance?" Angie asks. "Margot's great. I know you'll like her. If you had a—if you were seeing someone, I'd want to get to know them."

I can sense the Santa lady's eyes boring into the back of my head, and sweat is beginning to streak down my back beneath my T-shirt and sweater and winter jacket. "If you're not getting anything, we should leave," I say.

Angie shakes her head, looking annoyed. "Fine."

I'm boiling by the time I make it outside, and I peel off my coat in the frosty air. It feels good on the flushed skin of my face and neck. Angie stops on the sidewalk and starts texting again. I pull out my phone and glance at the time. It's still early. If I go home now, I'll be alone for the rest of the afternoon, while Angie flirts with Margot over fancy coffee drinks. I imagine sitting with them instead, but the idea of it turns my stomach.

"I'm going to meet Margot at Bradstreet Café in forty-five minutes," Angie announces. "You don't have to come, that's fine. I get that it's weird for you."

"It's not weird," I object, but Angie gives me a skeptical look before I even finish speaking. "Okay, fine, it's weird," I say, frustrated by the way Angie's watching me.

Her expression immediately softens. "I know," she says gently. A few flakes of snow settle on her hair. "I guess it *is* kind of weird to hang out with just the three of us. What if more people were there, like in a group?"

I let out my breath in a steamy exhale. "Maybe," I say grudgingly.

A flash of excitement lights up Angie's face and then is instantly snuffed, as if she doesn't want to show how much she wants this. "Okay, I was going to wait till you knew her better to tell you, but she told me she's having a Christmas party right before she leaves for break. It's going to be at her parents' summer house in Marblehead. It's just going to be her group of friends—and me. I want you to come too."

"I don't think I should just show up at Margot's party. She probably doesn't want me to come."

"She totally wants you to come!" Angie insists, but when I give her a doubtful look, she backtracks. "I'll ask her. I'm sure she'd want you to come."

"Yeah, well, if she personally invites me, I'll go." I'm certain that Margot will never do that.

Angie likes a challenge. "All right," she says confidently. "I'll get her to invite you."

While I'm washing dishes after dinner, my phone vibrates in my pocket. I rinse off a soapy bowl and set it in the top rack of the dishwasher to drain before I dry my hands and pull out the phone.

It's Margot. Angie gave me your number. I wanted to invite you to my party Dec. 16. Hope you can make it. 344 Atlantic, Marblehead.

I stare at the message until the letters start to look like unintelligible scratches. My right thumb is still damp, and it leaves a wet smear on the edge of my phone. The kitchen light buzzes, flashing briefly off and on again.

Dad comes into the kitchen. "Did the lights go off?" he asks, and flips the switch so that we're plunged into dimness once again. "Have to fix this," he mutters. "Jessica, you have to finish the dishes if you want your allowance. No halfway washed."

"I know," I say, and put my phone away. I turn the water on again.

"Don't let it just run like that—you're wasting the water," Dad says. "Plug the sink."

"It's plugged, but it leaks."

He makes a frustrated sound. "Does your mother know?"

"I don't know."

My phone buzzes again, but I wait until Dad leaves before I check it. This time it's a message from Angie.

Margot said she invited you to her party. Promise me you will come xo

THE WALLS OF THE COMMONS DINING ROOM ARE PANELED in dark wood, broken up by tall, paned windows that reveal the rapidly darkening evening outside. Chandeliers hanging above the long dining tables shed a warm glow over much of the room, but the corner where Emily and I take our trays is a pocket of shadows. It's the last arts exchange day of the fall semester, so we've been invited to stay for dinner again. I loaded my tray with a plate of stuffed shells with marinara sauce, french fries, a piece of apple pie, and a soda—stuff Mom never cooks at home. Emily eyes my dinner with suspicion. She went to the stir-fry station and got chicken and vegetables with rice.

"You like it?" she asks after I try my food.

The stuffed shells are oddly sweet. "It's okay." I squirt some ketchup onto my plate and dip a french fry in it. "Margot invited me to her party."

Emily raises her eyebrows and forks up some chicken. "Seriously?"

"Yeah. Did you get an invite?"

She snorts. "You've got to be kidding. No."

"I didn't think she'd invite me, honestly."

"Why did she? Because of your friend Angie?"

"I guess."

"What's the deal with you and Angie?"

"We're best friends," I say, avoiding Emily's gaze.

"And Angie is Margot's girlfriend?"

"Yeah," I say brusquely.

"You are not a fan of that."

I give up on the weird stuffed shells and focus on the fries. "Nope."

"Why not?"

"You're not a fan of Margot either. Do you have to ask?"

"I'm guessing your reasons for not being a fan of Margot are a little different from mine."

I keep eating french fries, even though they taste like sand. "So have you come up with any ideas for who's writing those letters to Ryan?" I ask.

She doesn't answer immediately. She pushes her rice around on her plate and studies me coolly. "Well," she says finally, "he's not Ryan's boyfriend."

"She has a boyfriend?"

"Yeah. Noah Becker. He's over there—you see that guy on the other side of the room in the blue sweatshirt, pushing his chair back?"

I twist in my seat and spot Noah right away, because Margot and Ryan are approaching his table with their trays. He's a sandy-haired boy, cute enough in an average way. "You don't think he wrote the letters?" I ask.

"No," Emily says. "He couldn't have. He's not the type. Noah's the opposite of someone who would do that. He's just this straightforward guy. Not stupid or anything, but there's nothing romantic about him. Whoever's writing those letters knows poetry."

"So she's cheating on her boyfriend with some mystery poetry guy."

"Yeah."

"Who do you think she's cheating with?"

"Somebody she has to keep a secret, obviously. Why, who do you think it is?"

I shrug.

Emily eyes me skeptically and takes a bite of her stir-fry. After she swallows, she says, "I have to say I wonder why she doesn't just break up with Noah. It's not like he's the hottest guy in school. I don't think she really even likes him that much."

I start in on my apple pie. The crust is a little soggy, but the apples are good.

"Although he is a senior, and his parents are pretty rich," Emily continues. "I think they're in banking or something. Maybe that's why she's dating him."

I think about the tone of the letters, the precision of the handwriting, the way he thinks about Ryan when he drives to and from school. "Don't you think the poetry guy is older?" I ask.

Emily's fork pauses in midair. There's a suggestion of a knowing smile on her mouth. "How much older?" she says.

"A lot," I say.

She puts her fork down. "Yeah. What boy our age is going to write letters like that?"

"No boy," I say. "A teacher."

Emily stares at me, and I see the idea catch fire in her, burning its way into the gleam in her dark eyes. She glances across the Commons at Ryan, and then back at me. "That's why she's with Noah. For cover."

It's pitch-black by the time I get back to West Bed High, even though it's only seven o'clock. I'm supposed to go straight home after the arts program dinner, but instead I continue walking past my house. The lights are on, and I see the flickering of the TV through the living room window. I take the trail into Ellicott Park.

The trees are bare now, and the sky is clear tonight, making it pretty easy to find my way to the hollow. I skid down one side and climb up the other, and then I take out my phone to turn on its flashlight. A twig cracks beneath my feet as I head for the fallen log. I kneel on the cold ground and bend over, shining the light into the dark.

I pull out the bag and open it. There are nine letters—one new—but the note with the scalloped edge is gone.

ANGIE'S WEARING A BLACK VELVET MINIDRESS OVER sheer black stockings and purple fake Doc Martens. She contorts her face as she leans toward the mirror over her dresser to layer on mascara. When she steps back she gives herself a critical look and fluffs her hair, causing her dangling sleigh bell earrings to jingle.

"How do I look?" she asks, pursing her lips at her reflection.

She looks like Courtney gave her a makeover, and I can't decide if it works or not. "You look amazing," I tell her.

She suddenly seems hesitant, and the Angie I know slips out from behind this girl's makeup. "I hope she likes it," she says.

"If she doesn't, she's an asshole."

Angie gives me a reproachful look in the mirror. "Thanks, I guess," she says.

The plan is for me to stay over at Angie's tonight after Margot's party. Angie's parents totally believe the story we made up: that we're going to a midnight screening of *The Wizard of Oz* with the other theater kids. It involves props and singing along, and it sounds absolutely awful, which makes it the perfect lie because Angie's parents would never go. We'll be back late, after they've already gone to bed, but they trust her.

The drive to Marblehead takes a little over an hour. Angie turns on Google Maps and follows the directions while I scan through the radio stations. It's all holiday music all the time. By the time we get to Marblehead, we've heard Mariah Carey's "All I Want for Christmas" three times. We pass a sign for Devereux Beach, briefly illuminated in the headlights, and continue past the empty parking lot onto a road flanked on both sides by the ocean. The Atlantic seems to simmer, barely visible but immense in its rippling blackness.

"It's supposed to snow tomorrow," Angie says as we turn onto Margot's street. "Good thing her party's tonight."

"Lucky us," I say. It comes out sounding more sarcastic than I intended.

"Well, I'm glad, even if you aren't."

"Sorry."

The street is lined with big houses. Some of them are dark, probably because they're summer vacation homes, but some have wide windows that reveal Christmas trees glittering with light. When Google tells us that our destination is on the right, I see a curving driveway leading slightly upward to a house that's blazing: Christmas lights are wrapped around the big front porch, and all the interior lights seem to be on. The gravel driveway circles around a fountain, and I count four cars. Angie parks at the end of the driveway and turns off the engine, but doesn't make a move to get out.

"You okay?" I ask.

"I'm nervous," she admits.

"Why?"

She inhales, then breathes out. "Because . . ." She shakes her head. "I just don't know her friends, you know? What if they don't like me?"

"Why wouldn't they like you?"

"Well, I'm not one of them."

I stare at the house. I see people behind the giant windows—Margot's friends. I don't see Margot. Wind buffets Angie's car hard enough to make it rock slightly. Angie shifts in place, the velvet of her dress whispering against the seat. She unbuckles her seat belt.

"I'm not one of them either," I say. "At least we'll be together."

She looks at me. Her eyes reflect the light from the house in glimmering pinpoints. She reaches for my hand and laces her fingers with mine.

The house is huge. The front entryway opens into an expansive living room done entirely in shades of white. Steps lead down from the living room into an even bigger kitchen and family room, with floor-to-ceiling glass doors onto a wide back deck overlooking a private beach. During the day the view must be spectacular, but at night, the only thing to see is the heaving black of the Atlantic beneath the matte black of the cloudy sky. Every time someone comes in one of those doors, the roar of the ocean crescendos like a lion's, only to be abruptly silenced by the double-paned glass.

At first, I trail Angie around the house, but it doesn't take long for Margot to separate her from me. There are only eight people at the party—not counting me—and they all seem to know one another. They absorb Angie with more enthusiasm than I expected, but they barely even glance at me. Once Angie looks in my direction while she's laughing at something someone else said, and the expression on my face must have startled her because she stops mid-laugh and gives me a concerned look. She starts to get up to come to me, but Margot's holding her hand and pulls her down onto the white couch beside her, and I can't see her anymore.

I find the drinks in the kitchen. There are a lot of them. The vodka is already open, so I pour some into a red plastic cup and add some cranberry juice and ice. I open the door to the deck and step outside. The wind scrapes over my face with breathtaking force. It smells like the coming snowstorm mingled with the briny scent of the ocean. I push through the wind to the railing and gaze down at the water. In the light from the house I see a strip of beach down below. The water is closer than I thought; dark waves crash onto the edge of the sand, leaving a white froth behind like soap suds. It's freezing out here, but I'm only outside for a minute before the doors open again and two people stumble onto the deck, laughing and cursing.

"I can't get this lighter to work!" the guy complains.

"Let me try," the girl says.

They don't notice me. I met them barely an hour ago, but I don't remember their names. They're shivering, and neither of them has a coat on.

"It's fucking cold," the guy mutters.

"I'll keep you warm," the girl says, giggling.

I head back to the door, and as I brush past them, the girl shrieks, "Oh my God, someone's out here!"

"It's that chick Margot's girlfriend brought," the boy says. "What are you, spying on us?"

I don't respond, going back inside and slamming the door behind myself. The kitchen is blessedly warm after the frigid deck.

Ryan is standing by the drinks, making something complicated with a shaker. She asks, "How is it out there?"

"Freezing." I take a gulp of my vodka and cranberry and head out of the kitchen.

I don't see Angie and Margot in the living room anymore. Somebody has started playing hip-hop over the house speakers, and the bass has been turned up so high it makes the floors shake. Two girls are beginning to dance drunkenly. They've taken off their heels, and their legs are bare beneath their glittery holiday dresses. Two boys sit on the couch where Margot and Angie were sitting, watching the dancing girls. They don't notice me as I walk right past them and up the stairs.

On the second floor, a long hallway lined with doorways splits the house. Half of them are closed, and I wonder if Margot and Angie are behind one of them. I imagine Margot's hand pushing up the hem of Angie's velvet dress, her fingers on Angie's thigh. I pause outside the first door, my heart pounding, but I can't hear anything over the music. I keep going, past a marble bathroom, past a room containing twin bunk beds. The door at the end of the hall is cracked, so I push it all the way open and enter a sprawling bedroom. It's empty. In an alcove on one side is a sitting area with a pink velvet love seat surrounded by windows. A king-size bed with a white tufted headboard sits on a dais across from the love seat. The bed is covered in a fluffy white down duvet and more pillows in more shades of pink than anybody ever needs. I go to the sitting area and peer out the window. In the distance a signal light blinks on and off, marking the edge of the land.

"You're not supposed to be up here."

I turn around, startled, to see Ryan standing in the doorway. She's holding a cocktail glass—a real one, the kind they put martinis in—and is wearing a silver minidress with a complicated neckline and no shoes. Her blond hair is pulled over her right shoulder, clasped with something that looks like diamonds. She takes a healthy sip of her cocktail.

"This is Margot's parents' room," she explains. "Off-limits."

I sit down on the love seat with my drink. The cushions are too soft, and I sink deeply into them.

"Margot's mom wanted to make it look like Vegas," Ryan says. "Did you see the bathroom?" She goes through the doorway on the left side of the bed and flips on the light. I glimpse pink marble and gold fixtures beneath a crystal chandelier. "It's so trashy," she says, almost in wonder. She leaves the bathroom and perches on the padded white bench at the foot of the white bed, facing me. "What are you doing up here?" she asks.

"Nothing." I take a sip of my drink.

Ryan is halfway finished with her cocktail. The lamplight glitters on the diamond studs in her ears. She crosses her bare legs, bobbing her foot up and down. Her toenails are painted hot pink. She gives me a knowing look. "You have a thing for your friend, don't you?"

I stiffen. "What?"

She leans back, elbows sinking into the soft duvet of the bed, the cocktail in her right hand perilously close to spilling. She gives me a hooded smile. "You heard me. Margot told me you're obsessed."

"That's bullshit." I take another drink. The cranberry juice is super tart, but it doesn't quite disguise the bite of the vodka.

"Don't be such a closet case," she says flatly. "I'm Margot's best friend. I know how this works." She sits up, finishes her cocktail in one gulp, and then leans forward, the empty glass dangling in one hand. "I bet you've had a crush on her for a long time. Isn't that why you became friends in the first place? And she's super nice to you, because that's who she is. Oh my God, Margot just goes on and on about how *nice* she is."

The sarcasm in Ryan's voice cuts more than what she's saying about me. "She *is* nice," I say.

Ryan laughs. "See? I don't know why you bother trying to hide it. Obviously you're totally whipped on her."

"I am not."

Ryan shakes her head. "Oh my God, what's the point? She clearly isn't into you. She's into Margot." She pauses, looks sour. "And Margot is definitely into her."

I take another drink. There isn't enough vodka for this.

"That's why she had this party. She doesn't really have permission, but it was so easy to get 'permission' from Margot's mom." Ryan makes air quotes with one hand, and then places the cocktail glass on the fur rug at her feet. She gets up and walks back toward the bathroom, but stops in front of another door. She pulls it open, revealing a walk-in closet. "Margot's mom is really kind of pathetic," Ryan says. "Last time I was here, she was drunk half the time, and the other half she was high. I bet she keeps some good stuff here." She steps up on a footstool in the closet so that she can reach the upper shelves. A shoebox tumbles down, spilling a pair of gold heels onto the floor, followed by a few scarves, floating in brilliant orange and fuchsia streaks through the air.

"Shit," Ryan exclaims. "Oh my God." She sounds genuinely surprised.

I watch her step down from the footstool, holding a black box. She sets it on the bed carefully, and the weight of the box causes it to sink into the fluffy duvet. She opens the box. I can't see it from where I'm sitting, so I climb out of the overly soft love seat and approach the bed.

The box contains a small golden gun. It doesn't look real.

"You should put that back," I say.

Ryan's eyebrows rise mockingly. "Oh! Finally, some words. For a while I thought you didn't speak English."

I stare at her, speechless.

She rolls her eyes. "I'm so sorry, was that racist?"

I head for the door. My legs are trembling.

"Oh, don't leave!" Ryan cries. "I was just starting to like you. Not like a lesbian, though."

Halfway between the door and the giant white bed, I turn back. "What is your problem?" I demand.

Ryan runs her fingers through the long tail of her hair. "I don't have a problem. You do, and you don't even know it."

"Know what?"

"The whole reason Margot's having this party is so she can screw Angie. Can you believe they haven't done it yet?"

The business-like tone of Ryan's words stuns me. As if Angie were an item on Margot's to-do list.

"It's not because Margot hasn't tried," Ryan says. "Your friend is kind of a prude, you know."

"Shut up," I choke out.

"I just thought you'd like to know your friend brought you here as her chaperone," Ryan says, pretending innocence. "She wouldn't come alone."

My fingers tighten over the plastic cup. I can feel it crack.

"You're neglecting your duty, though," Ryan continues. "Pretty sure Margot's getting some right now. Third door on the left down the hall. You wanna go watch?"

I hurl the red plastic cup at her. Ryan ducks out of the way, her mouth open in shock, and the liquid cascades out, splattering cranberry red across the white duvet, the white bench, the white rug, a brilliant explosion of color.

It's disappointingly unsatisfying. I'm shaking. I want to feel something crunch under my hand.

"Shit!" Ryan shrieks. "Margot's mom's going to kill you!"

My heartbeat pounds in my ears as I turn on my heel to leave. Behind me Ryan bursts into high, sharp laughter.

I don't know how many drinks I've had. I can't taste the vodka anymore, but Ryan is standing in front of me, wavering in my vision as if she were morphing in and out of reality. She's pointing her finger at me, leaning against the counter as she makes another of her fancy cocktails. She knocks over a jar of olives, and slick green spheres roll like eyeballs off the counter and onto the floor, olive juice dribbling in a thin greenish waterfall over the edge. She utters a shriek of surprise and grabs some paper towels, then squats down, her dress riding up over her thighs as she pats at the liquid. I can see down her dress from this angle. She's wearing a pink satin bra. A long silver chain with a pearlescent stone dangling on the end falls out of her cleavage, swinging like a pendulum.

She looks up at me, gives me a leer, and says, "See something you like?"

"You wish," I mutter.

"Too bad for you I'm straight," she says. Her voice sounds unnaturally loud, and it's probably because she has to talk over the music that's still blaring from the living room. "Not that you'd be my type anyway. You're too—" She waves her hand at me as she stands up with the olive juice–soaked paper towels. They flap, soiled and heavy, splattering juice in my direction. "What's with your look, anyway? You want to be a boy? Is that it?"

"You want to be a slut, is that it?" I retort.

She scowls at me. "What the fuck does that mean?"

"I know you're cheating on your boyfriend."

Her eyes narrow.

"I *know* you're cheating. I've read your disgusting love letters."

She freezes for an instant, panic in her eyes. Then she crumples up the damp paper towels and throws them toward the sink. They land with a plop on the counter, striking some of the beer bottles. "You haven't read *shit*," she spits at me.

"I've been to your stupid little tree in the woods." I step toward her and she actually takes a startled step back. I laugh. "You think you know everything about everyone, but I know your secret."

"Shut up."

"You hide those letters he writes you in that bag under the log. I've read them. I've read every single fucking one."

"Shut *up*!" she screams, and now panic has fully bloomed over her, spreading tomato red through her makeup and seeping like a rash onto her neck.

"*My darling,*" I mock her. "He thinks about you on his way to school. He thinks about you when he's working. He can't wait to be alone with you so he can fuck your flat underage ass."

She shoves me.

I stumble back in shock. There's more than fury on her face—there's hatred.

"Shut. The. Fuck. Up," Ryan orders. Behind her, two girls are hovering in the entryway to the kitchen, watching us with wide eyes.

"Why should I shut up?" I shout as loud as I can. "Shouldn't everybody know you're cheating on your boyfriend with your teacher?"

She picks up a beer bottle and throws it at me. She has terrible aim, and the bottle crashes onto the floor, breaking. Shards of glass fly all over while beer fizzes everywhere.

A girl in a red dress runs over to Ryan and pulls her back. "Ryan, Ryan," she says soothingly. "Oh my God, stop it. Ryan!"

Ryan throws the girl's hands off her and runs out of the kitchen, and I'm standing in a pool of beer facing two Peebs who look like they just noticed I'm here.

I stare at my alcohol-flushed face in the bathroom mirror while everything spins around me. I lean against the counter, trying to hold on to the slippery granite, and the music is still pounding, and behind me someone pounds on the door, fist against the wood, *thump-thump-thump*, and I don't open the door and eventually they go away, and I keep staring at myself until I stop wanting to throw up, until my heartbeat slows down, until I feel more like I'm swimming through mud than trying not to drown.

THE LEATHER BOX FROM MARGOT'S MOM'S CLOSET IS lying open on the marble kitchen island. I don't know what time it is. The gun glints in the light of the crystal chandelier hanging above. The back door opens, letting in a blast of freezing winter air. It's Angie, and she's not wearing a coat. Her eyes are red, and I can tell she's upset. I move toward her almost involuntarily. All I want to do is make sure that she's okay, and it doesn't even matter that she probably doesn't understand how much she means to me.

It's purer this way. She can take whatever she wants from me, whenever she wants it, because I'm her best friend.

Then Margot comes inside behind her, grabbing her hand. "Please don't go," she says. Angie doesn't pull away. She doesn't even see me.

Everything around me rocks, as if I were on a boat on the ocean. One of Margot's friends pushes past me toward the drinks. Someone rips open a bag of chips, sending them flying across the floor. I move out of the way and bang my toe against a stool, and then I stumble into the edge of the island, and the box is right in front of me. The gun is engraved with leaves and flowers, and it looks like a charm you might wear on a bracelet next to a miniature dagger and a coil of rope.

I reach for it. The metal is cool, and the gun is heavier than I expected. It's pretty. The vines seem to come alive, twining around the grip and the barrel, ending in the small dark muzzle: a silent, open mouth.

Someone says my name.

Ryan lunges toward me from the other side of the island. She screams, "You fucking liar! You tell him it's not true."

Across the kitchen Angie hears Ryan and glances in our direction. Her eyes widen and her lips form my name but I can barely hear her over Ryan's yelling. Angie marches over to me, demanding, "What the hell are you doing with that?" She pulls the gun from my hand. Her fingers are so cold from being outside it's as if they've been dipped in a bucket of ice. They still send an electric jolt all the way through my vodka-induced emotional padding. She gingerly places the gun back in the box as if she'd been handling a snake. "Let's go," she says.

It takes me a second to realize she wants to leave. With me.

As we start to go, Ryan picks up the gun. "I'm not finished," she declares, her finger on the trigger.

Margot grabs her arm, yanking the gun down. "Where did you get this?" she asks, her face white. "This is my mom's."

Angie takes my hand and drags me out of the kitchen and into the cream-on-white living room, where the music is blasting extra loud. A few people are dancing in a circle, drinks in hand. The giant TV above the gas fireplace plays a video on mute in which a black man with dreads and a bloody face walks away from a burning car. Several empty bottles of beer are tipped over on the white fur pelt that serves as the living room rug. There's no head attached, but I have no doubt it came from a bear. The fact that the rug has been decapitated makes it even worse. I'm fixated on the absent head, wondering what happened to it and whether there's some kind of dumping ground for discarded bears' heads. I picture them piled up in a pyramid formation in an abandoned city lot; the colors would be shades of blue and gray, the white heads shadowed, toothy jaws slightly parted.

Angie pulls on her coat, her scarf and gloves, and practically throws mine at me. I fumble with the zipper on my down jacket, tug on my wool hat. We are almost at the front door when Margot comes running after us. She pleads with Angie not to go, and Angie halts with one hand on the doorknob, turning back to look at her.

The two of them, at this moment, would make such a good panel. I could title it "Stay." Margo's hand is outstretched, her arm extended so that the sleeve of her white sweater slides up, exposing the delicate bones of her wrist. The sweater is practically see-through. Beneath it the outline of her black bra is clear, and the waistline of her black leather leggings hugs her flat stomach.

I get why Angie likes her. I don't want to get it, but I do, like a punch to the gut. Margot exudes this attitude that's somewhere between dominatrix and jock, and it should be annoying but for some reason it's not. She makes you feel like you want to please her, and she's turning the full force of that onto Angie now. She won't be able to resist.

Angie's expression is a little wary. She knows she's going to lose this game. Thick brown curls tumble over the flushed apple of her cheek. Her scarf is a slash of crimson around her throat, her coat swinging wide to reveal the arc of her waist. Her hips turn halfway to the door, but her torso twists toward Margot. Even if her legs are taking her away, her heart is bringing her back.

I've sketched Angie countless times, and every time I feel guilty for stripping her naked with my pencil, but that doesn't stop me from doing it again. I've never drawn Margot before, but she's a lot like Angie, physically. They're both tall, and I would start them as a series of oval shapes, their limbs long and graceful as they move toward each other in their dance of apology.

And then there's me, an extra in their drama, sweating in my down coat a few feet away. I'm a pile of bulging circles, half a head shorter than Angie, my thighs like squashed loaves of bread. Angie's always telling me I'm cute, but *cute* is a euphemism for "not sexy."

I turn away so I don't have to see them kiss. I can imagine it just fine on my own.

I fix my blurry gaze on a painting hanging over the side table in the front hall. It's a stroke of gold over indigo blue, the colors so vivid they make me feel light-headed. I take a step closer. The paint is thick, layered onto the canvas as if it had been spread like peanut butter. There are shadows of orange and vermilion beneath the gold, like sunlight sedimented into stone.

Angie and Margot have forgotten about me.

ANGIE'S CAR IS FREEZING COLD, AND SHE CRANKS THE heater up on high, but all I feel is drunk. Everything is a fog, a slurry, and I lurch against the door, my face sliding down the frigid glass, my breath an alcoholic mist.

"You know what's funny?" Angie says.

"What?"

"The reason Margot and I got in a fight is because she thinks I'm cheating on her."

Angie's words don't make sense to me. I can't remember her fighting with Margot, and the idea of Angie cheating on Margot is—"She thinks you're cheating?" I say, bewildered.

"With you."

The world seems to shudder. My insides slosh around as if I'd been liquefied. Despite the cold air still blasting through the vents, I'm dripping with sweat.

"I don't know if she really believes that, or if she's saying it to piss me off," Angie says, her words clipped. "The stupid thing is, she's half right. There is something going on between us, and it's not okay."

Angie's phone tells her to turn, and outside the window the Atlantic surges, the waves crashing against the edge of the road, and I feel as if it's going to swallow us, and maybe that would make Angie stop saying these things.

"I purposely don't mention Margot to you because I know how angry she makes you," Angie continues. "And I purposely don't mention you to Margot because it makes her mad too. Do you know how hard it was to get her to invite you tonight? And you act like I forced you to go there against your will. How do you think that makes me feel?"

My stomach roils. I roll down the window, and the biting winter air screams in. I gulp it down, tasting snow.

"Are you going to be sick?" Angie asks.

I don't answer, because if I open my mouth I don't know what's coming out. I clutch the door handle with clammy hands. The road ahead cuts a line through the dark, and tiny white flakes swirl in the beams of the headlights. I gag on the taste in the back of my throat and lean my head into the frigid wind, welcoming its lash on my flushed face.

Abruptly, Angie veers over to the side of the road, slamming on the brakes. The sudden deceleration causes a hot and nasty liquid to rise up in my throat, and I barely get the door open before I vomit vodka into the gutter. My head spins. I stumble out of the car, bent over, heaving. Snow dusts the edge of the street and strikes my face in tiny pinpricks.

Angie is behind me now, her hand on my back. "Are you okay?" she asks. She rubs my back, and the motion of her hand makes me sick again. "Oh my God, you shouldn't have drunk that much. Jess, are you okay?"

I sit up, blinking in the light of the dashboard. "What—where are we?"

Angie says, "We're almost home. You fell asleep. Or blacked out."

There's a disgusting taste in my mouth. I groan, wiping the back of my hand across my lips. My hand smells like puke and I recoil from my own fingers. "Did I throw up?"

"You don't remember?"

"I—no."

Angie sighs. "Yeah, you threw up. We stopped on the side of the road. You drank way too much."

There's judgment in her voice, and it pierces the fog around me. I shrink back in the seat. My throat hurts.

"Are you okay?" Angie asks.

"Feel like shit," I croak.

"Yeah, I bet."

We drive in silence through the lightly falling snow. As long as I don't move, the world doesn't spin. Angie's phone tells her to turn right, and I realize we're already back in West Bedford.

"I can't believe you," Angie says in a low, bitter voice. "I can't freaking *believe* you."

"What are you talking about?" I ask hoarsely.

I don't remember why she's mad. All I remember is her kissing Margot, and even though I didn't mean to watch, I can still see it as if it were happening right in front of me. White carpet—the house had white carpet. I suddenly remember the sight of cranberry juice splattering all over it, an eruption of color on a blank canvas. There's a weird buzzing in my head, nearly drowning out Angie's voice.

She turns onto her street. One of the houses has an inflatable

Santa on its front lawn, staked into the ground with ropes, but the wind is pummeling it backward, the plastic skin on Santa's face rippling like water. I feel like that Santa.

I see Angie and Margot standing in the foyer, arms around each other, and I'm dizzy, and I press the heel of my hands against my eyes, and I smell the vomit again and gag.

". . . the deal is with you and Ryan?" Angie is saying. "What the hell were you doing? I go into the kitchen and you have a freaking *gun*?"

"Ryan found it. Sh-she found it, not me." My voice sounds funny in my ears, as if I were shouting from the bottom of a well.

"I don't care who found it! You were being crazy tonight. I can't believe what you said."

"I didn't say anything!" I shriek, and Angie flinches. "I didn't say shit—what are you even talking about?"

Angie turns into her house's driveway and pulls the emergency brake, making the car jerk to a stop. "You accused Ryan of cheating on her boyfriend!" Angie cries. "How can you not remember? Ryan's boyfriend was *there*. And even if it's true, how would you know? You're—I don't know what's wrong with you."

She shuts off the car's engine, and the sudden silence makes her last few words sound shockingly loud. My stomach is still churning from the motion of the car, and everything I'm feeling is about to erupt out of my mouth just like the vodka. I try to contain it, I try to stuff it all back down, but I say, "What's wrong with me? What's *wrong* with me?" My voice rises. "What's wrong with me is *you*."

My lungs are heaving, and I really want to throw up again but I swallow the dregs of vodka that rise up in the back of my throat. I choke it back, and it tastes foul.

"You made me come tonight," I say, my words tumbling one over the other. "You ash-asked me to come. You made me promise. You made me. Did you ever think maybe I didn't want to?"

"You didn't have to come if you really didn't want to. You could have said no."

"I can't say no! I can't fucking say no to you!"

I open the door and climb out into the snowy night. I'm nauseated by the motion, and I have to pause for a second, gulping in the cold air, but then I shove the door closed as hard as I can. I start to walk down the driveway.

Angie's door opens and she calls, "Where are you going? You're supposed to stay over tonight."

I stop, turning back. The porch light is on, silhouetting her in the flying snow. "I don't think Margot would like that. Would she? What would you tell her?"

"Stop being a jerk. It's not like that."

"What's it like then? No, wait, don't tell me—I really don't want to know. I don't want to know anything about you and Margot. When are you going to get that? Stop telling me about her. I don't give a shit about her. Every time you tell me about her it makes me want to throw up. Don't you get that?"

She crosses her arms against the cold and comes toward me, but stops several feet away. "Why are you so jealous?"

"Why am I—" Her question makes me laugh hysterically. I'm shaking and laughing and all of a sudden I'm really, really cold, and I say, "Why? Jesus, Angie. Don't act like you don't know."

Angie doesn't move, and I'm shivering so hard it feels like all the liquor is being shaken out of me, and even if I'm crying, I can't tell because my face is half frozen. I turn around to leave and wait for Angie to say my name, to tell me to come back, but she doesn't say a word; and before long I'm at the end of the driveway, and then I'm on the sidewalk, and I'm walking, farther and farther away, and Angie doesn't call me back.

WAKING UP IS LIKE CLAWING MY WAY THROUGH SPIDER-webs. My mouth is dry and sticky at the same time, my tongue thick and swollen, my lips cracked. When I open my eyes, weak gray daylight fills my room. The blinds are open. On the floor beside my bed I see my jeans crumpled next to my shoes. There's an irregular, dark stain on the carpet around them, and the edges of the soles are crusted with dirt.

My head throbs. I reach for my phone, but it's not on the nightstand. I glimpse my coat on the floor just inside the door. I sit up carefully, and I'm not as dizzy as I thought I'd be, so I swing my legs over the side of the bed and walk gingerly toward the coat. My phone is in the pocket, but it's dead.

I go over to my desk and find the phone's charger and plug it in. It takes a minute for the phone to turn on again. I open my messages, but there's nothing new from Angie. I feel a stab of disappointment. I reread her message to me from yesterday before the party: *Should I wear the black or red?* She attached a picture of two dresses spread out on her bed. I sigh, closing the text, and notice a message above it from a number I don't recognize. I open it.

You're such a fucking liar.

It was sent at 2:21 a.m.

My heart thuds. I hesitate, and then I delete it.

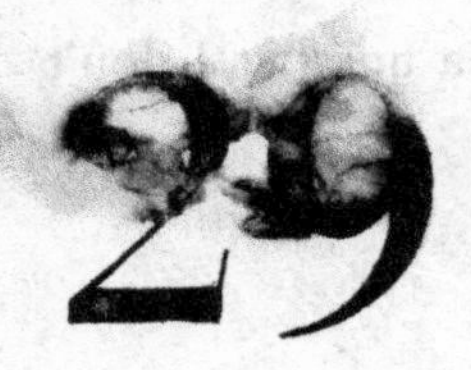

IT'S GOING TO BE A WHITE CHRISTMAS. THE SNOWSTORM from a couple of nights ago was followed by a blizzard that has blanketed Massachusetts under a foot and a half of heavy white flakes, and another storm is coming after this one. The news is a constant stream of weather reports with meteorologists trying to tamp down panic that this is going to be as bad as it was a few years ago, when it snowed almost constantly for over a month and didn't fully melt until June.

I flip through the channels, skipping past soap operas and talk shows and cooking shows. Every once in a while I glance at my phone to make sure I haven't missed Angie's call. A familiar face flashes by on the TV, causing me to backtrack to a local news channel.

"—girl has been reported missing. Police say that Ryan Dupree was last seen on the night of December sixteenth during a party she attended in Marblehead."

The picture of Ryan has to be a yearbook photo, because she's posed in front of a mottled gray backdrop wearing a prim, flowered dress, her blond hair spilling loose over her shoulders, a fake smile on her face.

"Ryan is a junior at Pearson Brooke Academy in East Bedford, but her family lives in Atlanta, Georgia," the newscaster says. "Her parents, who are currently unable to travel to Massachusetts because of the weather, have released a video appealing to their daughter to come home."

My phone rings, making me jump. I grab it, but I don't recognize the number. I toss it on the couch beside me, disappointed.

The news cuts to a video of two adults standing in the sunshine in front of a sprawling brick house. The warm sunlight is at odds with the expression of rising despair on the woman's face as she addresses the camera: "Ryan, if you're out there and you can hear this, please know that we love you and we miss you. Please come home. Whatever caused you to do this, we forgive you. Please come back." The woman's voice cracks, and she presses a hand over her mouth as she tries not to cry. The man puts his arm around her shoulders.

The voice-mail alert dings on my phone. Surprised, I pick up my phone, but I'm distracted by the scene on the news. Now it shows a reporter standing in front of the Pearson Brooke sign, the coat of arms half buried in a snowdrift. "East Bedford police say that Ryan's suitcase is also missing from her dorm room, which suggests she may have run away on her own. School officials are asking anyone who might have seen Ryan Dupree to call them immediately with any information."

When the report ends and the announcer moves on to the weather, I mute the TV and listen to the voice-mail message.

"This is Officer Steve Carroll of the East Bedford Police calling for . . . Jessica Wong. I understand you were at a party with

Ryan Dupree on the evening of December sixteenth. Ryan has not returned home, and I'd like to talk with you about the last time you saw her. Please give me a call back."

Officer Carroll sounds tired, even a bit grumpy. With the TV silenced, the house is unusually quiet. Jamie and Justin are upstairs, and Mom and Dad are still at work. I rub my fingers over the throbbing pulse in my temple. My knee jitters.

As I reach for my phone, it rings again. This time it's Angie.

I KNOW WHAT KESTREL'S ENDGAME IS. IT COMES TO ME IN the middle of the night while I lie awake, sleepless, listening to my sister's even breathing in the bunk bed over my head. When Justin's home, I have to move out of my room—which used to be his room—and back into the room I used to share with Jamie. If I were in my room, I would get up and turn on the light, but I can't do that now.

I have to leave. I slide out of the bottom bunk and grab my sketchbook and pencils from my backpack. I open Jamie's bedroom door quietly and tiptoe into the hall. The floor creaks as I walk past my room; the light's out underneath the door so even Justin must be asleep finally. I pad down the stairs on bare feet and go into the living room, where I turn on one of the lamps beside the sofa. It's chilly down here, and I wrap myself in a blanket. Settling into one corner of the couch, I open my sketchbook and flip to the back, where I've written a list of ideas for the rest of the Kestrel story. I jot my notes down hurriedly, trying to keep hold of that tenuous connection between what I saw in my head and what I'm scribbling with my pencil. When I finish, I read over my notes. I'm really excited by my new idea for the end, but it still feels incomplete. I'm missing something, but I'm not sure what. I flip back through my sketches and examine what I did earlier.

I left off on a scene with Raven and Kestrel together. Kestrel has come to Raven's dorm room to ask her why she's been following her. Raven doesn't want to admit the truth—that she thinks Kestrel is doing too much black magic. In one panel, Raven and Kestrel are face-to-face, eye to eye. I need to figure out what they say to each other, but I've drawn a blank. I've spent a long time sketching these two girls. Raven's in a tank top and pajama pants, her long black hair hanging loose over her bare shoulder. Her mouth is parted as if to speak, but the dialogue bubble over her head remains empty. Kestrel's in jeans and her bird T-shirt, her wavy hair pulled back in a ponytail, one eyebrow arched in expectation.

I could leave the dialogue bubble empty. The thing I want to do—the thing that makes my skin tingle in anticipation—is to draw them kissing. This was never in my original plans for Kestrel, but the more I've worked on the comic, the more it seems to lean in this direction. Kestrel and Raven are drawn to each other and simultaneously repelled by that attraction. They're supposed to be competitors, not girlfriends. And, of course, there's Laney.

She's in the hallway outside the half-open door, watching.

If Kestrel and Raven kiss and Laney sees them, all hell will break loose. Laney won't be able to hide her jealousy from Kestrel anymore. Kestrel will have to face the question of how she really feels about Laney. Their friendship could be ruined. I created these characters, but as I stare at the image I drew in my sketchbook, I realize I don't know how Kestrel feels. She and Raven are a matched pair. They're sexy together, like a real comic book. She and Laney, though, feel unbalanced to me. Laney will always be the odd one out.

Frustrated, I flip to a blank page. I start to sketch Kestrel and Raven walking through the woods, a scene I've already planned out. One of the Warden's jobs is to patrol the grounds around Blackwood Hall School, but because he's been injured recently, he sends Kestrel and Raven out instead. Some students have seen wolves in the woods, and the Warden suspects it's because Kestrel's spell drew supernatural predators to the hollow—a kickback that Kestrel didn't anticipate. On the left panel, I draw Kestrel and Raven walking down the trail, with Raven in the lead, her hair flying out in a black flag behind her. Kestrel follows, her gaze on Raven's back, her forehead furrowed into an expression of distrust. On the right panel, half hidden by tree trunks and shadows, I sketch the suggestion of wolves, teeth bared.

Kestrel and Raven don't know that Laney has followed them. She has also heard about the wolves, and because she can't protect herself with magic the way Kestrel and Raven can, she brings a weapon with her. In a close-up on Laney, I draw her shoulders hunched defensively, her eyes trained on the ground where Kestrel's and Raven's footsteps have left a trail. Normally I think of Laney as a dorky sidekick, but as I shade in her shock of short hair, I begin to see her differently. She's stocky but powerful, and she may not be gifted with whatever magical talents Kestrel and Raven have, but she isn't stupid either.

I put a gun in Laney's hand.

ON NEW YEAR'S EVE, ANGIE COMES OVER TO WAIT FOR the ball to drop on TV. This is the third New Year's Eve we've spent together, but I was surprised she wanted to do it this year. Jamie's at a sleepover at a friend's house, Justin went out with some girl he insists is not his girlfriend, and my parents went to bed at ten o'clock, so it's only me and Angie on the couch. We make hot fudge sundaes with cherries, but Angie eats barely a third of hers.

"Is something wrong with it?" I ask.

"Sorry, I'm just not that into it. I keep thinking about . . ." She pulls out her phone, but there are no new messages. "Sorry."

"It's okay. How's Margot?"

"She's fine. She had to go to some party with her parents in New York."

"Is she there?" I point at the screen full of revelers wrapped in scarves and hats, screaming up at the lights of Times Square.

"No. She texted me a picture. She's inside somewhere. It looks like a ballroom or something." Angie holds out her phone and shows me a selfie of Margot blowing a kiss at the camera. Behind her is a huge room hung with chandeliers and holly garlands, full of old people in suits and fancy dresses holding champagne flutes.

"Looks boring."

"Yeah." Angie takes her phone back but doesn't put it away.

We watch TV in silence. I keep an eye on the countdown clock, wondering what will happen at midnight. Angie's only a few inches away from me. She has taken off her shoes, curling her legs up on the couch. If I scoot toward her the smallest bit, we'll be touching.

At three minutes till midnight her phone rings. It's Margot on FaceTime. It looks like she's standing in a closet, because there's a rack of coats behind her.

"Hey!" Angie says, sitting up straight as she answers. "I was thinking about you."

"Hi," Margot says, smiling tightly. "Hi, Jess."

Angie glances at me. "Sorry, I'll be right back." She gets up and takes the phone into the kitchen, leaving me alone.

I watch the ball drop by myself. I hear the low murmur of Angie's voice in the next room, and Margot's tinny response. I gaze at the brown murk of Angie's sundae on the coffee table. I want to throw it against the wall and see the liquid drip down like shit onto the matching carpet.

When she returns, the phone is in her pocket. It's eight minutes into the New Year. I'm staring fixedly at the TV, where they've switched to Key West to show the drag queen dropping in her shoe. Angie sits down next to me, curling her legs up again. Then she lowers her head onto my lap, stretching out.

I freeze. She snuggles into me like a cat, oblivious to the shock that paralyzes me.

"I'm so tired," she murmurs. "I just want to go to sleep right here."

Her hair is spread over my legs, her cheek on my thigh. I gingerly touch her upper arm. The wool of her sweater is soft under my hand. "You okay?"

She takes a deep breath, relaxing against me. "Happy New Year, Jess."

SINCE OUR HOUSE IS ONE OVER FROM THE DEAD END where Ellicott Park cuts off the block, I have a clear view from the living room window of the two cop cars parked with their rear ends angled into the street. One guy in uniform stands outside the car on the left, talking into the radio on his shoulder. His breath steams out into the frigid air as he turns his head, eyeing the neighborhood. Dirty snow is piled everywhere, practically turning the sidewalks into tunnels. Standing a short distance away is a jogger wearing neon-orange running shoes and a thermal jacket marked with reflective stripes. He has a black dog on a leash, who keeps sniffing around the cop.

A gray sedan streaked with slush and dried mud drives past my house and parks behind the police cars. A guy in a charcoal wool overcoat climbs out of the passenger seat, and then an older woman wearing a knee-length blue down jacket gets out of the driver's side. He looks like he's going out to some fancy dinner, and she looks like somebody's mom. Neither of them is wearing a uniform, but the cop goes to meet them and acts like they're in charge. The jogger hovers nearby while his dog approaches the guy in the overcoat, who squats down to pet him.

Another vehicle pulls up behind the gray sedan: a white van with block lettering on the side that reads MEDICAL EXAMINER. The guy in the overcoat goes to meet the driver of the van, and as he walks he glances toward our house. I back away from the window, but I think he sees me.

The young guy in the overcoat is Lieutenant Kyle Griffin, and the older woman in the mom-issue parka is his partner, Detective Lieutenant Donna Cardoni. They rang the doorbell midway through dinner, and after Dad let them in, he made Jamie go up to her room while the rest of us—Mom, Dad, Justin, and me—squeezed onto the living room sofa, sitting across from the two detectives.

Griffin has a face straight out of the Boston suburbs: slightly asymmetrical with a crooked mouth and a dimpled chin; close-cropped brown hair that was probably redder when he was a kid; blue eyes. He could've been the older brother of any number of Irish-surnamed kids at my school. It takes me a while to realize that although he looks like he was born five miles from here, he doesn't have a Boston accent. Cardoni does, and she sounds uncannily like Angie's mom. She even looks a little like her: the pudgy chin; that tired look in her eyes; the ugly coat; and thick-soled shoes.

"We're sorry to interrupt your dinner," Cardoni says. "As you may have seen from the police vehicles across the street, we've been investigating a situation in Ellicott Park. Earlier today a jogger and his dog discovered the body of a young woman in the woods. We believe she may have been there for as long as two weeks, since right before the first big snowstorm that hit before Christmas."

Mom tensed up when Cardoni said the word *body*, and now she puts her hand on Justin's arm as if to assure herself the body isn't his. She asks, "What happened?"

Cardoni says, "We're not certain yet, ma'am, but we're investigating this as a homicide."

Mom gasps. "Is it safe here?"

"I understand your concern, ma'am. This is a very unusual discovery, so I think you and your children are safe, but I would understand if you want to take precautions, particularly for your youngest upstairs. Maybe don't allow her to play outside unsupervised for a little while."

"Do you know who died?" Dad asks.

Cardoni's gaze flickers in my direction. "We have some leads, but right now the victim is still unidentified. I can tell you the victim is a teenage girl."

"Is she from here?" Mom asks.

"We're not sure," Cardoni says. "We've only begun to investigate. One thing that would really help us is to get all of your contact information. We're talking to all your neighbors—everyone in the neighborhood—to ask about what they've seen and heard in the past few weeks around here. Since you folks live right across the street, anything you remember might turn out to be very useful." Cardoni looks at my father. "Can we start with you, sir? What's your name?"

"Of course," he says. "Anything to help. My name is Peter Wong."

"And what's your occupation, Mr. Wong?"

"I'm a pharmacist. At Walgreens."

As my dad speaks, I notice that he has a grain of rice stuck to his chin, probably from dinner. The sight of it makes me redden in embarrassment, and I look down to hide my face. The blue velvet-like fabric of the sofa has faded and thinned on the armrest next to me, leaving a lighter-blue bald patch where elbows have rubbed it for as long as I can remember. I put my arm on the armrest in an effort to hide the bald patch, but once I notice it, I can't stop noticing everything else about our living room that screams *cheap*. The living room carpet is regularly cleaned, but that can't disguise the fact that it's an ugly shade of shit brown. The coffee table that divides us from the detectives—who are sitting in mismatched plaid armchairs Mom found at a garage sale—has a wood veneer that's peeling up at one corner. The only new thing in the room is the TV, and in the context of the rest of the house, it looks completely out of place. Dad got up before dawn on Black Friday to fight his way through holiday shoppers at the mall to get it. At night he and Mom watch Chinese TV on it, piped in through an internet streaming box that Uncle Dennis brought back from China.

I hear Mom tell them her name and occupation—Esther Wong, medical assistant—and her accent, always more apparent than my dad's, seems unusually strong tonight as she overexplains her work hours, her commute, and when she's at home. It's obvious that she's freaked out by the detectives, but she still wants to make a good impression by answering every question in as much detail as possible. She's trying too hard, like she often does, overcompensating for her accent and for not entirely understanding how things work here. Like when we had a bake sale in elementary school, and everybody else's mom brought cookies and cakes, but my mom brought fried rice. Or how when she learned some kids gave their teachers gifts at the holidays, she showed up with a tacky box of Ferrero Rocher from Walgreens—sale sticker still attached—rather than a gift card to Target.

When the detectives move on to questioning my brother, I'm relieved.

"I'm a sophomore at MIT," my brother says in response to Cardoni's question.

"He's going to be an aerospace engineer," Dad says proudly.

"He's very smart," Mom adds, patting him on the knee while he stiffens. "Full scholarship!"

Cardoni looks suitably impressed, asking Justin, "Are you home for the holidays?"

He looks uncomfortable. "Yeah. I got home a few days before Christmas." He's gotten thinner over the past semester, and I wonder how hard he's working to maintain his grades. Mom and Dad might praise him in front of strangers, but at home, they constantly push him to do better.

"Do you happen to remember the date you returned?" Cardoni asks.

"The . . . twenty-first, I think. Yeah. I remember the roads were still pretty bad after that first blizzard."

"Thank you." Cardoni finally looks at me, her expression bland but expectant. "And what's your name, dear?"

"Jessica Wong. I'm a junior at West Bedford High."

"How old are you?"

"Sixteen."

"You're about the same age as the victim, we think," Cardoni says. "Have you heard of any of your friends or classmates going missing lately?"

Both detectives look at me now, and I drop my gaze to the floor. The detectives are still wearing their shoes, even though they left slush stains on the carpet. My parents only allow important white people to get away with that in our house. I answer, "Yeah, I've heard."

"You have?" Mom says, startled.

"What have you heard?" Cardoni asks.

I rub my palms over my jeans, and then I tuck my hands under my thighs to prevent them from moving. "Just that—that this girl from Pearson Brooke disappeared. People are looking for her."

"How did you hear about the girl?" Cardoni asks.

"Um, on the news. It was before Christmas."

Cardoni nods. "Do you remember anything else about this girl? Her name?"

I hesitate. I look up at Cardoni, whose face is blank. "Ryan," I say. "Her name is Ryan Dupree. I talked to someone about this before—a police officer from East Bedford."

Griffin begins to flip back through his notes.

Mom says in surprise, "You talked to a police officer? Why didn't you tell us?"

"It wasn't a big deal," I say. "He was just asking if I knew where she went. I didn't."

Cardoni glances at Griffin, who is now scrolling quickly through something on his phone. Cardoni frowns.

"Why would a police officer ask you?" Mom demands. "How do you know this girl?"

"I don't, not really," I say. "We weren't friends or anything. I just know her from Brooke. You know, that arts program."

Mom sighs in relief. "Oh, that program."

"What program?" Cardoni asks.

Griffin puts down his phone and returns his attention to me. He seems a little frustrated.

"She does an art program at Pearson Brooke," Dad explains, also looking relieved. "Jessica draws pictures."

"Her teacher thinks she is very talented," Mom says. "She makes very colorful pictures of monsters and superheroes. Like Superman?" She sounds almost apologetic.

I shrink back into the couch.

"It's free—the arts program," Dad adds. "It's good for her to have some exposure to—to connections at that school, for college."

Cardoni smiles at me while Griffin writes something down. "That's wonderful that you're an artist," she says.

"She's really good," Justin says quietly.

I glance at him in surprise, but he doesn't acknowledge me.

Griffin, who has been silent since he first introduced himself, finally speaks up. "You're pretty close to the park here. I bet it's a good place to hang out with your friends. When I was your age that's the kind of stuff we'd do for fun, you know? Chill out, party a little. Do you or your friends ever do that?"

Dad says immediately, "Jessica wouldn't know. She doesn't go into the park."

"Jessica is a good girl and isn't friends with kids who do that," Mom insists. "She studies at home. Does her—her art."

I wince. Cardoni is looking at Mom, but I'm sure she noticed my reaction. "Of course," the detective says. Griffin opens his mouth, but before he can speak Cardoni continues, "Thank you for taking the time to talk to us tonight. You've been very helpful, and I just have one more question before we go. Have any of you been in Ellicott Park in the last two weeks?"

"No," Dad says dismissively. "It's too cold to go to the park. None of us have gone to the park."

"I think so too, sir," Cardoni says. "But I have to ask each one of you to speak for yourselves."

Mom shakes her head decisively. "No. I haven't gone to the park."

Justin says, "No." He cracks a smile at her and adds, "Plus, I hate nature."

Everybody laughs nervously, and then it's my turn. "No, I haven't been in the park." My knee is bouncing, and I force it to stop moving.

Cardoni reaches into her pocket and pulls out a business card, placing it on the scratched coffee table between us. She turns it around to face me, looking at me directly while she says, "This is my card. If you think of anything that might be of help, you give me a call or a text, okay? Anytime."

"We will, Detective," Dad says.

Cardoni holds my gaze for another moment, then stands up. She turns to my parents. "Thank you for your time. We appreciate it."

Mom nods vigorously. "Of course, anything we can do to help."

Cardoni gives me one last glance. "Anything at all—it doesn't have to be big. Sometimes we see things that don't seem important at all, but it's not your job to determine if it's important. That's what we're for."

I LIE AWAKE LISTENING TO JAMIE'S BREATHING. SHE TOOK the news about the body in the woods pretty well, but Mom made it sound like no big deal. "Somebody died in the park," she said, "so the police had to do some work there today. You stay away from the park."

Jamie went to sleep without a problem, but I can't stop thinking about it. I want to know how the jogger found her. Did his dog smell it? Had some of the snow melted? What had the jogger seen first? A hand, fingers blue from the cold. Her hair, long strands like wet straw trampled in the snow. Maybe her necklace catching the light.

I picture the girl on the ground, her body weighting down layers of damp, dead leaves as the snow falls in soft heavy flakes over her, covering her mouth, her eyes, drifting into her nostrils. If that jogger hadn't found her today, she might have lain there beneath the drifts until spring came, undiscovered, frost spreading across her skin in blue veins, her lips turning purple. When spring finally arrived, the snowmelt would soak through her dress and dampen her hair, making her look as if she'd drowned, and the water would run down her cheeks like tears.

THE FIRST DAY BACK AT SCHOOL, EVERYONE'S TALKING about the body in the park. Some people think she was a prostitute; others think she must have been a junkie. Nobody asks for my opinion, so I don't mention that the cops came to my house.

After school I meet Angie at her locker and wait while she packs up her stuff. She's wearing a blue cable-knit sweater that I remember from last winter, cords, and waterproof boots. Her hair is pulled back in a simple ponytail, and the only makeup she has on is lip gloss. She looks like my friend again.

We leave school together without saying anything, but before we're out of the parking lot, a car honks behind us.

Margot.

As the Mini pulls up beside us, she unrolls the passenger side window and leans toward it. "Angie, is your phone dead?"

Angie looks puzzled. "You tried—oh, I turned it off during last period. Sorry, I forgot to turn it on again."

Margot briefly scowls. "Well, I have to talk to you. Do you want a ride home?"

Angie glances at me, causing Margot to look at me too.

"Hey, Jess," Margot says shortly.

"Hey," I answer.

"Sure, we'll take a ride," Angie says. "Jess is coming over."

Margot doesn't look pleased. I smile at her, which makes her look even more irritated.

Angie opens the car door and flips up the front seat so I can climb in the back. I take off my backpack and slide it in, then crawl into the small space. Margot's messenger bag is on the floor behind her seat. It looks a lot like the bag in the park that's stuffed with Ryan's love letters. Once Angie climbs in and shuts the door, Margot pulls into the street with a rough jerk of the wheel. I'm thrown to one side and scramble to find the seat belt.

"What's going on?" Angie asks. "Is something wrong?"

Margot accelerates down the quiet street, and I dig my fingers into the edge of the leather seat to hold on.

"It's all over the news," Margot says tersely. "You didn't see?"

"No, I—I didn't see."

Margot reaches for Angie's hand, and their fingers intertwine, resting on Angie's leg. I look outside as the wind knocks over a wooden reindeer, one of its thin cable tethers whipping through the air.

"Ryan's parents arrived today to identify the body," Margot says.

"Oh my God." Angie sounds subdued. "This is . . . I feel so bad for them. Are you . . . How are you doing?"

Margot's jaw tenses. "I don't know." She turns into Angie's driveway and leaves the engine running. "I need to talk to you," she says to Angie. Her eyes flicker back to me. "Alone."

"Sure, of course," Angie says. She opens the door and climbs out. "Jess, why don't you go inside? I'll be there in a minute." She offers me the keys to the front door.

I climb out of the Mini and take Angie's keys. Margot gives me a cool look. "Thanks for the ride," I tell her.

Angie gets back in the car and shuts the door, turning to face Margot. I swallow the anger that rushes through me and head up the path to Angie's front door, sliding the key into the lock with clumsy fingers. The house is silent and feels empty. I drop the keys on the hall table and go upstairs to Angie's room. Her laptop is on her bed. I grab it and sit down on the floor, then open the computer and click on the internet. It doesn't take long to find it. The *Boston Globe* has a story titled, PEARSON BROOKE STUDENT, 16, FOUND DEAD IN EAST BEDFORD WOODS. It's accompanied by the same yearbook photo the news showed when Ryan was missing, her face frozen permanently in that fake smile.

> EAST BEDFORD—The body of a teen girl that was discovered by a jogger and his dog in Ellicott Park, a wooded area between West Bedford and East Bedford in Essex County, on January 2, has been identified. She was Ryan Dupree, a 16-year-old boarding student at Pearson Brooke Academy. The death is being investigated as a homicide, according to a statement released by the Essex County District Attorney. The cause of death has not yet been verified.
>
> Originally from Atlanta, Dupree was reported missing on December 17 after she failed to check into her flight home for the holidays. Dupree was initially presumed to be a runaway, because her luggage was missing from her dorm room and friends reported her as being upset the last time they saw her.
>
> Pearson Brooke Academy issued a statement early

> **Wednesday morning, describing Dupree as "a bright and dedicated student, a valued member of the girls' field hockey team, and a star on our Model UN." A hotline for tips relating to Dupree's disappearance and death has been established and police urge anyone with information to contact them.**

There are several other stories online, but very little additional information. Someone has already set up a Facebook memorial page for Ryan. Reading strangers' theories about how they think she was killed is like sinking slowly into quicksand, but I can't stop myself. *I heard she was strangled. No, she was raped. She was raped and strangled.* A couple of commenters are quick to link her death to the murders of other girls in New England over the past couple of years—a prostitute, a meth addict, a homeless teen—who were also found in wooded areas.

When Angie enters the room, I look up guiltily. Her eyes are red, as if she's been crying. She sits down on the floor beside me and leans her head on my shoulder.

I hold my breath. She stays.

I extricate my arm from between us and slide it around her. She shudders, inhaling deeply. I tentatively stroke her shoulder. She begins to cry, softly at first, but then the sobs seem to overflow out of her, making her body shake. I put both my arms around her and hold her, and her hair smells like her new peach shampoo and she's warm and trembling, her face wet against my neck.

"I'm sorry," she mutters between sobs. "I'm sorry."

"It's okay." I feel like I've been given a gift that I've wanted for years, but now that I have it, it's nothing like I expected. Angie's not supposed to be crying when I hold her.

She reaches for the box of tissues on her nightstand and pulls out a bunch of them, wadding them up to wipe off her face. Her laptop has slid to the floor, and as I pick it up to move it out of the way, she stops me. "Wait," she says. "Let me see that."

It's still open to the Facebook memorial page. "You shouldn't read that," I warn her, but she grabs her computer and settles it onto her lap. I watch as she scans the page, then scrolls to read more of the comments. Her puffy eyes widen. I see the screen reflected in her irises.

She closes Facebook deliberately. She blows her nose and throws the tissues toward the trash bin by her desk. They miss and land on the floor. She pulls her knees up, wrapping her arms around them. "Margot says they canceled school today at Brooke and brought in all these counselors to talk to people. She says the police will be there tomorrow to interview all of Ryan's friends."

"Really?" I want to reach out to Angie, to touch her again, but she's holding herself close now, shutting me out.

"She says the police will want to talk to us too," Angie says. "They want to talk to everyone who was at the party."

"But I've already talked to them."

"I know, but we have to talk to them again. Margot says the detectives are going to call our parents tonight. They're doing all the interviews at Brooke because most of Ryan's friends are there, and probably because none of the Brooke parents want their kids to go to the police station. So they think it's easier if we just go there too."

I rub my hand over the back of my neck. "When are we supposed to go there?"

Angie looks drained. "I don't know. They're calling our parents. You know what that means."

"What?"

She gazes down at her knees with an expression that is part despair, part anger. "It means I have to tell my parents I lied about where we went. And when they ask why, I have to tell them I've been lying to them for years. I have to tell them about Margot."

THE CALL COMES WHILE MOM IS MAKING DINNER. I HEAR the phone ring from the living room, where I'm doing my homework on the couch. She answers the phone, then turns off the vent hood over the stove. There's a long silence. Dad asks her what's going on, and she says, "It's the police," and then my dad seems to take the phone from her because he says, "Hello? This is Peter Wong."

I put down my pencil and stop pretending like I'm doing math. I hunch over and listen to my dad's side of the conversation.

"What did she do?" he asks. "A party? When?"

A pause. Someone pulls out a chair, scraping it over the floor.

"This is just for information? What time?"

I check my phone, but there's no message from Angie. I wonder if the police called her parents before mine.

"All right. Tomorrow at one. Yes, she will be there."

My mom exclaims in Chinese, "What happened? Why do they want to talk to her? They already talked to her!"

"They have new questions," my dad answers. I hear his

footsteps across the kitchen floor, and a moment later they become muffled on the living room carpet. "Jessica," he says.

He stands in the doorway with my mom hovering beside him. She looks scared; he looks confused. "Yeah?" I say.

"The police called," Dad says. "They want to interview you tomorrow because they say you knew the girl who was in the park. They say you were at a party with her the night she disappeared."

"You told us you didn't know her," Mom says, bewildered.

"I barely knew her," I say.

"You lied to us," Mom says. "Where was this party?"

"We—Angie and I went to a party at Margot's house."

"Who is Margot?" Dad asks.

"She's a friend of Angie's. She goes to Pearson Brooke."

"A friend of Angie's," Mom mutters. "I told you, Angie is a bad influence on you. She makes you lie to your parents—"

"Angie didn't make me lie! I lied on my own, okay?" My face is hot now, and in the corner of my eye I see Jamie coming down the stairs.

"What's going on?" she asks in a small voice.

"Go back to your room," Dad orders her.

Her face turns white, and she runs back upstairs.

Dad lets out a long sigh. He rubs a hand through his hair and says, "Jessica, you can't lie like this. You can't lie to us."

"You're grounded," Mom says curtly. "No more going to Angie's house."

"Mom—"

"She's a bad influence on you," Mom insists. "She makes you do things. You are like a servant for her, not like a friend! Every time she calls you, you go and do what she wants."

"That's not true—"

"You think I don't see?" Mom continues. "I see the way you act with her. I see every time. Jessica, you—you are my daughter. I want you to be happy. If you are lesbian, it's okay. But you don't lie to your parents. You don't let your friend control you like that. You have to tell the truth."

I can't breathe. Mom is looking at me like I'm someone to pity.

"Tomorrow I will take you to the interview," Dad says.

"I can go by myself," I choke out.

"No," Dad says, and for the first time he looks like he might explode. I shrink back into the couch. "I will take you," he says again. "I will be there. You will tell the police the truth. No more lying."

PART TWO

TRANSCRIPT OF INTERVIEW OF MARGOT ADAMS

<u>Present:</u>

DC: Detective Lieutenant Donna Cardoni, Massachusetts State Police

KG: Lieutenant Kyle Griffin, Massachusetts State Police

NS: Neera Singh, Pearson Brooke Academy Dean of Students

MA: Margot Adams, witness

Det. Lt. Donna Cardoni (DC): Today is Thursday, January 5, and we are at Pearson Brooke Academy, in Rice Hall. The time is 9:03 a.m. I am Detective Lieutenant Donna Cardoni of the Massachusetts State Police, assigned to the Essex County District Attorney's Office. Also in the room is my partner—please state your name.

Lt. Kyle Griffin (KG): Lieutenant Kyle Griffin, also with the Massachusetts State Police.

DC: We are joined by a representative of Pearson Brooke

Academy, who will be observing. Please state your name and spell it for the record.

Neera Singh (NS): Neera Singh, Dean of Students. N-E-E-R-A S-I-N-G-H.

DC: We are interviewing—could you please state your name for the recording?

Margot Adams (MA): Margot Adams. That's Margot with a t—M-A-R-G-O-T. Adams, A-D-A-M-S.

DC: Thank you. Please tell us who you are, Margot.

MA: I'm a student at Pearson Brooke. I'm a junior.

DC: Thank you. For the record, this interview is entirely voluntary, and if you choose to end this interview at any time you may do so. This interview is being recorded. You're nodding. Please remember this is an audio recording, so all your answers must be spoken aloud. Is everything I've said okay with you?

MA: Yes.

DC: Okay. Let's begin by addressing your relationship with Ryan Dupree. How did you know her?

MA: She was my friend.

DC: How did you two meet?

MA: First year at Brooke. She was on the same floor of my dorm.

DC: Part of the goal of these interviews today is to get a better idea of who Ryan was as a person. Can you tell us about Ryan? What was she like?

MA: She . . . she was . . . [inaudible]

DC: I understand this must be hard for you. Take your time.

MA: She was . . . a really good friend. She was loyal. She supported me through everything.

DC: How would you describe Ryan?

MA: Um . . . opinionated? It's so weird to—to try to summarize her personality. She just always had an opinion. She wasn't scared to say what she was thinking. I guess some people weren't comfortable with that, but I thought it was . . . I always knew where I stood with her. I liked that.

DC: I know you two were close. Did you and Ryan have other close friends?

MA: Sure. But Ryan was . . . We were best friends.

DC: When I was a teen, my best friend and I knew everything about each other. You must have shared a lot of secrets with Ryan.

MA: Yeah.

DC: Can you think of any of your friends who might have been angry with her for any reason?

MA: [inaudible] I don't know.

DC: Why don't you tell me about your other friends. Did you have a group you'd, for example, eat lunch with every day?

MA: Yeah.

DC: And who were they?

MA: Well, there's Noah, Ryan's boyfriend. And his friend Jacob, and Jacob's girlfriend, Krista. Plus Li-Hua and Brian and Ayesha.

DC: Tell me more about Noah. When did he and Ryan start dating?

MA: Last spring. They got together in April.

DC: Did they get along? Sometimes relationships can be stormy when you're a teen.

MA: Of course they got along. He wouldn't have killed

her! Even if they got in a fight, he's not that kind of guy. He's not violent.

DC: I'm not saying he is. I'm just trying to get an idea of who the people were in Ryan's life.

MA: I know people say the boyfriend is always the number one suspect, but he couldn't be a suspect. He would never hurt Ryan.

DC: Okay. Tell me more about these other friends you mentioned—Jacob, Krista?

MA: Jacob is Noah's best friend. What do you want to know about him? He's just a normal guy.

DC: He isn't close to Ryan?

MA: No. She thought he was kind of an idiot.

DC: Did he know that?

MA: I don't know.

DC: What about Krista and the other girls?

MA: What about them?

DC: How close were they to Ryan?

MA: We were all friends. But none of them knew Ryan as well as I did.

DC: Did Ryan have any enemies?

MA: [inaudible]

DC: Can you repeat that?

MA: I said I don't know. If other people were jealous of her, it was their problem. She didn't do anything to them.

DC: Who do you think was jealous?

MA: Maybe Ayesha. She had a crush on Noah last year. I think they went to the winter formal together, but then he started dating Ryan.

DC: But you all still hung out together?

MA: Yeah.

DC: Would Ayesha do that if she was still jealous?

MA: You'll have to ask her.

DC: Okay. Are there any other friends you think we should know about? People from Ryan's life we should talk to?

MA: I don't think so.

DC: When you talked with the East Bedford police back in December, you told them that the last time you saw Ryan was at a party at your parents' house in Marblehead. Were all these friends at the party?

MA: Yeah.

DC: Looking at the notes from that interview, I see that there were nine people at the party besides yourself. Ryan, Noah, Krista, Jacob, Ayesha, Brian, Li-Hua, Angie, and Jess. You didn't mention Angie and Jess when I asked about your friend group. Why were they invited?

MA: Angie's my girlfriend. Jess is Angie's friend, and Angie made me invite her.

DC: She made you. Why?

MA: She really wanted Jess to come. Probably because she hadn't met most of my friends and didn't want to be alone.

DC: It sounds like you didn't want to invite Jess.

MA: I—well, I feel like Jess has a crush on Angie. So, no, I didn't want to invite my girlfriend's friend who has a crush on her.

DC: Sounds uncomfortable.

MA: What does this have to do with Ryan?

DC: Did Ryan know Angie and Jess?

MA: Of course. She knew I was dating Angie. She's met them both. I mean, she met them both before.

DC: Okay. What I'm trying to do is reconstruct the last time you saw Ryan, and that involves thinking back to the feelings you had at the time, as well as sort of mentally walking through the place where you last saw her. Why don't we talk about that first. Tell me about the house where you had the party. Can you describe it for me?

MA: You'll see for yourself when you go look at it. My stepdad told me you're going to search it.

DC: Well, we'd like to get your perspective on it too.

MA: What do you want to know? It's my family's beach house. It's in Marblehead. We don't usually go there in the winter because it's too cold. My mom and stepdad bought it four years ago right after they got married. My mom hired an interior decorator who did everything in white. White furniture, white carpets, everything. My brother thought it looked ridiculous but he hates our stepdad so he blamed our stepdad for our mom's weird white fetish.

DC: Where's your brother now? Is he at Brooke with you?

MA: No, he's in college. NYU.

DC: You were saying that you don't use the house in the winter very often. If that's the case, why did you decide to have your party there?

MA: Um, because it's empty.

DC: Your parents weren't at the party?

MA: No.

DC: Were there any adults present at the party?

MA: No.

NS: [inaudible]

KG: Ms. Singh, did you want to add something?

NS: Yes, yes, I didn't know—Pearson Brooke did not know that there were no adults present at that party. We granted permission for students to stay overnight based on our belief that there would be adults present. Margot's mother emailed us.

DC: All right, Ms. Singh, thank you for that. I'm sure that's something you're concerned about, but right now we are focusing on Margot's experiences. You're welcome to follow up on that on your own time. For the record, Ms. Singh is nodding. Margot, you were saying no adults were present at the party. Did your parents know you were going to have a party at their house?

MA: Um, yeah. My mom emailed the school, like Ms. Singh said.

DC: Okay. She wasn't concerned about you and your friends being out there alone?

MA: No, why would she be? It's Marblehead. Nothing ever happens there. We're not kids.

DC: All right. Let's move on to the party itself. Can you walk us through what happened? Start from the beginning—or even before the party started—and what you and Ryan did that night.

MA: Ryan and I got there early to set up, around five o'clock. We had to stop at the store on the way to buy stuff—soda, chips, snacks, you know.

DC: What store did you go to?

MA: Um, Whole Foods. Why?

DC: I'm looking for details, no matter how small.

Sometimes they can jog your memory. So please tell us about everything you remember, even if you think it's irrelevant. So you went to Whole Foods. What then?

MA: We got to the house, we put out the snacks. We got sushi at Whole Foods for ourselves and we ate that for dinner before anyone else got there. We prepped the bedrooms, because some of our friends were staying overnight.

DC: Who was planning on staying overnight?

MA: Everyone except Angie and Jess. All the Brookies had to stay overnight because we can't be out past curfew unless it's a parent-sanctioned overnight event.

KG: Everything okay, Ms. Singh? You look like you want to say something.

NS: [inaudible] I'm fine.

DC: Margot, when did your friends start to arrive?

MA: Around eight.

DC: And what happened after that?

MA: We . . . we partied.

DC: What do you mean by "partied"?

MA: Haven't you ever been to a party, Detective?

DC: Not since my youth. Humor me.

MA: We played music. We danced. We ate chips. We talked. A variety of board games were available.

DC: Sounds very wholesome.

MA: We're Pearson Brooke students, not gangsters.

DC: Was there drinking?

MA: Yeah, some.

DC: Did anybody become intoxicated?

MA: I can't remember. Maybe.

DC: And what about Ryan?

MA: What about her?

DC: Did she drink?

MA: A little.

KG: I don't want you to feel like we're out to get you, Margot. Everybody drinks when they're a teen, even if adults like to pretend it doesn't happen. It's okay, nobody's going to penalize you for being normal. We're just trying to put together a three-dimensional picture of what was happening the last night that Ryan was seen. Can you say more about the party? Maybe we should back up a little. Let's go back to when your friends arrived. What was it like?

MA: Um, Noah arrived with Jacob and Krista first. I think Ryan let them in, because I was still in the kitchen putting out the food. Brian and Ayesha and Li-Hua got there a little bit afterward. They brought beer with them.

KG: What was the mood like?

MA: The mood? I guess it was happy, positive. The semester was over, most people were going home the next day, so this was a chance to have some fun. [inaudible] It wasn't supposed to turn out like this.

KG: Of course not. When did Angie and Jess arrive?

MA: Not that much later.

KG: What happened when they arrived?

MA: I introduced Angie to my friends. They all thought she was great—she is great. We hung out in the living room, we talked. Normal stuff.

KG: What about Jess? Did she join you?

MA: I think so, at first anyway. After a while she went somewhere. I don't know what happened to her. I was—I was pretty much focusing on Angie.

KG: Sure. You were having a good time.

MA: Yeah.

KG: How did you meet Angie?

MA: At the Creamery. It's this ice-cream shop in East Bedford? She works there. I saw her there last spring, and this fall when I came back to school, she was still working there. I thought she was cute. I asked her out. I don't know why you're asking about Angie, though. She didn't even really know Ryan. She goes to West Bedford High, not Brooke. Besides, we spent most of the night upstairs in my room. We missed most of what was going on downstairs.

KG: About how long were you upstairs?

MA: I don't know. A while. An hour or two, maybe. Are you going to ask what we were doing?

KG: Playing cards?

MA: Right. I won.

DC: When you went back downstairs, what was going on?

MA: People were still partying.

DC: How about Ryan? What was she doing?

MA: I don't remember. Probably she was hanging out with Noah. Didn't you already talk to him? He probably has a better idea than I do.

DC: Yes, we've talked to him. You know, looking back on my notes, he says that Ryan got into an argument with Jess at the party.

MA: Oh. Yeah, I think that's true.

DC: Do you remember anything about it?

MA: I wasn't there at the time. I heard about it later.

DC: What did you hear?

MA: Just that Jess said some stuff that really pissed Ryan off. Obviously I never got a chance to ask Ryan about it. I think Jess is kind of a jerk, honestly.

DC: Why?

MA: She's obsessed with Angie, so she hates me and all of my friends. For a while she was practically stalking Angie. Angie was so upset about it. I can't believe they're still friends.

DC: How do you think Jess felt about Ryan?

MA: I just said she hates me and all of my friends, including Ryan. I remember now, they said Jess accused Ryan of cheating on Noah. I don't know why Jess would say that. She doesn't know any of my friends. She doesn't even go to— Well, she's in the Brooke Arts Exchange Program, actually.

DC: What's that?

MA: It's this program for lower-income students. They come to Brooke to take art classes. Jess is one of them.

DC: Do you think she might have learned something about Ryan while she was at the arts program? Something that would make her think Ryan was cheating on her boyfriend?

MA: I guess it's possible. I've seen Jess at Brooke with this girl Emily Soon. Emily's a Brookie. Emily definitely does not like Ryan.

DC: Why not?

MA: There was a lot of drama between them last year. Emily was a sophomore transfer student, and when she got here, she became friends with Ryan and me. We thought Emily was great, until she started being a bitch about stuff.

DC: What stuff?

MA: She started being judgmental about who I was dating, and I thought maybe she was homophobic, but it turns out she had a crush on me and was really jealous. Total internalized homophobia. Ryan called her out on it, and they got in a huge fight. I'm pretty sure Emily's been holding a grudge ever since. You should talk to her.

DC: Good idea. Thanks. Let's get back to the party, though. You say you heard that Jess and Ryan had an argument. What happened afterward?

MA: Well, Jess and Angie left.

DC: When?

MA: Around midnight. I remember because Angie had to get home before one a.m.

DC: What did you do after she left?

MA: I went to bed.

DC: Even with the party still going on?

MA: Yeah. I was really tired.

DC: You weren't concerned that your friends were still there?

MA: Why would I be? I trust my friends.

DC: It just seems unusual for the host of the party to go to sleep before the party's over.

MA: Look, Angie and I had a fight, okay? I was upset. I didn't want to deal with people anymore, so I went back up to my room and I fell asleep. I don't know what happened at the end of the party, because I was asleep.

DC: What did you fight about?

MA: Why does it matter? It has nothing to do with Ryan. Angie and I just argued. That's all.

KG: You may be right. It probably has nothing to do with Ryan. Do you know when Ryan left the party?

MA: No. [inaudible] I'm sorry, I wish I did.

KG: Let's talk about the next morning. What happened then?

MA: I woke up after nine. I went to the room where Ryan was going to sleep, but it was empty, so I went downstairs to look for her. She wasn't there, but neither was Noah, so I figured she went back to Brooke with him. He had to go back to the dorm to get his stuff before going to the airport. I think they were going to go together.

KG: What did you do once you realized Ryan was gone?

MA: I had to clean up the house, and I remember now it snowed a lot overnight so I had to shovel a path to the trash bins. Jacob helped me before he and Krista left. That was probably around eleven. Brian, Ayesha, and Li-Hua left around then too. After that I cleaned up—somebody got cranberry juice all over my mom's white duvet, so that was ruined. My mom's kind of a freak about her white stuff, so I tried to bleach the duvet. I think I was doing that for a while. It didn't really work. But I was still trying to clean it when Ryan's parents called me.

KG: About when was that?

MA: It was the afternoon by then. Maybe around three. They said she had missed her flight and she wasn't answering her phone. They wanted to know if I knew where she was, but I didn't. That's when I called Noah, but he was on a plane so he couldn't answer. He didn't call me back till later that night, and he said he hadn't talked to Ryan since the night before. He went back to school really early the morning after the party.

KG: Was he concerned about not having seen Ryan?

MA: Not really.

KG: Do you think it's unusual that Ryan's boyfriend hadn't said good-bye to her before leaving for Christmas vacation?

MA: I—I didn't really think about it. Sometimes Ryan—I mean, it definitely never occurred to me that she might have been murdered. I just thought other people had talked to her, and probably Noah thought the same thing, and when you get on a plane you can't use your phone, so I don't know.

DC: When did it become obvious that nobody knew where Ryan was?

MA: By that night we knew. I talked to everyone by then, and they all told me they hadn't driven Ryan anywhere. It's weird because she didn't have a car so somebody had to have taken her away from Marblehead.

DC: It sounds like you have some theories?

MA: Well, somebody's lying? Or someone else came and picked her up.

DC: I want to go back to this fight that Jess and Ryan had. I know you said you weren't there, but what do you think about the idea that Ryan was seeing someone other than Noah?

MA: [inaudible]

DC: What was that?

MA: She wouldn't cheat on Noah. She's not like that.

DC: You're sure?

MA: She's my best friend! Was my best friend. I would know.

DC: Okay. Is there anything else you'd like to tell us? About Ryan, or about the last time you saw her?

MA: You should talk to Emily. She hates Ryan. And ask Jess about that cheating thing and how she'd know.

DC: Noted. Anything else?

MA: No.

DC: Then that concludes this interview. Thank you.

[End of recording]

JESSICA WONG REACHES FOR THE DOOR TO RICE HALL, but someone on the inside pulls it open first. Kim Watson, the arts program director, is on the other side.

"Jess!" Kim seems confused for a moment. "We don't have the program today. Are you here to talk to admissions?" Rice Hall houses the admissions department as well as the conference room that the police are using.

"No, I'm here to talk to the police."

"Oh." Kim's eyes flicker to the man behind Jess, and she steps back to let the two of them enter the building. Hovering in the vestibule, she says, "I didn't know you knew Ryan."

"I was at the party the night she disappeared," Jess replies, not meeting her eyes.

"I'm so sorry to hear that," Kim says.

"I didn't really know her. I'm sorry for—for all of you at Brooke, though."

"Thank you," Kim says, then looks at the man with Jess. "You must be Jess's father." She holds out her hand, and he steps forward to shake it. "I'm Kim Watson, director of the Pearson Brooke Arts Program. Your daughter is very talented."

"That's—that's good. I'm Peter Wong."

"Great to meet you," she says. "Jess, I picked something up for you over the holidays. A flyer for an event I think you'd be interested in. Why don't you come to my office so I can give it to you before I forget? And, Mr. Wong, that way you can see some of Jess's work and what she's been up to here."

"He doesn't need—"

Mr. Wong cuts Jess off. "We have to go into the interview."

"They're running a bit late," Kim says. "I came in for an interview myself. I was Ryan's house advisor, and they told me I'd have to come back later. Why don't we go in and check how long the delay will be?"

"I don't know," Jess says reluctantly. "They said we should be here at one."

"You'll have plenty of time," Kim insists. She opens the interior door and briskly leads the way down the hall to the admissions desk, where the staff have been keeping track of the police interviews. Mr. Wong joins Kim at the desk while Jess hangs a few steps back. Kim asks the admissions clerk to call when the police are ready for Jess. While Mr. Wong gives them his cell phone number, Jess pulls Kim aside.

"I don't think this is a good idea," Jess whispers.

"Why not?" Kim asks.

"He—my parents aren't interested in my comics." Jess shakes her head slightly. She looks uncomfortable. "He's not going to get it."

Kim says in a low voice, "If you really don't want to show him, we don't have to. But I think he'll be very impressed. Why don't we just show him the final color panels from last semester? Nothing in progress."

"Jessica?" Mr. Wong says, hovering behind Kim. "Miss—"

Kim gives Jess a questioning look. Jess glances behind Kim at her father, who seems puzzled. "Okay, fine," Jess relents.

Kim turns to Mr. Wong with a smile. "Kim," she says. "Please call me Kim. Let's go. We'll have you back in plenty of time."

Kim ushers them out of Rice Hall and into the arts center next door. She takes them directly to her office on the ground floor, which Jess has never seen. One wall of the room is entirely covered with eight-by-ten oil paintings of mushrooms in every color from dirt brown to neon green, a kaleidoscope of *Alice in Wonderland* hallucinations. Mr. Wong eyes the mushrooms skeptically as Kim searches through a stack of papers on top of her desk for the flyer she wants to give Jess.

"Here it is," she says, and hands it over.

It's an ad for an event at MIT featuring the author and artist of the *Yellow Empress* comics.

"Do you know this series?" Kim asks.

"No," Jess says.

"I think you'd really like them," Kim says, and turns to look through the bookshelf behind her. "The art is right up your alley, and the storytelling is a great twist on origin stories."

She hands Jess issue one of *Yellow Empress*, which depicts an Asian woman dressed in an elaborate yellow silk gown and a multitiered headdress, heavy with glittering jewels. She's also carrying a bloody knife, crimson streaks running down the handle and over her fingers.

"You can borrow that," Kim says. "And you should go to the event. It's free."

Mr. Wong, who is standing behind Jess reading the card, says, "It's at MIT? Jessica's brother is at MIT."

Kim beams at him. "That's wonderful. Maybe Jess can go with her brother."

"She should focus on her schoolwork first," Mr. Wong says.

Small square photos of *Yellow Empress*'s author and artist, Chen Ning and Erin Mei Tan, are inset on the back of the card. Jess tucks the card inside the comic. She takes care not to crush the issue's soft paper cover.

"Of course," Kim says to Mr. Wong. "Has Jess shown you what she's been working on during the arts program?"

"No," Mr. Wong answers.

"Well, let's go upstairs to Studio B and take a look," Kim says.

Mr. Wong glances at his watch. "We should go back."

"Five minutes, Mr. Wong. And it's all right if you're a few minutes late. You won't get detention." Kim gives him a winking smile. When he doesn't respond, she adds hurriedly, "Besides, I know you'll enjoy seeing them."

Kim shows them out of her office and up the stairs to Studio B. Someone has left a papier-mâché elephant on the table, half painted in hot pink and yellow, its trunk arcing up in an exaggerated curve. They go to the cubbies where Jess stored her materials, and Kim gives Jess an encouraging smile when she hesitates. She glances back at her father. Mr. Wong looks at the pink-and-yellow elephant with exactly the same expression he had when he saw Kim's collection of mushroom paintings.

"Let's lay them out here," Kim says, taking the portfolio out of the cubby.

"Wait, I—"

But Kim has already opened it on the nearest worktable, and is pulling out the three color printouts.

"It's just the beginning," Jess tells her father. "There's a whole story after this. This just sets it up."

The first two pages are a spread of several panels that begin with a wide establishing shot of the Blackwood Hall School campus, which Jess drew like a map. Each of the subsequent panels zooms in, first at medium range on a brick building—the dorm the girls live in—and then on the entrance hall inside, where someone is carrying a suitcase up the main stairs. A stained-glass window above the landing depicts a girl standing proudly on a hill, the wind blowing her hair back. The panels on the right-hand side show the same girl—Kestrel—first opening the door to her dorm room; then standing just inside the dorm room meeting her roommate, Laney; and finally, a close-up on Kestrel's face, lit up with anticipation. The third page depicts Laney and Kestrel's first meeting in four equally sized panels. Laney is shy at first, but Kestrel is outgoing and enthusiastic, and soon they are lying on their stomachs on the rug, looking at a laptop together.

"I think the story that Jess is putting together is so fascinating," Kim says. "It's an origin story—like the beginning of Superman, you know? But it's so much more than that. And she has a wonderful style. The characters are so lively. I love the way she fuses manga-inspired art with American webcomics. Like Clamp meets *Lumberjanes*."

Mr. Wong studies the printouts with his hands folded in front of him. "They remind me of your grandfather," he says to his daughter.

Jess looks puzzled. "What do you mean?"

"My father—he was a painter."

"He was? I didn't know that."

Mr. Wong shakes his head. "You knew, but you forgot. When you were very little, he came from China to help take care of you and Justin. Your mother and I had to work, so he lived with us in Boston for a year."

"Oh, right."

"He would draw pictures for you," Mr. Wong says. He looks at his daughter with a combination of pride and sadness. "Adventure stories. You were very young, but you liked them."

Jess lowers her gaze to her comics. The color printer rendered the images with a shiny gloss. They seem to glow beneath the lights.

"That's wonderful," Kim says. "Do you have any of those pictures anymore?"

Mr. Wong frowns, reaches down to touch the edge of one of the printouts, straightening it on the table. "I don't know. Maybe, in the basement." He glances at his watch again. "We should go back. Thank you for showing me, Miss—Kim." He turns to head for the door, and adds, "I like your pictures, Jessica."

TRANSCRIPT OF INTERVIEW OF ANGELA REDMOND

Present:

DC: Detective Lieutenant Donna Cardoni, Massachusetts State Police

KG: Lieutenant Kyle Griffin, Massachusetts State Police

AR: Angela Redmond, witness

JR: Jim Redmond, parent to Angela Redmond

Det. Lt. Donna Cardoni (DC): Today is Thursday, January 5, and we are at Pearson Brooke Academy, in Rice Hall. The time is 12:37 p.m. I am Detective Lieutenant Donna Cardoni of the Massachusetts State Police, assigned to the Essex County District Attorney's Office. Also present is my partner.

Lt. Kyle Griffin (KG): Lieutenant Kyle Griffin, Massachusetts State Police.

DC: We are interviewing Angela Redmond, and because Angela is a minor we also have her father, Jim

Redmond, present. Mr. Redmond, can you please state your name for the recording?

Jim Redmond (JR): Jim Redmond.

DC: Can you spell that, please?

JR: J-I-M R-E-D-M-O-N-D.

DC: Thank you. Angela, could you do the same?

Angela Redmond (AR): Angela Redmond. But you can call me Angie. Oh, A-N-G-E-L-A R-E-D-M-O-N-D.

DC: Thank you, Angie. You understand that this interview is entirely voluntary, and you're free to leave at any time? Since this interview is being recorded, please be sure to state your answer out loud rather than nodding your head.

AR: Yes, okay.

DC: We've asked you to come in today because we understand you were at a party on December sixteenth, the night that Ryan disappeared. We'd like you to tell us about your experiences at the party that night. I want you to tell us in your own words everything that happened that night, from start to finish. Just try to remember how you were feeling—whether you were excited or nervous, you know? And no detail is too small. Even tiny details can help. Don't worry about trying to determine whether something is important or not. That's our job. Your job is just to tell the whole story as completely as you can. All right?

AR: Okay.

DC: Great. You can start whenever you're ready.

AR: Okay, um, the night of the party, I was—I was a little nervous. I didn't really know Margot's friends, and I wanted to make a good impression. I, um, I spent a lot of time trying to figure out what to wear. Are you sure you want to hear this?

DC: Absolutely. No detail is too small.

AR: Well, I texted Jess to help me pick a dress. Jess is my best friend. She liked the black one better, so I put that on and got ready. Jess came over to my house around seven because I was driving us both to the party. I told my parents we were going to see *The Wizard of Oz* with some of our friends, so they didn't know we were going to Margot's. I shouldn't have done that, I know. I'm sorry, Dad.

JR: I know, hon.

AR: Anyway, Jess came over and I drove to Marblehead. When we got to the party, Margot introduced us to her friends. I don't remember all their names, but they seemed nice, especially Ayesha. Her parents' house is really nice, like something you see on TV. I remember there was a lot of white—white sofas, carpets, but it didn't look like a hospital. It looked—expensive. The whole house looked expensive. I felt a little weird because Margot's friends were all dressed up like they were going someplace fancy, and I was—I mean, I was wearing a dress but I wasn't nearly as dressed up as they were, and Jess wasn't dressed up either. It was like they got all dressed up for some special event but I didn't understand the dress code.

KG: It must be a pretty different culture over at Pearson Brooke. Hard for a girl from West Bedford to figure out.

AR: Well, they were all nice to me. After we got there,

Margot and I hung out in the living room with her friends for a while. Later, we—Margot and I—um, we hung out in her room for a while, upstairs. When we went back downstairs, most people were still in the living room, but I went out on the deck for a little bit. The house has this big deck that overlooks a private beach. It was dark, so you couldn't see much, but I just wanted to get some air. I was—Margot and I had a fight. I wanted to get outside, cool off. But Margot followed me, and we ended up fighting outside too. It was so cold. I remember it was really windy, and it had started to snow a little. I didn't have my coat on and I kept trying to go back in but Margot was trying to convince me to—to come out to my parents. Margot's been pushing me to do it since last fall. She thought I was ashamed of it or something, but I wasn't. I'm not ashamed of it.

JR: You could've told us, hon.

AR: You, yeah. Not Mom.

DC: Angie, what happened after you argued with Margot?

AR: I—I went back inside, and I saw Jess in the kitchen with Ryan. They were arguing. I could see that it was bad. Jess looked really upset. So I decided it was time to leave. I got Jess and we started to leave, but then Margot apologized, so we stayed a little while longer. Not that long, because I had to get home by one a.m. We probably left around midnight, and I remember it was snowing then, and I was a little worried about the roads, but it wasn't that bad. Jess was supposed to stay overnight at my house, but she—we kind of argued on the drive back, so she ended up walking home from my house. I got home a little before one. My parents heard me come in. I said hi to them and then went to bed. That's the end.

DC: Thank you. I'm going to ask some follow-up questions to clarify a few things. You said that you were nervous going to the party because you hadn't met Margot's friends before. But what about Ryan?

AR: Oh. Yeah, I met Ryan before, but only a few times, like in the park once or when Margot and I stopped by her dorm once. I didn't really know her.

DC: In the park. You mean Ellicott Park?

AR: Yeah.

DC: When was that?

AR: It was back in September. One night we met up with some friends—Jess and I—and Margot brought Ryan.

DC: Can you tell us more about this? Do you and your friends meet in the park often?

AR: Um, we sometimes hang out in the park in the summer. At night. We—we talk and stuff. That's all, Dad, I swear.

JR: You think I didn't hang out in the woods when I was your age, hon? It's okay.

DC: Angie, you were saying—about when you first met Ryan?

AR: Yeah, I had just met Margot at the Creamery, and we'd been messaging each other, and I said I was going to be at the park that night. Since Brooke is so close, she said she might come too. That was the first time I realized she—she liked me.

DC: Did you ever meet up in the park again?

AR: No.

DC: When was the next time you saw Ryan?

AR: Probably a few weeks later? Once Margot had to go back to her dorm to get her phone because she forgot it, and I went with her and Ryan was around. She seemed nice. We didn't really talk much because Margot and I were supposed to go to a movie.

DC: Did you talk to Ryan much at the party in December?

AR: Only in a group with other people. And then, like I said, I was—I went upstairs with Margot, so I missed a lot of the party.

DC: You said that when you came back inside after being out on the deck, you saw Ryan arguing with Jess. Let's go over that again. What did you see when you came inside?

AR: I—I saw them at the kitchen island facing each other. They both looked pretty angry.

DC: Do you think they'd been drinking?

AR: I . . . yeah.

DC: Had you been drinking?

AR: No! I had to drive home. I'm not stupid. My dad can tell you—I was sober when I got home. But Jess—I think she drank way too much. I think it was really hard for her to be there.

DC: Why?

AR: She didn't know anyone, and I was busy with Margot, so . . . she was kind of on her own.

DC: Okay. Jess and Ryan are in the kitchen. How did you know they were fighting?

AR: It was obvious. Ryan was telling Jess to take back what she said about her.

DC: And what was that?

AR: I didn't hear it directly but Jess accused Ryan of cheating on her boyfriend, and she said it basically right in front of him. Noah was at the party. It must have been awful to hear that. So I get why Ryan was mad.

DC: When we talked to Noah, he said that Jess had a gun in the kitchen. Do you remember seeing that?

AR: Um . . . yeah, now that you say that, um, yeah, I remember that. When I came inside she was holding this gun. It was gold, really shiny. It looked fake, really. I didn't think it was important, that's why I didn't mention it. But I told Jess to put it down and that's when I tried to get her to leave, but Margot apologized, and then we stayed a little longer.

DC: Okay. Do you know where this gun came from?

AR: No, I have no idea.

DC: Were you curious? Did it seem surprising to see your best friend holding a gun?

AR: Of course, but it was all—it was just a weird night, and I was upset with Margot and I just wanted to leave.

DC: Okay. You said that you and Jess argued on the drive home. What was that about?

AR: It was so stupid. She was so drunk, and I told her it was not okay for her to spread those rumors about Ryan when she couldn't have any idea if it was true or not. She got really sick on the ride home. I had to pull over, and she threw up. I felt really bad for her. She does this sometimes. She drinks because she's nervous, and I really worry about her.

DC: Why do you think Jess couldn't know if the rumor about Ryan was true or not?

AR: Uh—I guess I just didn't believe it. Jess doesn't know Ryan. How could she possibly know anything like that about her?

DC: We're almost finished here, but I want to go back briefly to the moment you came back into the kitchen from the deck, when you saw Jess holding that gun. How do you think it looked to Margot?

AR: To Margot? Um, I—I guess Margot was behind me, so she probably saw the same thing I did.

DC: Can you walk me through that? Pretend that you're Margot seeing the situation, and describe what you see.

AR: Okay. If I'm Margot coming into the kitchen, I see Ryan and Jess at the island. Oh, there are some people behind them—some of their other friends. I don't remember who. Maybe Noah. Noah and one other girl. So Margot comes into the kitchen, sees Ryan and Jess standing facing each other. I think the gun is in a box on the island between them. Ryan is telling Jess to take back what she said, that she would never cheat on Noah. And then Jess picks up the gun. She's not pointing it at anyone, she just picks it up like she's looking at it. And I—Margot sees me go over to Jess and tell her to put the gun down. Jess doesn't do it at first so I take it out of her hands and put it back in the box. And then I—Margot sees me grab Jess's hand and tell her we have to leave. And then we walk out of the kitchen, and Margot follows us. But she doesn't follow us immediately—now, I remember. I think she probably stopped to talk to Ryan. Jess and I are already at the door, with our coats on, before Margot catches up to us. And then she apologizes for what she said to me. I thought she was—pretty sincere. So I forgave her. That's all. Then I drove home with Jess, and when we got back, Jess went to her house and I went to bed.

DC: Is there anything else you'd like to tell us? It's not a trick question. I always ask everyone if there's anything they want to say that we didn't ask about. You've been really forthcoming and we appreciate it.

AR: No, there's nothing else I want to say.

DC: Do you have any questions for us?

AR: No.

JR: I do. Does my daughter need a lawyer? I can get a lawyer.

DC: That's up to you, sir, but Angie's only a witness at this point.

JR: At this point. Is that going to change? She didn't do anything. She lied to us, and that's not going to go unpunished, but that's all.

DC: I can't predict the future, Mr. Redmond, but as of now, your daughter is only a witness. It's your right to consult with legal representation if you wish. Is there anything else I can answer for you?

JR: No.

DC: Then that concludes our interview.

[End of recording]

ANGIE REDMOND'S FACE IS PALE AS SHE LEAVES THE conference room, eyes downcast. As she brushes past Jess in the hallway, she shakes her head almost imperceptibly. Mr. Redmond nods to Mr. Wong as the two men pass each other. Jess says nothing and heads into the conference room with her father behind her.

It looks nothing like a police interrogation room. The long oval table is made of polished dark wood, surrounded by wooden chairs imprinted with the Pearson Brooke crest. There is no lock on the door; there is no two-way mirror on the wall. There are three tall windows flanked by dark blue draperies overlooking the snowy quad, where footprints leave meandering trails across the white. Jess takes off her coat and hangs it on the back of a chair, then takes a seat with her back to the windows, facing the detectives. Her father sits beside her.

"Mr. Wong, Miss Wong. Thank you for joining us today," Cardoni says. She's wearing small silver hoop earrings, the remnants of lipstick, and a slightly wrinkled, unfashionable blue suit with no lapels over a cream-colored shell. "We appreciate you coming in voluntarily," she says. "As a reminder, you're free to leave at any time."

Cardoni flips to a new page in her notebook and turns on a digital recorder set in the center of the table. Griffin gives Jess an encouraging smile. He's dressed in a crisp dark gray suit over a light blue shirt and a dark blue tie that looks like it's fresh off the rack.

Jess side-eyes her father as Cardoni drones through the formalities. He is sitting up straight, frowning as he pays attention. Jess slouches back against her chair's wooden spindles, draping her hands over the armrests.

". . . no detail is too small," Cardoni is saying. "So please tell us everything you remember, starting with when you left for the party."

Jess blinks. "I . . . I didn't really want to go. Angie wanted me to go. She made me promise to go with her, so I did."

The basic facts of the night are straightforward. Angie drove them to Marblehead. Jess had a terrible time while Angie disappeared upstairs with Margot. Jess drank too much and got sick on the way back. Angie and Jess argued, so Jess went home instead of spending the night at Angie's house. Her story takes only a few minutes, and as she finishes, she glances at Griffin, who is spinning his pen through his fingers. Cardoni flips through her notes.

"You haven't mentioned Ryan," Cardoni says. "How well did you know her?"

"Not well."

"Had you met her before the party?"

"Um, once or twice. We barely talked."

"We've spoken to several other people who were at the party,"

Cardoni says, "who say that you argued with Ryan and made a very personal accusation at her."

Jess presses her back against the spindles of her chair, and the crossbar digs into her spine. "Is that what they say?"

"Jessica, tell the truth," Mr. Wong warns her.

Cardoni's eyes flicker to Mr. Wong, then back to Jess. "Can you tell us what happened? From your perspective?"

Griffin shifts in his seat, eyeing his boss for a second, then scribbles something in his notebook.

"Jessica?" Cardoni prompts.

"From my perspective," she says flatly, "Ryan was kind of a bitch to me. So I told her about some rumors I heard."

"What did she do?" Cardoni asks.

"She was just a bitch. What does it matter?"

"Watch your language," Mr. Wong says.

"You wanted the truth," Jess shoots back.

Mr. Wong exhales and shakes his head.

Griffin leans forward and stops playing with his pen. "Let's back up a little, okay? How about we walk through the party from the beginning again. You said you didn't want to go to the party in the first place. Why did you go?"

"Because Angie asked me to go," Jess answers, looking at Griffin. "She's my best friend."

He nods. "And you do that stuff for your best friend."

"Yeah."

"So it must have sucked to do this thing for your best friend—going all the way to this party where you don't know anyone—and when you get there it's totally boring, right?"

"Yeah. It was a stupid party. All they were doing was drinking and watching videos."

Griffin laughs shortly, shakes his head. "Rich kids. What dumbasses."

Cardoni purses her lips but stays quiet.

"If I were you, I would've gotten a couple of drinks right away," Griffin notes with a slight smile.

Jess eyes her father.

"It's completely normal," Griffin assures her, keeping his gaze on her and not on Mr. Wong. "We're not looking to bust anyone for drinking. You had a couple drinks, right?"

Jess tucks her hands beneath her thighs and sits up slightly. "Yeah."

Mr. Wong rubs a hand over his eyes.

"What was Angie doing while you were trying to survive this party?" Griffin asks.

Jess fidgets. Her chair creaks. "She was with Margot. I didn't see her for most of the party. I mean, I guess she and Margot were, you know, together."

Griffin nods blandly. "So what did you do while your best friend abandoned you?"

Jess relaxes a little. "I walked around the house. It was a big house. That's when I ran into Ryan. I went into an empty room and was just sitting there, minding my own business, and then Ryan came in and started talking to me, saying stuff that pissed me off. So I threw my drink at her."

"I bet that felt good," Griffin says.

Jess shrugs.

"When you threw the drink at her, were there other people around?"

"No. That was upstairs. It was just Ryan and me. That's when she found the gun."

Cardoni pauses in her note taking and looks at Jess.

"There was a gun?" Mr. Wong interjects.

Jess ignores him.

Griffin says, "The gun was upstairs?"

"Yeah."

Griffin and Cardoni briefly trade glances.

"It was in Margot's mom's room," Jess says. "Ryan found it in the closet."

"How did that happen? Can you walk us through that?" Griffin asks.

"Um, I was in Margot's mom's room. That's where I was when Ryan came in. We were talking—or Ryan was saying that shit about—sorry—she was talking about how Margot's mom's decorating was trashy. She went into the walk-in closet and was looking around—I think she was looking for pills or something—and when she came out, she had the gun."

"What did it look like?" Griffin asks.

"The gun? It was gold," Jess says. "I remember it looked like a toy."

Cardoni says, "Several people saw the gun downstairs in the kitchen. How did it get downstairs?"

"I don't know. I don't remember."

In the silence, the sound of Cardoni's rollerball scraping across her notebook seems unnaturally loud.

"Okay," Griffin says. "Let's go back a little. What happened after you threw the drink at Ryan upstairs?"

"I left," Jess says. "I went down to the kitchen. I think I got another drink. I wasn't driving or anything."

"Do you know how many drinks you'd had by then?" Cardoni asks.

Jess stiffens. "No."

Mr. Wong exhales loudly again.

"When was the next time you talked to Ryan?" Griffin asks.

"Um . . . later? I don't know exactly when. It was in the kitchen. She—she came up to me and said—I can't remember exactly what happened, I was—my memory's a little fuzzy." Jess rubs her damp palms over her jeans.

Griffin nods. "Some people who were at the party say they saw you arguing with Ryan in the kitchen. Do you remember that?"

"I remember yelling at Ryan. I was just really pissed about what she said to me, so I—I said I knew she was cheating on her boyfriend."

"How did you know that she was cheating?" Griffin asks.

"Because I found these letters some guy had been writing to her. Love letters. The guy wasn't her boyfriend."

Looking at Jess, Cardoni stops taking notes again.

Griffin says, "Tell us more about the letters. What did they say? Where did you find them?"

"They're in the park. Ellicott Park. Ryan hid them in a bag under a log. I found them by accident last fall, when I was sketching in the park. I overheard Ryan and Margot talking about them nearby. So after they left, I went and read them. Ryan's totally seeing some guy who's not her boyfriend."

Jess pauses, watching the detectives watching her. Cardoni's gaze is focused and sharp, like a mother alert for any hint of a lie; Griffin's is open and expectant, like a friend's.

Jess says, "I think the guy Ryan was seeing is a teacher."

Griffin's expression immediately tightens. "Where are the letters now?"

"I don't know, probably still in the woods." Jess hesitates, then offers, "You want me to take you to them?"

"That would be very helpful," Griffin says. "How far away is the location?"

"Not far. Like a ten- or fifteen-minute walk into the park."

"We would like to see the letters, but I have a couple more things to ask," Cardoni says.

Griffin looks impatient.

"What?" Jess asks.

"Did you touch the gun at Margot's house?" Cardoni asks.

"Did I touch it? I—" Jess's forehead wrinkles. "I think I did. It looked like a joke, not a real gun." She meets Cardoni's gaze directly. "Why?"

Cardoni doesn't blink. "Did you see anyone else handle the gun? Besides you and Ryan?"

Jess shakes her head. "I don't remember."

"What did Ryan say to you that made you so upset?" Cardoni asks.

Jess goes very still. Her fingers clutch the edge of her seat. "What does it matter?"

"Just trying to get a full picture of what went on," Cardoni says.

"I don't think it's relevant," Jess says.

Griffin says, "It's okay, it's just between us."

Jess narrows her eyes at him. "Between us and the digital recorder."

He smiles tentatively. "And we'll keep that private."

"Tell the truth, Jessica," Mr. Wong says.

Jess doesn't look at her father. Cardoni continues to watch Jess calmly, pen in hand, while Griffin shifts in his seat. Finally Jess says, "Do you want to see the letters or not?"

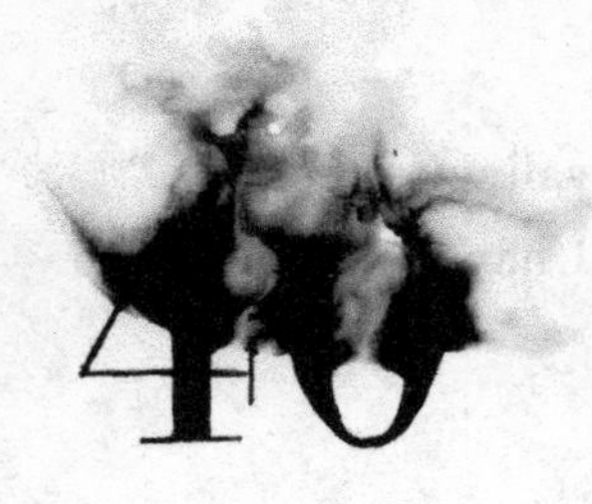

40

JESS'S FATHER DRIVES THEM BACK TO THEIR NEIGHBORhood in West Bedford, the detectives following in their sedan.

A block away from their house Mr. Wong says, "You didn't tell us about the gun."

Jess clenches her teeth. "I forgot."

"How could you forget about that?"

She doesn't respond. She stares out the window at the snow-covered houses, many still ornamented with sagging Christmas decorations.

"Don't lie again," he says.

"I'm not, Dad."

He shakes his head as he pulls into their driveway. "You need to—"

She climbs out of the car before he finishes his sentence and slams the door behind her. The detectives are parking their sedan across the street in front of the trailhead with the defaced sign.

"Jessica," her dad calls.

"I have to go meet them," she says, not turning around. "Are you coming or not?"

She hears his footsteps crunch across the snow behind her as he follows her across the street.

"It's this way," Jess says to the detectives, and heads into the park.

Last night's snow covered up the icy crust that formed over the past week, making the trail deceptively even looking. It's only mid-afternoon, but the winter light coming through the bare branches is watery and gray, already hinting at the approaching dark. The snowfall of the past several weeks has blown in drifts against the boulders and hills, like ocean waves frozen in mid-surge.

Jess misses the white oak that marks the way to the hollow because its bulbous roots are hidden under the snow, and has to double back. When she strikes off the trail, her father and the detectives follow. Cold clumps of snow slip into the low tops of her sneakers. She scrambles down the side of the hollow, slipping into the drifts, and then climbs awkwardly up the other side. Snow encrusts her jeans up to her knees.

At the top of the hill she goes directly to the place where Ryan hid the bag. She kneels as Griffin joins her. Cardoni and Mr. Wong are slower to climb to the top. Jess starts to paw the snow aside, uncovering the fallen log that has nearly disappeared beneath the white. When she clears off the log, she leans over to peer into the gap beneath it. She sees nothing but darkness, so she thrusts her hand beneath the log, her fingers scraping the frozen ground. She almost misses the end of the leather strap because it's farther back than it was last time. She has to tug hard to drag it out, but at last, it pops free. She shakes the dirt and snow off, then holds the leather messenger bag out to the detectives.

Griffin takes it in a gloved hand. "Thanks. The letters are in here?"

"Yeah."

Behind Griffin, Mr. Wong is staring at something on the ground, something yellow—a fluttering piece of plastic bag, as if he'd rather look at trash than his daughter.

Griffin hands the bag to Cardoni, who is also wearing gloves, while he takes out a camera and snaps photos of the log. Then Cardoni places the bag on the log, unbuckles it, and looks inside. She removes a handful of folded letters and sets them on top of the bag. The camera clicks repeatedly as Griffin photographs them. Jess counts nine letters, all written on the same plain white paper.

Mr. Wong has gone over to the piece of trash and is picking it up from the ground, except it's not a bag, it's a piece of tape. As it unravels, the words printed on it jump out in stark black on yellow: POLICE LINE DO NOT CROSS.

Jess gets to her feet, snow falling in clumps from her jeans. The detectives notice that she is looking at her father. About ten feet away, Mr. Wong holds the crime scene tape in his hand. The snow is uneven near him, as if parts of it had been shoveled aside into mounds, then covered over with new snowfall. Mr. Wong looks shocked.

"Is this the place where the girl was found?" he asks.

Cardoni steps toward him, hand outstretched to take the police tape. "I'm sorry, sir. Yes, it is."

AFTER DINNER, JESS GOES UPSTAIRS TO HER BEDROOM and closes the door. She sits at her desk and takes out her phone, but then hesitates, her finger hovering over the home button.

Finally she sends a text to Emily. *Talked to cops today. Took them to the park. They have the letters now.*

She waits for a response. When Emily doesn't answer immediately, Jess drags out her history book and attempts to do the worksheet that was assigned earlier that day, but she has a hard time focusing. She doodles trees in the margins of her worksheet until the entire page is engulfed in a forest of oaks, bare branches cutting across the questions.

When her phone rings, she almost jumps out of her chair.

"Hi," Jess says, answering the phone.

"Hey," Emily replies. "I got your text."

Jess drops her pencil. "Yeah?"

"Did you tell them I know about the letters too?"

"No."

Emily exhales. "Okay."

"Do you still have the photos you took?"

Jess hears the sound of a door closing before Emily answers. "Yes. Why?"

"The one that Ryan wrote—it was on fancy paper, remember? It wasn't there anymore. I think the guy took it."

There's a beat of silence. "And I have a picture of it," Emily says.

Jess picks up her pencil again and begins to doodle a hollow log at the bottom of the page. "You could send it to the police. Anonymously."

"I don't want to get involved in this. I really did not like Ryan, but this is insane. People are saying she was shot. Is that true?" Emily sounds frightened.

"The police didn't tell me. Where did you hear that?"

"There are rumors. And there's this Facebook page where a lot of people are posting theories."

"Oh yeah. I've seen it. How do you know what's true?"

"Some of Ryan's friends said there's been an autopsy, and the results say she was shot."

"Like a suicide?"

"No, supposedly the angle means it couldn't have been suicide."

Jess's pencil scratches a hole in the paper. "Really?"

"Yeah. Everybody's scared to go in the park now. What if it was some crazy serial killer?"

Jess flexes her fingers around the pencil. "What if that teacher she was seeing had something to do with it?"

"No, he couldn't have. He's all into poetry." But Emily sounds doubtful. "I mean, I don't *think* he would be—his letters are so . . ."

"Romantic?"

"I know what you're thinking, that any teacher who would sleep with a student is probably a jerk, but—"

"No, I was thinking he definitely is a creepy asshole," Jess interrupts. "Statistically speaking the person who killed her was probably her boyfriend or some guy she was having sex with. That letter from Ryan could help the cops find him."

"How? It doesn't say who he is. We don't even know if he's really a teacher."

"But it proves that Ryan was seeing him. They could match her handwriting to that letter. And their relationship was clearly shady." Jess takes a deep breath. "Look, I know you don't want to get involved. But don't you think the cops should have all the evidence they can get?"

TRANSCRIPT OF INTERVIEW OF KIMBERLY WATSON

Present:

DC: Detective Lieutenant Donna Cardoni, Massachusetts State Police

KG: Lieutenant Kyle Griffin, Massachusetts State Police

KW: Kimberly Watson, Faculty Advisor

Det. Donna Cardoni (DC): Today is Friday, January 6, and we are at Pearson Brooke Academy, in Rice Hall. The time is 8:49 a.m. I'm Detective Lieutenant Donna Cardoni of the Massachusetts State Police, assigned to the Essex County District Attorney's Office. Also present is my partner.

Lt. Kyle Griffin (KG): Lieutenant Kyle Griffin, Massachusetts State Police.

DC: We are interviewing Kimberly Watson this morning. Can you state your full name and occupation for the recording, please?

Kimberly Watson (KW): Kimberly Anne Watson. I'm an art teacher here at Pearson Brooke, and I'm also the faculty advisor for Fischer Hall, the dormitory where Ryan lived.

DC: How do you spell your name? Is it the normal way?

KW: K-I-M-B-E-R-L-Y. Anne with an E. Watson like Sherlock.

DC: Thank you. As you know, this interview is entirely voluntary, and you're free to leave at any time.

KW: Understood.

DC: Great. We've asked you to come in today to help us get to know Ryan a little better. Can you tell us how you knew her, and how you'd describe her?

KW: I knew her about as well as the average resident in Fischer Hall. Because I knew I was coming in for this interview I looked at her records, and she did miss curfew once during sophomore year. I issued her a warning, and she didn't miss any more curfews. The only other times I had administrative interactions with her were when she had to show parental permission to leave campus for events that went past curfew. That happened a couple of times, including the night she disappeared last December.

DC: Did any of these interactions strike you as unusual?

KW: No. She was really pretty average, and certainly not a troublemaker.

DC: How would you describe her as a person?

KW: Well, I didn't know her that well. She ran pretty much in the middle of the pack of girls at Fischer Hall. She didn't reach out to me personally—I do develop closer relationships with some of the girls sometimes, but Ryan never needed much attention. I don't think she was a wallflower, but she wasn't the most outgoing girl either. I honestly think she was a little shy. She was close friends with Margot and Krista, who also live in Fischer Hall. Margot's certainly more outspoken than Ryan was, and Krista always struck me as a very happy girl—bubbly, even. Ryan was the quiet one of those three, at least in person. Last year I heard that there was some tension between Margot, Ryan, and a sophomore transfer who lived in a different dorm, but a lot of that happened online. It's hard for us to keep track of what these girls get into online. I'm sure you understand. The technology moves faster than we do. Often these girls get into difficult relationships with each other online that can be very hurtful emotionally. It didn't seem unusual to me, though.

DC: You sound hesitant.

KW: No, it's just—it's a tragedy that Ryan was—is dead. I don't want to sound uncaring about her, but I admit she—sometimes she was a little cold. I don't think that justifies anything remotely like what happened to her, but she wasn't a friendly girl. She and Margot were close, and maybe that's what contributed to that feeling in me. They both sort of kept other people out.

DC: Girls can be very intense with each other. Do you think their friendship was unusually close?

KW: I don't know. I remember being so close with my girlfriends when I was a teen, you know? There can be a manipulative aspect to it that goes beyond loyalty to—to—I'm not sure what I'm getting at. Sorry. I don't want to put the wrong impression in your mind. Ryan was a good girl, not a troublemaker, and had close friends.

DC: Did you hear of a rumor that Ryan was cheating on her boyfriend?

KW: No. I didn't know her well enough to hear anything like that. I couldn't even tell you who her boyfriend was.

DC: Did you ever teach Ryan? Was she a student of yours too?

KW: No. I teach a few art classes, including a general introductory survey and some studio art classes, but Ryan wasn't interested in art. I also run the Pearson Brooke Arts Exchange Program, and we ask for Brooke students to volunteer to be buddies with outside students, to sort of help them through the Brooke world. Ryan didn't volunteer for that either, so I've never had much academic interaction with Ryan.

DC: Since you run the arts exchange program, do you know Jessica Wong?

KW: Yes, I—actually I saw her here yesterday right before you interviewed her. I didn't know she was going to be interviewed. She said she was at the party the night that Ryan disappeared.

DC: Yes. Can you tell us about your impressions of Jessica?

KW: Well, she's very talented. She goes to West Bedford High School, and her teacher there submitted some of her work to the arts exchange program. Jess draws comics. She's working on a really wonderful project this year. I'm very excited about it.

DC: Can—

KG: What's she working on? I used to read a lot of comics.

KW: Oh—Well, it's an origin story, sort of like a superhero comic, but with a twist. It's about three girls at a boarding school. It's obviously inspired by manga, but also media like *Buffy the Vampire Slayer*. And Jess has a unique voice. It's this fantastic exploration of identity and jealousy and first love—all really juicy things. And her artwork is great. She needs some more development, but she's young. If she continues to work on her art, I think she could be a professional artist.

KG: Sounds interesting. Identity and jealousy. Can you say more?

KW: It's about three girls. There's something of a love triangle going on between them, and a power struggle as well. Who gets the girl, who gets to be the superhero, all that. I think she's heading for sort of a dark conclusion, although I'm not sure what it is yet. It's a battle between good and evil with magic, though, so I expect somebody's going to die.

KG: Really? Can you show us the comics?

KW: I—why do you want to see them?

KG: We're just trying to get a sense of who Jess is.

KW: Well, I'm not sure that Jess's comics would be relevant in this situation. I'm afraid that what I said may be leading you in the wrong direction. You can't draw conclusions on somebody's personality based on the art they make. It's subjective.

KG: Don't you think the art can reflect someone's state of mind?

KW: Maybe initially, but a lot of work goes into it—it's not just a direct one-to-one expression of feelings, and it's not pure stream of consciousness either. I'm not sure how much you know about this process. At the arts exchange program I'm really encouraging these young artists to explore their innermost fears and bring that out in their artwork, but in order to encourage them I have to be open to them expressing things that people might normally repress as too negative or too harsh or simply too much. So whatever Jess is working out in her art is not necessarily related to her everyday real life. They're exaggerations. These themes are bigger than life on purpose.

KG: I'm sorry, I don't have an art degree. What themes are in her comics?

KW: I really don't think they're relevant to your investigation.

DC: I think we're getting off track here, but Lieutenant Griffin's suggestion is a useful one. I understand that art isn't a one-to-one expression of real life, but I do think it could show us something about Jessica. We'd like to see the artwork.

KW: I—I'm not going to show you Jess's work without her permission.

DC: I understand your hesitation, but it's in your interest to help us out. Sometimes the most irrelevant-seeming thing can lead to a real development in the case.

KW: I just don't see how that could be true. They're comics.

DC: Then it shouldn't hurt anyone for us to see them.

KW: I'll have to think about it.

DC: Please do.

KW: Is that all for today? I have to get to class.

DC: Sure. Here's my card. We'll follow up about Jessica's comics.

[End of recording]

IN STUDY HALL, JESS IS SUPPOSED TO DO HER MATH homework, but she pulls her Kestrel notebook out of her backpack instead. She flips through her sketches until she reaches the thumbnails for the climactic scenes. The flyer that Kim Watson gave to her falls out onto the table, and Angie, who is sitting beside her, picks it up.

"What's this?" Angie asks.

"An event that Kim at Brooke told me about. I think I'm going to go."

"Sounds cool."

"Yeah."

"How come you didn't invite me?" Angie wears an expression of false hurt, lower lip slightly pouting.

"I—I didn't think you'd want to go."

"Of course I'd want to go." Angie adds in a low voice, "We're trying to be normal again, right?"

Jess glances around the room. There are six tables, five of them filled with four students each. She and Angie are seated alone at the table farthest from the door. One girl is watching them from across the room. When Jess meets her gaze, the girl drops her eyes guiltily.

Yesterday when Jess returned to school after taking the police into the park, everybody seemed to be watching her, as if they'd be able to glean gossip about Ryan simply by staring. When she and Angie are together, it's even worse. Two West Bed girls at a Peeb house party—the rumors coil around them like rope.

Angie nudges Jess's thigh with her knee and leaves it there. Jess's leg seems to pulse at the spot where Angie's knee touches her.

"We should go," Angie says. "It'll be fun." She adds under her breath, "Besides, I need a break from this place." Her cool expression briefly dissolves; she looks spooked.

"My parents are only letting me go because my brother is going with me."

"That's okay," Angie says. "I don't mind if Justin goes."

"You're not going out with Margot?"

Angie pulls her knee away. She indicates the date and time of the event on the flyer. "Not on Sunday afternoon." She looks at Jess and adds, "I'm all yours."

"My parents don't want me to hang out with you anymore," Jess blurts out.

"What? Why?"

"They said you're a bad influence on me."

"A bad influence?" Angie's forehead wrinkles.

Jess says quickly, "I don't agree."

Angie spins her half-chewed ballpoint pen on the table. "You don't?"

Jess misses the pressure of Angie's knee on her thigh. Angie gazes down at the spinning pen.

"No." Jess reaches out and stops the pen. It's pointing straight at Angie, who raises troubled eyes to Jess. Her face is snow white, contrasting sharply with the purplish lipstick she's begun to wear regularly. "I promise," Jess whispers. "You don't have any influence on me at all."

Angie's mouth twitches. "You promise."

"Yeah." Jess picks up Angie's pen and takes Angie's left hand in hers.

"What are you doing?" Angie asks.

"Hold still," Jess says. She lowers the pen to the back of Angie's hand and draws a heart with a banner across it, like a tattoo. Angie's skin reddens around the pressure of the ballpoint, but she doesn't object. In the banner Jess inks in two words.

I promise.

THE TWIST FOR THE END OF KESTREL'S STORY DAWNS ON Jess while she sifts through the pages she has sketched, looking for the ones that she wants to polish before scanning. She stops at the drawing she sketched in the park the afternoon she found the love letters. It's a page of vignettes: the trees, the boulder, a hand lying outstretched on the ground. The hand is hers—slightly stubby fingers, chewed nails. The smudges around the fingertips that might be dirt could just as easily be pencil.

It has nothing to do with Kestrel, but there's something about the hand—her hand—that triggers a strange feeling inside her, like an itch on a wrinkle in her brain.

Kickback. An equal and opposite reaction.

She sees Kestrel in a blue-tinted gale emanating from the Doorway, her hands uplifted, fingertips glowing white. She sees Raven catching the kickback to Kestrel's spell, her body contorting in pain, her mouth in a grimace.

She sees Laney in the murky gray shadows between the trees, her gun like a gold coin in her hand.

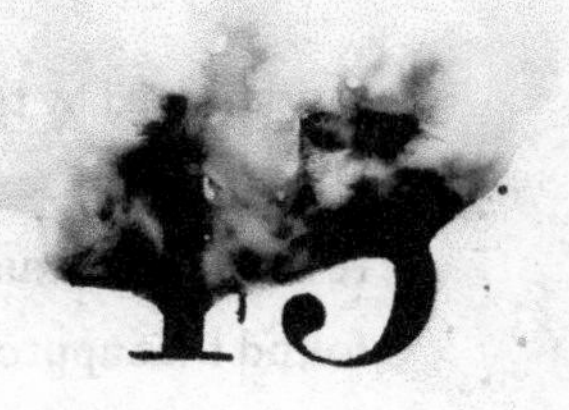

North Shore Sentinel—January 12

Prep school teacher–student romance possibly linked to homicide

By Kerry Loughlan

EAST BEDFORD—Pearson Brooke Academy, a prestigious boarding school north of Boston, has fired a popular English teacher, Jonathan Krause, 34, for engaging in a sexual relationship with Ryan Dupree, the 16-year-old girl who was found dead in neighboring Ellicott Park earlier this month. Their relationship was discovered in the course of the investigation into Dupree's death, but Massachusetts State Police deny that Krause is a suspect at this time.

Pearson Brooke, whose prominent alumni include Massachusetts Senator Daniel Clarkson and actress Mia Bryant, was one of dozens of New England private schools investigated by the *Boston Globe* last year for multiple allegations of sexual abuse. Although there is no definitive research on sexual abuse at private schools, a federal study found that approximately 10 percent of K–12 students in public schools have been subjected to unwanted sexual attention. During the *Globe* investigation, Pearson Brooke acknowledged that it had settled a sexual misconduct lawsuit involving a teacher who worked at the school from 1984–89 and had inappropriate relations with at least two teenage boys.

The relationship between Krause and Dupree was documented in a series of letters, including one or more which the police received from an anonymous source. The letters reportedly reveal that Dupree's teacher encouraged her attachment to him and promised to take her on weekend trips away.

"We are shocked by the news that Jonathan Krause was engaged in this relationship with Ryan Dupree, and he has been terminated from his position at Pearson Brooke immediately, without severance," said Cheryl Donovan, Pearson Brooke Academy's Head of School, in a statement. "Our thoughts and prayers remain with Ryan's family, and we continue to cooperate in any way we can with the police."

Students described Krause as a charismatic and engaging teacher with boyish good looks and an open, friendly nature. "He was always really nice," said one Pearson Brooke student who had enrolled in his Modern English Poets class. "He was really sympathetic and seemed to care about everyone. This whole thing is really sad."

Other students characterized Dupree as the possible

aggressor. "Ryan wasn't exactly a nice girl," said one classmate. "I can see how she might have manipulated him into being with her."

But Pearson Brooke faculty and administrators emphasized that the responsibility fell on Krause, not on Dupree, who was a minor. "She was only sixteen," said one faculty member. "[Krause] took advantage of her, and his behavior is shameful."

Police declined to draw a clear connection between the illicit relationship and Dupree's death, but a source close to the investigation confirmed that Krause was visiting family in Ohio the night that Dupree disappeared, and did not return until Jan. 2, thus providing him with a solid alibi. However, the investigation has also uncovered significant tension between Dupree and an unidentified fellow student regarding her relationship with Krause, which may have played a role in Dupree's death.

Krause, who left his apartment in East Bedford on Jan. 10, has not returned to the area since then. He did not respond to several requests for comment.

JESSICA'S FATHER PULLS INTO A PARKING SPACE FACING the commuter rail station in West Bedford. "Your brother will meet you at North Station," he says.

Jess unbuckles her seat belt and reaches for the door. "I know, Dad."

"You go only with your brother to the event, and then you come back. You know the train schedule for tonight?"

She opens the door, letting in a draft of cold air. "Yes, I know. You gave me the schedule." She climbs out of the car and into the chilly afternoon.

"Jessica!"

She turns back to look at her dad before she closes the door. "What?"

He shakes his head at his daughter, then waves his hand in resignation. "Call us if you need anything."

"Bye, Dad." She pushes the door closed and starts to walk toward the platform, but she doesn't hear the car pull away. She glances back; her father is sitting in the car watching her, and makes no move to leave. Down the platform a girl in a puffy blue coat straightens away from the wall where she was leaning, glancing in her direction. Jess turns away from her and stands facing the empty tracks, pulling her phone out to send a text. *He's still here, prob waiting for train. Don't come over.*

The frigid air freezes the insides of Jess's nostrils. By the time the train comes five minutes later, she's bouncing on her toes to keep warm. She looks over her shoulder at her dad and waves at him as the conductor steps out onto the platform. Inside the train, the heat is on full blast and she pushes back her hood as she moves down the aisle toward the next car, looking for the girl in the puffy blue coat. Finally Jess sees Angie enter the car from the opposite end. She waves at Jess as the train starts to move.

They meet midway, and Angie flashes a grin at Jess. "He didn't see me, did he?"

"I don't think so," Jess says, and they slide into two empty seats together. Angie's cheeks are rosy from the cold, and when she pulls off her wool hat, static electricity makes some of her hair stand straight up. "Your hair," Jess says, laughing, and Angie makes a face and tries to flatten it down.

"You sure your brother isn't going to tell?" Angie asks.

"He's not gonna tell," Jess assures her. Outside the windows, bare trees whip past as the train speeds toward Boston.

"Do you think—" Angie cuts herself off as her phone dings. Frowning, she pulls it out of her pocket and checks the message. Her forehead furrows as she starts texting back.

"What's wrong?"

"It's Margot," Angie says, still texting.

Jess eyes Angie's phone. "Something wrong?"

Angie shakes her head briefly. "She's just worried. She doesn't like that I'm going with you to this thing."

"Why not?"

Angie sends her message and looks out the window. "Why do you think?"

The heart that Jess drew on Angie's left hand has faded. Angie's nails are bitten short, the skin around her fingertips red and rough. She doesn't normally bite her nails.

The phone dings again, and Angie looks at it immediately, her mouth drawn into a tight line. "I'm sorry," she mutters. "I'm turning off my phone after this." She responds to Margot's latest text and then depresses the power button, putting her phone away. She turns to Jess with a forced smile. "This is going to be so fun," she says. "I'm so excited to get away from everything for a little while."

Jess asks, "Are you sure you're okay? Is Margot upsetting you?"

Angie's false smile vanishes. She shakes her head and looks down at her hands. "Let's just have fun, okay?"

Justin is sitting on one of the wooden benches near the Dunkin' Donuts inside North Station, staring at his phone. He doesn't see Jess until she's standing right in front of him. "Justin," she says.

He starts in surprise, looking up at Jess and then at Angie beside her. "Hey," he says. "Angie, hey. What're you doing here?"

Angie smiles at him. "I'm coming too!"

"You can't tell Mom and Dad," Jess warns him.

Justin looks a little puzzled. "I can't—why?"

"Just don't tell them Angie's here. Please."

He shrugs. "Okay, whatever." He stands up. "You ready?"

"So ready," Jess says.

He shoots her a puzzled look, but nods. "Okay. Let's go."

"You don't have to go to the event if you don't want," Jess says as they walk through the station toward the exit.

"Are you saying you don't want me to go?" Justin asks.

"No, if you want to go, that's cool. I just know that Mom and Dad are making you babysit me and it's not really necessary. Angie and I can go on our own if you just show us where it is."

He considers the two girls and says, "I told them I'd call when we get there."

"Oh my God, really? That's so stupid! I'm not twelve!"

He shakes his head. "No, but someone just got murdered in the neighborhood, Jess. Be real. They're a little freaked-out."

"They're just trying to prevent me from having a life," Jess grumbles.

"I think they're just realizing you actually had one," he says.

At the exit, Justin holds open one of the doors. "Thanks," Angie says, walking through.

Justin grabs Jess's arm for a second, and she looks at him. "What?"

"You okay?" he asks.

Jess frowns. "Yeah, why?"

"You know you can tell me if something's going on, right?" He lowers his voice. "With your friend?" His eyes flicker toward Angie, who has stopped and stands waiting a few feet away, trying to look like she's not listening.

Jess doesn't meet her brother's gaze. "Nothing's going on," she says gruffly. "Let's go."

The building where the event takes place is a six-story glass box with a curving roof near the Charles River. Inside, a multistory atrium is crisscrossed by stairs painted in bright primary colors, and as Justin takes Jess and Angie to the glass elevators, they walk past a steel mesh sculpture hanging in midair like a space-age snakeskin. Jess stands at the rear of the elevator, gazing down at the rapidly receding ground floor. "What do they do in here?" she asks, her breath misting the glass wall.

"They build totally insane stuff," Justin says. "Robots and prosthetics and all sorts of cool things."

On the sixth floor, signs for the event direct them into a circular auditorium that looks like the interior of a flying saucer. Several rows of seats arc to face the front of the room, while a curved wall of windows at the rear overlooks a terrace with views of the Boston skyline. The city lights have begun to come on in the fading daylight.

Two of Justin's friends have saved seats in the second row on the left side. The audience is mostly college students, and about half of them are Asian, like the two speakers. Chen Ning, the author of the *Yellow Empress* comics, is small boned and petite, dressed in an asymmetrical lime-green dress and knee-high, chunky brown boots. Her long black hair is loose over her shoulders, and she wears a wide, hammered silver necklace that looks like a collar. Erin Mei Tan, the illustrator, is taller and huskier. Her black hair is shaved on one side and dyed blue on the other, partly spiked up and partly trailing over one shoulder. She wears jeans and sneakers and a black-and-white plaid shirt, along with a fluorescent-pink tie.

"Queer," Angie whispers in Jess's ear.

"Which one?" Jess whispers back.

"Obviously blue hair is queer, but I don't know about the other one."

"Since when have you become such an expert?"

Angie grins but doesn't reply because Chen Ning, who introduces herself as Nina, has begun speaking. The two women have a slide show to accompany their presentation, in which they talk about their collaboration on *Yellow Empress.* Images are projected onto a giant screen behind them, beginning with black-and-white storyboards that they worked on together. In a series of slides they show the development of the main character in the initial concept stage—cycling through various historically inspired costumes—and how the art development supported and inspired the character development.

"We never thought *Yellow Empress* would get this big," Erin Mei Tan says, laughing a little. "We thought it was just this weird little webcomic that had its little Asian internet niche, you know?"

"And now we're on a tour!" Nina says. She has a slight Chinese accent. "My parents never expected this. I think they are a little shocked, actually. They wanted me to be a doctor. I was even premed in college."

Erin says, "That's because Nina came to the US as a kid. Her parents are Taiwanese immigrants. Mine are Chinese Filipinos from Daly City. I think they gave up on the Asian American dream for me when I got my first tattoo at fifteen."

Laughter ripples through the audience, and someone calls out, "What do they think of *Yellow Empress*?"

Erin smiles. "You know, I think they're very proud. They probably thought I'd end up working at my uncle's restaurant, so I've actually become an overachiever." She spreads her hands out as if to say *who, me?* "And look at me now—here I am at MIT. Someone take a picture so I can show my parents!"

"Can I borrow ten bucks to get the collectors' edition?" Jess asks her brother.

"Don't you already have it?" he says.

"No, I got them from the library. Plus this has character concept sketches, and I want it signed. I'll pay you back."

He hands over a twenty. "Bring me the change."

"Thank you!"

Jess and Angie head over to the sales and signing line, which snakes around the edge of the auditorium. As they approach the front, though, Jess starts to hang back, checking the time on her phone.

"I don't know if there's enough time," Jess says. "We have to catch the train back."

"We are not going until you get that signed," Angie says. "We're almost there, anyway."

"If we miss the train—"

"We're not going to miss it." Angie puts her arm around Jess's shoulders, steering her forward. "You're not getting out of this."

Chen Ning is first at the signing table. She smiles at Jess and Angie as they approach, and Jess hands over the comic book with a yellow Post-it on which she wrote her name.

"Jess?" Nina asks.

Jess nods mutely. Nina signs across the cover with a flourish, then passes the book over to Erin, who clicks her Sharpie open and adds her signature in metallic silver ink.

"Jess is an artist too," Angie says.

"That's great," Erin says. The edge of a tattoo peeks out from the collar of Erin's shirt. She asks Jess, "What do you draw?"

"Um . . ." Jess flushes self-consciously.

"She draws comics," Angie says. "She's super talented. Did your parents really think you'd end up working at your uncle's restaurant?"

Erin grins. "Yeah, they really did."

"Did you ever take any art classes or did you teach yourself?" Angie asks.

Jess tries to edge away from the table, but Angie shoots her hand out and grabs Jess, not letting her go. Erin's eyes flicker to their hands, then to Jess's pink face.

"I did take some art classes," Erin says. "I took a few years off after high school and then went back to art school. What are you thinking about doing?"

"Um, I don't know," Jess mumbles. "I haven't thought about it."

"Don't worry, you'll figure it out," Erin says. "Everyone does. You have plenty of time."

Nina leans toward them and adds, "I'll give you my advice, okay? Don't be premed if you don't want to be a doctor."

Erin laughs. "Wise words."

ANGIE AND JESS BOLT OUT OF THE T STATION, TAKING THE stairs two at a time. "You said we weren't going to miss the train!" Jess says.

"We're not going to miss it," Angie insists.

She grabs Jess's hand as they run toward the station across the slippery street. Snow whips into Jess's eyes and stings her face. A car honks at them long and loud as they dodge traffic. They skid into the train station a minute before the scheduled departure time, but as they round the corner to the vaulted waiting room, they're confronted by a throng of people clustered beneath the giant departure board overhead. Jess looks up at the board, and all of the scheduled trains now have the same word listed in the status column: CANCELED. A voice repeats over the PA system: "Due to weather-related incidents and the oncoming winter storm, all remaining trains for the evening are canceled. The MBTA regrets the inconvenience. Due to weather-related incidents . . ."

Breathless from their sprint, surrounded by other angry travelers, Angie and Jess gape at the board above.

"What are we going to do?" Angie asks.

Jess realizes that she and Angie are still holding hands.

Justin meets them at the Kendall T station, his hands in his pockets and his wool hat pulled low over his forehead. The snow falls in heavy, wet flakes that quickly pile up against the curb. "Thanks for letting us stay with you," Jess says.

"Well, one of you is going to have to sleep on the floor, so don't thank me yet," he answers.

It's a ten-minute walk to Justin's dorm through the snowstorm. Inside, they stamp their feet on the already damp entry mat, and Angie shakes crystals of snow out of her hair. Justin leads them up an echoing set of stairs to the third floor, then down the hall to his suite. He and his two roommates share a triple that includes a common area with a kitchenette and a bathroom. Justin's room is the smallest, but it's a single; his roommates share a bigger room on the other side of the common area. In Justin's room there's only enough space for one twin-size bed, a desk, and a dresser. The floor next to the bed is covered by an old rag rug he brought from home.

He takes a spare blanket from the closet and tosses it to Jess. "That's all I have but I'll see if Derek has clean sheets. I can give you a towel for a pillow."

"Really?" Jess says. "Jeez, thanks."

"I told you. Be grateful, because I have to sleep on the couch." Justin gestures to the lumpy gray-and-tan plaid sofa in the common room, which looks like it was dragged up from the street.

A tall, skinny Asian guy pokes his head out from the other bedroom. "Justin, what's up?"

"This is my little sister Jess," Justin says. "And her friend Angie. They're staying overnight because the trains were canceled. Jess, Angie, this is Derek."

"Hi," Jess and Angie say in unison.

"Hey," Derek says.

"Derek, you have extra sheets?" Justin asks.

"Maybe," Derek says.

Justin goes into Derek's room while Angie glances around the tiny space. "Why did I think MIT would have fancier dorms?" she asks.

"I think Justin got a bad lottery number," Jess says. Her phone vibrates. It's her parents. "Hi, Mom," she answers.

"Are you at Justin's?" her mother asks.

"Yes, I'm here."

"Let me talk to him."

Jess goes out into the common area. "Justin, Mom wants to talk to you!"

He emerges from Derek's room with some blankets and sheets, and trades the bedding for Jess's phone. "Hi, Mom," he says. "Yes, she's here. Yes, everything's fine. I'll take her to the train in the morning."

Back in Justin's room, Angie perches on the edge of the bed, scrolling through something on her phone. She glances up when Jess returns with the sheets and pockets her phone. "I'll sleep on the floor," Angie says. "I'm not supposed to be here, anyway."

"Don't be stupid. You're sleeping on the bed. I'll sleep on the floor." Jess pulls off Justin's quilt and peels off his sheets, dumping them in a pile in the corner. She grabs the clean bottom sheet and shakes it out over the mattress. The fabric flies up, hiding Angie for a moment, and when it floats down she's holding the other end of it and giving Jess an odd look, almost as if she were embarrassed. "What?" Jess asks.

Angie looks away and tucks in the sheet. "Nothing."

Jess lies on her stomach on Justin's floor, one blanket beneath her and one on top, reading the *Yellow Empress* comic. It's late, but she's wide-awake and supremely aware of Angie lying in the twin bed right next to her. She tries to focus on the comic instead of on Angie's breathing. The art is intricate and lush; Erin Mei Tan has drawn every embroidered detail of the empress's golden robes. It's the kind of comic that reveals more of itself every time you read it.

Angie rolls to the edge of the bed and hangs her head over the side. "How is it?"

Jess glances up at her. "It's good. I've read them before but it's cool to see it all collected together. It's . . . different."

"What do you mean?"

"It feels bigger than most comics. There's a big landscape. It's not just focused on one city, like Gotham, you know? It's set all over China."

Angie throws the quilt off and joins Jess on the floor, lying on her stomach on top of the blanket. Jess scoots over to make room, but there isn't much room to give, so Angie is touching her all along her right side. Angie's only wearing a white T-shirt borrowed from Justin over her underwear. It's blue, printed with white bowling pins.

"Go back to the beginning," Angie says. "I want to read it."

Jess flips back a few pages and lets Angie read in silence. Jess lies down on her side, pillowing her head on her bent arm. She is still wearing her long-sleeved tee, but she took off her jeans beneath the blanket. She tries not to look at the curve of Angie's ass, at the way the light turns her bare legs golden.

"Are you staring at my bowling pins?" Angie asks, her gaze still focused on the comic.

Jess flushes. "What? No."

"Let me under." Angie wriggles beneath the blanket. "I'm cold."

Jess doesn't say a word. She doesn't move, and she doesn't breathe as Angie flips through the pages of *Yellow Empress*. Angie's legs slide against hers. They're smooth and soft, and they raise tiny electric shocks all over Jess's skin.

Angie tucks her hair behind her ear. Her eyes flicker to Jess. "You're watching me read."

"No I'm not," Jess lies.

The desk lamp that Jess angled over the comic book now spotlights Angie, the red highlights in her brown hair, the shine of her lips as she licks them. Her leg moves again, her thigh skimming Jess's. Skin to skin, they hold still.

This isn't a mistake, an accidental brushing of hands. This isn't a tentative flirtation. This is on purpose. Jess feels the decisiveness of Angie's thigh with every shallow breath and each thudding heartbeat.

Angie leans toward her. At first Jess doesn't understand. She freezes when Angie's lips brush against hers. They're so soft, like nothing else Jess has ever felt. She has never kissed anyone before. She doesn't know how to do it, how to move her shoulder out of the way between them, how to kiss her back without banging their front teeth together. But Angie does. She presses against Jess, and they're already lying down so there's nowhere to go but closer. The floor is a hard plane beneath Jess's back. It's a shock to feel Angie's breasts against her arm, and then against her chest.

Angie doesn't stop. Her hair hangs down over the two of them in a cascade, blocking out the light and tickling Jess's cheek. Her mouth is warm and insistent. She tastes like the toothpaste she rubbed over her teeth before they went to bed. Jess hesitantly touches Angie's back, skimming her fingers across her shoulder blades. Angie trembles, and Jess feels it deep in her bones, an answering shiver as if they were connected by the breath they exchange.

Abruptly, Angie pulls back. The suddenness of it leaves Jess gasping. She blinks, dazed.

"I'm sorry," Angie mumbles.

"What—"

"I'm sorry." Angie scrambles away from Jess, the blanket falling off the two of them. She wipes a hand over her eyes, leaving a damp trail on her cheek.

Jess raises herself up on her elbow, her heart hammering. "What's wrong?"

"I'm sorry. I shouldn't have—I shouldn't. I'm so sorry." Angie gets to her feet and climbs back into the twin bed, lying down with her back to Jess.

Jess rises to her knees. The air is cold on her bare legs. "Angie, what's wrong?"

Angie's shoulders tremble, but she doesn't turn around.

"Did I do something? What's wrong?"

In a broken voice, Angie whispers, "Everything."

Jess lies awake in the dark, her body rigid. She listens to Angie's irregular breathing and knows that Angie's not asleep either.

Jess waits until there are no sounds from the common room, until she's certain that her brother is asleep. Then she quietly peels off the blanket and pulls on her jeans and socks, pocketing her phone. Angie doesn't say a word as Jess gets up and leaves.

She tiptoes past the couch where Justin is sleeping. She goes into the bathroom and shuts the door, locking it before she feels for the light switch. The fluorescents bathe the room in cold white light. In the mirror she is hollow eyed and startled looking, her mouth a plum-colored slash that doesn't look like it's ever kissed anyone.

She backs into the corner, where the door meets the wall. She slides down to the floor, wrapping her arms around her knees. She leans her head against the towel hanging from the towel bar above her. It's slightly damp. She turns her face into it, grimacing, her body shuddering silently as she cries.

Everything.

Later, she takes out her phone and sets the alarm for five in the morning, making sure it's set only to vibrate. She pulls the towel down and balls it into a makeshift pillow. She curls up on the cold tile floor and closes her eyes against the fluorescent lights. The bathroom smells faintly of Lysol and toothpaste.

40

AT FIVE IN THE MORNING JESS WAKES UP TO THE VIBRAtion of her phone in her pocket. She blinks in the harsh bathroom light, then gets to her feet. She avoids looking at herself in the mirror. She turns off the light and pads softly across the common room, past her still sleeping brother, and back into his bedroom.

Angie is breathing evenly now. Jess lies down on the floor and pulls the blanket over herself, fully dressed. She closes her eyes and waits until she hears her brother's alarm go off. Then she gets up, folds the blankets, and carries them out to the common room.

Justin is sitting up on the couch, looking sleepy. "Morning," he mumbles.

"Hey," Jess answers. She takes a seat on the other end of the couch, dropping the blankets between them. She checks the time on her phone. "We have to go soon, right?"

He blinks at Jess. "Yeah. Soon." He points to her phone and adds, "You need to fix your cracked screen. It's not going to last much longer."

"Are you going to pay for it?" Jess asks.

He rubs his eyes. "I'll see if I can find someone who'll do it for you."

When Angie emerges from his room, she doesn't look at Jess as she heads to the bathroom. Her hair is mashed down on one side, her face a little puffy. Jess doesn't know if Justin notices that she and Angie barely talk to each other that morning, but when he leaves them at North Station, he hugs only Jess. "Take care," he says.

Angie stands to one side awkwardly. "Thanks for letting us stay with you," she says.

Because of the overnight snow, some of the trains still aren't running, including the train to West Bedford. Instead, there's a bus. Jess and Angie climb on board and take two seats beside each other; Angie sits by the window and Jess takes the aisle. Jess puts in her earbuds, but discovers that her phone is dead. She leaves the earbuds in, and Angie says nothing until they're almost at West Bedford.

"I'll wait to get out last," she says.

"Why?"

"So your dad doesn't see me."

"Oh. Right."

When the bus stops outside the train station, Jess gets up, and Angie says, "I'm really sorry."

Passengers are already pushing their way down the aisle. Their row is up next. Jess sees her dad's car outside the window in the parking lot. There's no time for her to respond. She steps into the aisle.

SCHOOL IS CANCELED BECAUSE OF THE SNOW. AT HOME, Jess goes upstairs to her room and plugs in her phone, waiting for it to turn on.

The phone dings as a text comes in. Jess picks it up eagerly, but it's not from Angie. It's from Emily.

Somebody posted a video of you from the party. What's going on?

Jess texts back: *What video?*

A moment later Emily sends a link to a jerky phone video taken during Margot's party. Jess sits on the edge of her bed to watch it. It's startling to see the living room in Marblehead with its white sofa and giant TV. It looks so much more average than Jess remembers. A bunch of people cluster together on the sofa—almost everyone at the party. The sound is tinny, but the person who's shooting the video says clearly, "Move in closer, Noah." Margot, who is sitting on one end of the sofa, waves at someone off-screen. Angie walks in front of the camera and perches on the edge of the couch beside Margot. Her arm snakes around Angie's waist and tugs her closer, and then the phone bounces, and in the background Jess sees herself standing against the wall across the room, watching the people on the couch.

Someone has edited the video. It slows down to linger on Jess. She's holding a red plastic cup, and her face is flushed, her cheeks almost as red as the cup. She's scowling at the group on the sofa, eyebrows drawn together in one thick, unattractive line. She takes a slow-motion sip out of the cup, and a dribble of cranberry liquid leaks out over her chin. She doesn't seem to notice. She stands there like a slob.

And then the speed of the video increases again, and the camera cuts Jess out of the frame as it's propped up on a table. Ryan emerges from behind the camera. She approaches the group on the sofa, and because there isn't any room left, she lies down across everyone's laps, her silver dress bunching up on her thighs. Angie tries to scoot out of the way as Ryan's bare feet touch her knees. Everyone smiles, though Angie's smile looks a little forced. Then the video ends and loops back to the beginning.

Below the video, which was posted by someone called lexyling, is a string of comments from people Jess doesn't know. At least some of them seem to be Peebs.

sarahoy: *Azn chick at the back has a hate on for Ryan. You can tell by her eyes.*

Jaden34: *Who is she???*

Calliery: *West Bed student. Heard she comes to Brooke for arts exchange program*

Jaden34: *Why is she at M's party?*

Calliery: *She's friends with M's gf*

sarahoy: *Heard from Noah she threatened Ryan.*

Calliery: *Yep she waved a gun at her!!!*

Jaden34: *What r the cops doing they need to arrest her*
lexyling: *U guys don't know shit*
Jaden34: *@lexyling why do you know anything?*
lexyling: *I know Ryan's family*
sarahoy: *really???*
lexyling: *Asian girl totally flipped out at Ryan, threw bottles at her and everything. Ryan was so freaked out!!*
janeser: *ryan was a bitch*
sarahoy: *@janeser so disrespectful stfu*
Jaden34: *So why aren't the cops arresting her? WTF?*
lexyling: *They need EVIDENCE not just rumors but I heard they are getting some*

Jess's hand clenches around her phone. The crack lengthens another quarter inch. She keeps reading.

sarahoy: *Like what?*
lexyling: *I can't say*
Jaden34: *Bullshit. Tell us*
janeser: *ur a liar if u don't tell*
lexyling: *It's info that only Ryan's family knows, I can't tell, but there is some*
Calliery: *Who r u @lexyling? I know everyone who was at that party and nobody's talking. Who r u?*

There's no further response from lexyling. When Jess googles the username, she doesn't find anything except for the account used to make these comments. There's no photo attached; only a generic gray person icon. She watches the video again, even though it makes her nauseated to see how ugly she looks. She pauses on her face, examining the sneer on it, the droplets of cranberry juice on her chin like thinned-out blood.

She closes the video and drops her head into her hands, the phone pressed against her temple. She swallows. Her skin is hot, her heart racing.

She calls Emily.

"What's going on?" Jess demands when Emily answers. "Who are these people and where did they get this video?"

"Are you okay?" Emily asks.

"No! This is fucked up. Who posted the video? Who's lexyling?"

"I don't know, but probably Margot or one of her friends under a fake name. She's used sock puppets before."

"You think it's Margot?"

"Maybe." Emily sounds wary. "Why does it matter? I thought it was all just a bunch of BS."

"Of course it's a bunch of BS!" Jess is so agitated she jumps up, but the phone is still plugged in and the cord yanks her back down to the bed. "I just—she's saying shit about me."

Emily says tersely, "Welcome to my life. You just have to ride it out."

"Do you know who the other people are? Sarahoy or this Jaden person?"

"I don't know. I'm not like an internet detective."

"Can you find out? I have no idea who any of them are. Don't you know any of them?"

"I know who janeser is," Emily admits.

"Who?"

"Me. I'm janeser. I don't know who the other people are. Probably Brookies."

Jess's phone beeps in her ear and she pulls it away to see that Angie is calling. "I have to go," she says. "Please tell me if you figure out who they are, okay? Especially lexyling." Jess doesn't wait for her to answer before switching to Angie's call. "Angie?"

"What's going on?" Angie asks immediately. "Courtney texted me a link to some video—"

"Courtney? How did she get this?"

"I don't know, but I don't think that's the main problem here," Angie says. "I guess you've seen it too."

"Yeah, Emily told me."

"Well, maybe I should ask Margot—"

"No," Jess cuts her off. "Don't ask her anything."

"Why not? Maybe she knows these commenters and can get them to stop. I don't like what they're saying about you." Angie sounds indignant.

"You don't like it? How do you think I feel?" Jess snaps.

Angie exhales. "Jess. I'm sorry. Let me help."

Jess grits her teeth. "No. I've got it. I'll deal with it." She hangs up before Angie can respond.

LIEUTENANT GRIFFIN IS STANDING WITH KIM WATSON IN the hallway outside Studio B at Pearson Brooke. Jess sees him as she comes up the stairs with the other Arts Exchange students. As Kim waves them into the studio, she says, "Jess, hang back for a minute, please."

Jess shifts her backpack on her shoulder and eyes the detective. "What's going on?"

Griffin takes a couple of steps toward Jess and extends his hand. "Hello, Jess."

She looks at his hand for a second, and then reaches out with her own. "Hi," she says.

"Lieutenant Griffin would like to see some of your Kestrel comics," Kim explains. "I told him that I wouldn't show them to him without your permission. Would you be all right with that?" Kim's face is blandly neutral; she doesn't even smile encouragingly. "I'll be with you the whole time," Kim continues when Jess doesn't answer. "And if you're uncomfortable with anything, you can let me know."

"I thought it would help me get to know you a little better," Griffin says. "Since you're a key witness."

Jess glances behind him down the hallway. "Where's your partner?" she asks.

"Detective Lieutenant Cardoni had something else to follow up on," Griffin says.

"I was thinking that we could take your portfolio into the lounge," Kim says, "so we don't disturb the other students. It shouldn't take long—just a few minutes."

"I guess," Jess says grudgingly.

"Great," Griffin says. "I really appreciate it."

They walk through Studio B and past the other students to the storage room, where Jess takes her portfolio off the shelf and carries it into the lounge. The most recent exhibit has been removed, and the room is now a long blank wall facing the floor-to-ceiling windows. One folding table stands at the far end, and Jess sets her comics down on the beige plastic surface. When she opens the portfolio, the color printouts seem to leap out in screaming contrast.

"Wow, this is cool," Griffin says, sounding overly enthusiastic.

"I'll wait over there," Kim says, pointing to a bench in front of the windows. "Let me know if you need anything."

"Thank you," Griffin says.

He and Kim trade quick glances, and Kim nods her head slightly. Jess's hand freezes on the edge of the first panel, one of the three printouts she showed her dad.

"Kim told me your comic is set in a fantasy boarding school?" Griffin says. "Is it like Pearson Brooke?"

Jess watches Kim take her seat, just far enough away to give them a false sense of privacy. "Not unless you think Pearson Brooke is magical."

Griffin laughs, and it almost sounds real. "Some people would. But I know the magic here is made of money."

Jess's fingertips are warping the edge of the printout. She drops it to avoid ruining the paper, and immediately Griffin moves it aside to reveal the next page, which shows Kestrel's arrival.

"Is this the main character?" he asks. "Kestrel, right?"

"Yeah." Jess takes off her backpack and sets it on the floor. "Kim told you about her?"

"A little. But I want to hear your perspective. What's her story?"

Haltingly, Jess explains the background of the Blackwood Hall School and the Kestrel story line. Griffin nudges her along, dropping in compliments as they flip through the black-and-white panels. The panels she drew over Christmas break aren't in the portfolio yet, although she brought them with her today. She makes no move to take them out of her backpack. The comics in the portfolio end with a scene in the woods where Kestrel and Laney are doing a spell to open a Doorway to Faerie.

"I really like the background here," he says, studying the last panel. "Did you base it on something from real life or do you make it all up?"

"The story's all made up. I mean, it's about magic."

He turns to face her, leaning against the table and slouching a bit, all casual. "I'm just asking because the woods you're drawing—they're so realistic. They look a lot like Ellicott Park, you know?"

"Well, I live right across the street from the park," she says, not hiding her sarcasm.

He smiles a little, acknowledging her tone. "Obviously. And what about the characters? Where do you get your inspiration for them?"

"I don't know," she says dismissively.

He studies her for a second, as if he were trying to find a crack in her wall. Jess looks right back at him, not giving an inch. His expression grows more somber, and he says, "I think we may have gotten off on the wrong foot. I'm not trying to trick you into anything. But you should know that there have been some developments in the investigation, and they concern you."

"You don't really want to see my comics," Jess says flatly.

"No, I do." There's a brief flash of embarrassment in his eyes. "But primarily so that I could talk to you in a less—less formal setting."

Jess glances at Kim Watson, but she's engrossed in reading her phone—or at least pretending to be engrossed in it. "What do you want?" Jess asks the detective.

He settles himself against the table, acting relaxed again. "We've talked to a number of your friends who were at the party that night. They're—"

"They're not my friends."

He grimaces slightly. "Okay. Sorry. We've talked to several of the other people who were at the party. The funny thing about parties is that everybody's sort of having their own private party, if you know what I mean. I remember going to parties that I thought sucked, but other people who were there had an awesome time. Maybe they drank a little more than me, or vice versa." He smiles at her, but when she doesn't respond, his smile dies. "The point is, everybody we talked to gave sort of different stories about what happened, but everyone circles back to one event. That's you and Ryan arguing in the kitchen. Some of them disagree on who said what exactly, but they all saw you or heard about it right after. And several of them saw you pick up the gun."

"So what? I already told you about that."

Griffin gives Jess a concerned look. "We believe that the gun you handled the night of the party was the gun that was used in Ryan's death."

Jess begins to put her comics back into the black cardboard portfolio. It's a loan from the Brooke art department, and the bottom edge is worn soft from sliding on and off the shelf.

"Jess," Griffin says, "do you know what happened to the gun that night?"

"No."

"Do you have any idea who might know?"

She can't seem to fit her papers back into the portfolio. She has to remove them and restack the sheets. "Why would I know that?"

"I get the sense that you see more than you let on."

Startled, she looks at him. "What do you mean?"

He nods at the comics. "You're pretty observant. You have to be to do what you do."

She doesn't respond and goes back to closing up the portfolio.

"I saw the video online," he says. "The one from the party, with you in the background."

"I don't know who put that online," she says quickly.

"We're going to find that out," Griffin says.

"You are?"

"Absolutely. Whoever put that online is trying to draw attention to you, which makes me wonder why. It also makes me wonder if you know something."

She gives up trying to close the portfolio's clasps. "What could I know? They're not my friends. None of them even talked to me the whole night—except for Ryan, and she was a bitch to me." Jess looks directly at the detective. "I don't care if she's dead."

Griffin acts sympathetic.

"That doesn't mean I would do anything to her," Jess adds.

"Of course not. You told us that you left the party with Angie around midnight, right?"

"Yeah. We had to get back by one a.m."

"When you got back to West Bedford, did you go home immediately?"

"Yes. I already told you all this."

"Did Angie drive you back to your house directly?"

"No, she went back to her house. I walked home from her house."

"This was around one in the morning?"

"Yes. Like I said."

"What route did you take when you walked home?"

Jess's forehead furrows. "What do you mean? Like what streets?"

"Yes."

"The regular ones. Hawthorne to Birch Street to Ellicott."

"Your house is on Ellicott, right across from the park, right?"

"Yes. Why?"

"Did you see anything that night when you were walking home? The neighborhood must have been pretty quiet. You were probably one of the few people out at that time."

She shakes her head. "I don't know. I don't remember anything. It was late and I was—I was drunk. I wanted to get—get away."

He doesn't say anything. She picks up her backpack from the floor. "If there's nothing else you want to ask me, can I go?"

He straightens up. "Sure. Thanks for talking to me, Jess." He pulls a business card from his pocket and holds it out to her. "The reason I asked if you saw anything—anything at all, it might have seemed totally normal to you—is because we think that time of the night is a very important part of figuring out what happened to Ryan. If you remember something, will you call me? It would be really helpful to us."

She takes his card. "I don't remember anything."

"But if you do, please let me know. Anything at all."

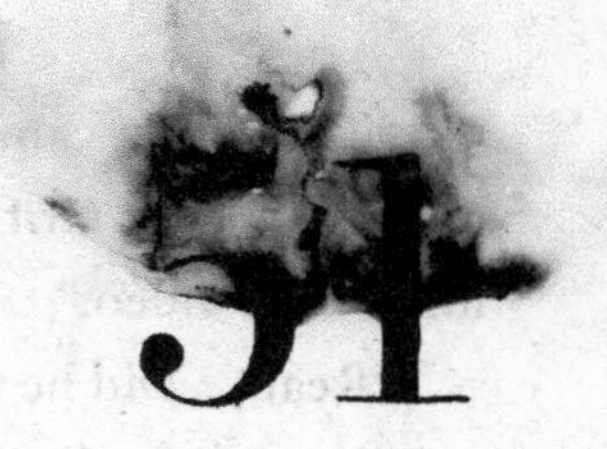

ANGIE IS IN THE PROPS CLOSET BACKSTAGE, STANDING ON tiptoe and reaching into a box on a high shelf. Her hoodie rides up as her arm stretches, revealing the skin of her lower back. Jess, standing outside the door, watches Angie pull a magic wand out of the box. It's made of a wooden dowel wrapped in purple and silver ribbons, with a tinfoil-covered star stuck to the end. Angie makes a note on a clipboard resting on a lower shelf and then turns to replace the wand. She starts when she sees Jess in the doorway.

"Jesus!" Angie says. "You scared me."

"Sorry," Jess says.

Angie puts the wand away. "What's up? You wanted to talk?"

There isn't much room in the props closet. All the walls are lined with shelves, and the shelves are jammed full of boxes and miscellaneous items—a fake skull in a Plexiglas box, a horn cup, a stack of witch hats. Jess edges into the closet, nudging a box of scripts out of the way. The crowded space smells like mothballs and makeup.

"The police came to Brooke earlier today," Jess says. "That guy, Lieutenant Griffin, said that he's trying to find out who uploaded the video."

"Really? Did he have any leads?"

"He didn't tell me if he did." Jess tucks her hands in her pockets. "Did you talk to Margot about the video?"

A flash of irritation crosses Angie's face. "No. You didn't want me to, so I didn't. Is that all you wanted to know?"

"No, I . . ." Jess takes another two steps into the props closet, and Angie takes one step back—the only step she can take. Her foot bumps into a garishly painted pirate chest on the floor behind her. "I don't want things to be weird between us," Jess says. "I mean, any weirder than they already are."

Angie tugs down the bottom of her hoodie. "It'll be okay," she finally says, but she doesn't sound convinced.

"Are *you* okay?" Jess asks.

Angie shakes her head briefly. "I'm fine. It'll be fine. How was Brooke today, other than the police thing?"

Jess blinks. "It was fine."

"See? We just have to let things get back to normal." Angie rubs at her eyes.

Jess stares at her. "Normal?"

"Yes. Normal," Angie says. Her voice is a little tight.

Jess takes one more step toward Angie, closing the space between them. She touches Angie's forearm, tugs one of her hands free. Angie lets Jess take her hand, their fingers interlacing.

"What are you doing?" Angie whispers.

"What are *you* doing?" Jess responds. "You've been my best friend since—"

"I'm still your best friend," Angie interrupts.

"Is that all?"

Angie meets her gaze. She looks tired and scared. "Jess . . ."

"Why did you kiss me?"

Angie looks down. Her hand is limp in Jess's grip. "We—I was—" She takes a deep, shaking breath. "I shouldn't have done that. I promised Margot that—I promised. I'm so sorry, Jess. You will always be my best friend. Always." She pulls her hand away, and Jess doesn't resist. "I wish things were different," Angie says, and then slips around her and out of the props closet.

THE LAMP CUTS A CIRCLE OF LIGHT OVER JESS'S DESK. Her eyes are gritty from lack of sleep, and the back of her neck aches from stooping over her sketchbook. Two pages are full of sketches of Raven's face, each one fine-tuning the angle of Raven's eyes and the lines of her mouth. Jess refers to the character sketches as she works on the two-page spread that will be the climactic scene in Kestrel's story.

It's set in Kestrel and Laney's dorm room, but the twin beds and dressers stand amid rocks and undergrowth. A tree grows in the lower-right corner of the room, pushing against the edge of Laney's desk. Leaves whip around the room on currents of wind represented by swooping gray lines, and gather in a pile against a boulder erupting from the floor near Laney's bed. On the right side of the spread, Kestrel faces Laney. Jess draws Kestrel with a slightly feral expression, lip curled hungrily as she reaches for Laney. The two girls are close, divided only by the gutter between the two pages. Jess draws Laney leaning toward Kestrel, her eyes closed. Above her—almost emerging from Laney's body—Jess adds a third, ghostly figure.

Her hand starts to cramp. She flexes her fingers a few times and continues. The specter soon takes Raven's form. Her long hair floats in a cloud around her face, and her lips are slightly parted as if she's speaking, but her eyes are hollow and unseeing. Jess draws a tiny circle in Raven's forehead and darkens it. She adds a trickle of blood running in a black line from the bullet hole down the ghostly girl's cheek.

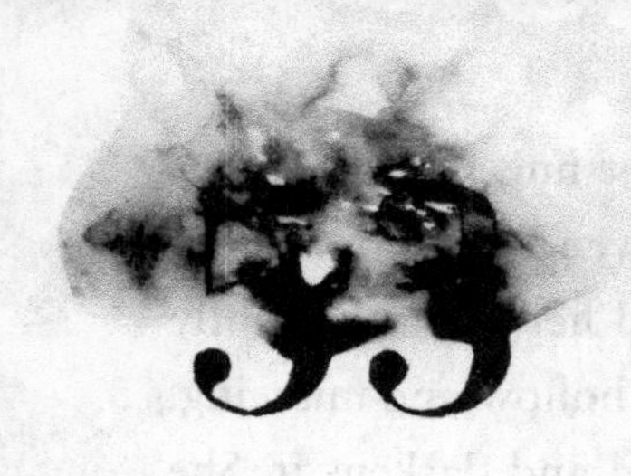

LIEUTENANT GRIFFIN'S CAR IS PARKED ACROSS FROM West Bedford High School. Jess crosses the icy street quickly, and by the time she reaches the passenger side he is already leaning across the front seat, opening the door. She slides her backpack off and climbs into the heated interior.

"I think we should drive somewhere," Jess says.

"Okay. Where?"

"Just away from here. Everyone's going to be leaving school in a second and I don't want anyone to see me." She wedges her backpack on the floor between her feet and reaches for the seat belt. "Thanks for coming," she adds.

"No problem." He pulls the car away from the curb and turns down the next street, heading in the direction of Ellicott Park. "What did you want to talk about?"

"I remembered something."

"That's great."

She side-eyes him, but he seems intent on driving. "I didn't think this was important earlier, but now . . . I think maybe it is.

The night that Ryan—that night after the party, after I got home, I got a bunch of texts from Ryan."

"You did?"

"Yeah. I was already at home by then. They woke me up. It was confusing at first because they didn't come from Ryan's phone. They came from Margot's phone."

He turns down the next street. "What do you mean?"

"I mean Ryan wasn't using her own phone to text me. I didn't understand at the time, but now I think it's probably because she didn't have my number. Margot did, though."

"Why?"

"Because she had to invite me to her party and Angie gave her my number. Anyway, the point is, I think Ryan was using Margot's phone to text me." Jess stops talking and glances at Griffin. When she doesn't continue, he catches her eye.

"What were the texts about?" he asks.

"They were about the letters in the park."

"What about them?" Griffin pulls the car to a stop on the side of the road and leaves the engine running.

"Well, earlier that night at the party she basically denied that they existed. But when she texted me, she accused me of taking them. So I was confused—I was half asleep anyway, but my phone kept buzzing and I didn't understand what was going on at first. I couldn't understand why Margot was texting me and saying that I took her letters. Then I realized it wasn't Margot, it was Ryan using Margot's phone. And Ryan said that she went to go get the letters, but they were gone. She accused me of taking them." Jess pauses, looking out the window. Griffin has driven them to the edge of Ellicott Park. The bare tree limbs are blanketed with snow.

"When we talked the first time," Griffin says, "the day you brought us to the park, you didn't mention any of this."

Jess turns to face him. "I sort of forgot."

He raises his eyebrows but doesn't say anything.

"I mean," she amends, "I forgot that she said the letters were gone. I remembered that she texted me but it didn't seem relevant. I just told her to fuck off and went back to sleep. To be honest, I didn't really remember what she texted until I took you to the park to show you the letters, and then they were there anyway. So I figured Ryan had been lying."

He doesn't take his eyes off her. "Do you have the text messages on your phone?"

"No. I deleted them. I didn't want to keep them around. They were kind of mean. But the stuff Ryan texted isn't the point. Don't you get it? Ryan was in the park that night. She was texting me from the park accusing me of taking her letters, and she was texting me from Margot's phone. So Margot had to be with her." Jess unbuckles her seat belt and moves her hand to the door latch. "And the letters were back—if they were ever gone in the first place—by the time I took you to get them. The only people who knew those letters existed were Ryan, that dude she was sleeping with, Margot, and me. I didn't take them, so that leaves the dude and Margot. If the dude took them, why would he put them back after Ryan died? It had to be Margot."

"Why would Margot have taken the letters?" Griffin asks.

"I don't know, because she's a bitch? Anyway, that's what I figured out. I thought you might want to know, since I read online that Ryan was shot in the chest so somebody had to be there to shoot her. And if Margot was there, it seems pretty obvious to me what happened." She opens the door to get out of the car.

"Jess," Griffin says.

"What?"

"We found out who posted that video from the party."

She turns back. "Who?"

"Margot."

The color drains from Jess's face.

"So I'm really glad that you told me about the texts—and your theory—but it's pretty obvious that you and Margot don't exactly get along. Why should I believe you?"

Jess gives him a withering look. "You don't have to believe me. It's the truth. Why don't you get Margot's phone records? Can't you check her location data or something and find out where she was? I didn't like Ryan, but I don't think she deserved to die." She slams the door behind her.

JESS IS ALMOST AT THE TRAILHEAD ACROSS FROM HER house when she spots the blue Mini parked on the side of the road. She pauses beside the car. The neighborhood is quiet, and nobody is on the sidewalk except for her. The brief ride she got from Griffin put her a couple of blocks ahead of the rest of the school traffic. The trail into Ellicott Park is still snowy, but it's been packed down a bit over the past few days. Jess steps off the sidewalk and into the park.

She has barely gone twenty feet down the trail when she sees a girl in a maroon parka in the distance, walking toward her. The girl sees Jess too.

"What are you doing out here?" Jess calls.

"Taking a walk. What are you doing here?"

"I live over there. I saw your car."

Margot glances behind Jess. The street is visible through the naked tree trunks. "I'm meeting Angie in a minute," she says.

"How are things with you two?"

Margot's eyes briefly widen. "Seriously?"

"Angie's my best friend. Of course I'm serious."

Margot smirks. "What do you really want to know? You want to know what she likes?"

Jess almost smiles back. "I know what she likes."

Margot's smirk disappears for a second, but then it returns. "She told me about MIT. Staying over in your brother's room. She told me it was a mistake, that she felt sorry for you. Did you know that?"

Jess's face burns.

Margot laughs. "You didn't know that."

"You better be treating her right," Jess says tightly.

"That's rich. What do you think I'm doing?"

"You don't get it. Angie's my best friend. We've known each other for way longer than you've known her. We have a history. That doesn't get erased just because she started seeing you a couple months ago."

Margot crosses her arms. She takes a step toward Jess, head cocked. "You really want to get into this?"

Jess doesn't flinch. "I'm already in it. You seem to forget that. Don't."

Margot looks disgusted. "What are you talking about? Angie's my girlfriend. You stay the fuck away from her." She gives Jess a once-over, lip curling. "Let me give you some advice. She's not into you. You need to move on."

Margot shoves past Jess, her boots crunching across the snow. Jess turns to watch her leave, to watch the plume of Margot's breath streaking behind her like a ghost.

TRANSCRIPT OF INTERVIEW OF MARGOT ADAMS

<u>Present:</u>

DC: Detective Lieutenant Donna Cardoni, Massachusetts State Police

KG: Lieutenant Kyle Griffin, Massachusetts State Police

MA: Margot Adams

Det. Lt. Donna Cardoni (DC): It is 10:23 a.m. on January 20, and we are at the East Bedford Police Department in East Bedford, Massachusetts. I'm Detective Lieutenant Donna Cardoni of the Massachusetts State Police. Also present—please state your name for the recording.

Lt. Kyle Griffin (KG): Lieutenant Kyle Griffin, Massachusetts State Police.

DC: We are joined by Margot Adams. Please state your name for the recording.

Margot Adams (MA): Margot Adams. Margot with a T.

DC: Margot is sixteen years old and is here voluntarily, on her own initiative. Margot, can you confirm this?

MA: Yes, I'm here voluntarily.

DC: And why did you choose to come to the station today?

MA: You left me a message saying you had some follow-up questions. I thought I'd come in and answer them.

DC: Since you're a minor, we'd prefer to wait for parental consent, but you've said your parents aren't available?

MA: My dad is in New York. My mom is—I don't know where she is. I tried calling her but she didn't answer. Do you want to talk to me or not? I didn't think it would be this big of a deal.

DC: We just want to make it clear that you're here voluntarily and you can leave at any time. Do you understand?

MA: Yeah, sure.

DC: Okay. Would you like some water or some coffee or anything?

MA: Some water, maybe.

KG: I'll get it.

DC: For the record, Lieutenant Griffin has left the room. Margot, we're very sorry to ask you to relive this difficult experience, but as you know, some additional information has come to light and we need to get your perspective on it. Since we first talked with you a couple of weeks ago, we've learned that your friend Ryan Dupree was involved in a relationship with Jonathan Krause, a teacher at Pearson Brooke. Why didn't you tell us about this earlier?

MA: I didn't think it had anything to do with—with anything.

DC: So are you saying you did know about Ryan's relationship with Mr. Krause?

MA: I—yeah, I knew about it.

DC: How did you find out about it?

MA: Ryan told me.

DC: When did she tell you?

MA: Last fall. Sometime in September, I think. She'd been seeing him for a few weeks by then. She was—she was really excited. In love.

DC: Let the record reflect that Lieutenant Griffin has returned.

MA: Thanks for the water.

KG: No problem.

DC: You said Ryan was in love with Mr. Krause. Did the fact that he was her teacher bother you?

MA: No. He's not that old.

DC: He's more than twice her age.

MA: Well, he didn't look that old. Not any older than you.

DC: For the record, Margot has just indicated Detective Griffin.

MA: How old are you?

KG: I'm 30.

MA: So Mr. Krause was like a couple years older. You look about the same.

DC: If their relationship didn't bother you, why didn't you tell us about it?

MA: I'm not stupid. I know that you—that adults—don't think it's okay. Ryan knew too. We both knew that if it got out that she was seeing Jon, people would freak out, and he might lose his job. She didn't want to do that to him, and Ryan was my friend, so I supported her. That's why I didn't tell you guys about him. It had nothing to do with Ryan's death—obviously, since he wasn't even in Massachusetts when she died. And now he has lost his job, just like we knew would happen.

KG: What did you think of Jonathan Krause?

MA: Like as a teacher?

KG: Sure. And as a—a human being.

MA: He was nice. I had one English class with him last year—Modern Poetry. He was a good teacher. He was funny in class.

KG: So you liked him?

MA: Yeah, I guess.

KG: Why "I guess"?

MA: I didn't really have an opinion on him. Ryan's the one who was in love with him, not me.

KG: How did you feel about Ryan continuing to date her boyfriend, Noah?

MA: That was her decision.

KG: You had no opinions?

MA: Sure I had opinions, but Ryan had the right to do whatever she wanted.

KG: Even if it meant lying to Noah?

MA: Look, Noah's a nice guy. I feel really bad for him, I do. But it's not like he's innocent. He was all into Ayesha. Didn't you hear that he and Ayesha hooked up the night of the party? That's why he never bothered to say good-bye to Ryan. He was occupied. So it's not like he would care that Ryan was with Jon. I don't necessarily think cheating is justified, but Ryan was in a tricky situation. She couldn't let anyone know about Jon, so having Noah around was a good cover.

DC: You said that Noah and Ayesha hooked up the night of the party. Do you think Ryan had any idea?

MA: I don't know.

DC: Did she notice that Noah wasn't paying attention to her?

MA: I don't know. Like I told you before, I spent most of the night with Angie.

DC: Noah told us that he was upset when Jess accused Ryan of cheating on him. Given what you've said about Noah and Ayesha, do you believe him?

MA: Sure. I bet that's why he hooked up with Ayesha later. I don't blame him. Finding out someone's cheating on you is rough.

KG: It sounds like you've been in that situation.

MA: No.

KG: Have—

MA: I told Ryan that she shouldn't cheat on Noah, though. I felt like it wasn't right.

DC: What did Ryan do when you told her this?

MA: She didn't like it. I think we argued.

DC: Did you disagree often?

MA: Not often. Sometimes. We were friends. Sometimes we didn't see eye to eye. No big deal.

DC: When was the last time you talked to Ryan about this?

MA: About Noah? Probably the night of the party. Yeah. After what Jess said, it came up.

DC: Can you tell us more about that conversation you had with Ryan?

MA: I don't remember much of it. It was late. Angie went home, I was tired, Ryan was drunk and really upset. I took her outside to cool off. I think she got into a fight with Noah. Yeah, I remember now. After Angie left, Noah asked Ryan about what Jess said, but then Ryan got really mad so I made her come for a walk with me.

DC: Where did you go?

MA: Outside. Just down to the beach, not far.

DC: What did you talk about?

MA: I told her she should break up with Noah so he didn't start asking questions. I didn't want her relationship with Jon to be exposed, because that would have totally messed everything up, you know? I didn't want to deal with her if that happened.

DC: What do you mean by "deal with her"?

MA: Just that Ryan gets really dramatic sometimes. I love her—I loved her—as a friend—but she could get upset, more upset than necessary.

DC: What did you do after you took the walk with Ryan?

MA: We—I already told you about this last time.

DC: I'd like to go over it again.

MA: Is that why you wanted to talk to me? I thought you had different questions. I don't really remember much about that night. It was a weird night.

DC: Well, try to think back. You're on the beach with Ryan having your heart-to-heart. In the freezing cold. You've told her that she should break up with Noah. What did she say?

MA: I don't remember. She was upset, that's all. I don't remember what she said.

KG: When we talked to you a couple of weeks ago, you said that you went to bed after Angie left.

MA: Yeah. That's right.

KG: Why didn't you mention going for the walk with Ryan?

MA: I don't know, I guess I forgot. It's not a lie. I talked to Ryan and then went to bed.

KG: Was that walk the last time you saw Ryan?

MA: I—I guess so.

KG: After the walk, what did you do?

MA: You know what I did. I went to bed.

KG: When did you wake up?

MA: In the morning.

KG: Are you sure?

MA: Yes. Why are you asking me this?

DC: We've learned that your car was at Pearson Brooke early in the morning of December 17. Your keycard was used to access the parking facility there at 1:43 in the morning. Did you drive Ryan back to school?

KG: We have people looking at security camera footage from the entrance to Pearson Brooke right now. It's in your best interest to tell us the truth. We all want to find out what happened to Ryan, and you can help us. We're not interested in punishing you for having an unsupervised party or for sneaking out after curfew or anything like that. We only want to find out what happened to Ryan.

MA: I—I need to use the bathroom. Can I go?

DC: Sure. Of course. It's down the hall on the right. This recording is being paused at 10:51 a.m.

[Break in proceedings]

DC: It is 10:59 a.m. and we are resuming recording of this interview with Margot Adams. Picking up from where we left off, we were discussing the use of your parking pass in the Pearson Brooke parking lot early on the morning of December 17. Why—

MA: I have to backtrack a little. I was trying to avoid getting involved in this, but it's true, I was there. I drove to Pearson Brooke. I got there at whatever time the parking lot says I did. One forty-something. I drove Ryan there because she wanted to go back to Brooke and she doesn't have a car, and she acted like she would steal somebody's keys and drive herself there if I didn't. She was really drunk. I didn't think she should drive.

DC: Why did Ryan want to go to Brooke?

MA: Because Jess said at the party that she had read Ryan's letters. The letters she wrote to Jon Krause. Ryan was really upset about that and she wanted to go get the letters to make sure they were still safe.

DC: Did Ryan have any reason to believe they were not safe?

MA: Ryan was really upset, okay? She just wanted the letters.

DC: Where were the letters?

MA: Ryan kept them in Ellicott Park. There was this tree where she and Jon would leave notes for each other. Ryan kept hers there so nobody at school would find them.

DC: How did you know about the letters?

MA: She showed them to me back when she first told me about Jon in the fall.

DC: Okay. So early in the morning of December 17, you drove Ryan back to Brooke so she could go and find her letters. What happened then?

MA: I went back to Marblehead.

DC: Are you sure about that?

KG: The parking lot also requires you to scan the card to exit. The records show that your car was parked there for a little over an hour.

DC: We also know that your phone was in the Pearson Brooke area for about two hours that morning. We just want to find out what happened to Ryan. We know you can help us, Margot. Maybe you saw something that you're afraid to share, but you don't have to be afraid. She was your best friend. She'd want you to help her.

MA: Best friend.

KG: Is something funny?

MA: Everything.

DC: Are you all right?

MA: Oh my God. You've got to be fucking kidding me.

KG: What?

MA: Not you. Oh my God. Okay.

DC: It would be a lot simpler if you would be honest with us. Help us find out what happened to your friend.

MA: I—She wanted to go get her letters. I told her it was a bad idea. It was too late, too dark, plus it had started snowing. But she insisted. She was really drunk, and she was really mad about what Jess said. So I agreed to drive her back to Brooke. We went into the park together. We—shit.

DC: Do you want some more water?

MA: No. When we got to the tree where she kept the letters, they were gone. The bag she put them in was there, but it was empty. She was really pissed off, and she thought Jess took them, so she wanted me to text Jess and get her to bring the letters back.

KG: Why did she want you to text her? Why not text Jess herself?

MA: She didn't know Jess's number. I—I had it. She used my phone and texted her.

KG: Did Jess respond?

MA: Yeah. She . . . she basically told Ryan to fuck off, which only made her even more mad. That's when [inaudible] That's when she took out the gun. My mom's gun. She must have taken it from the house. It was in her coat pocket. She said that she was going to go to Jess's house and make her give the letters back. I tried to convince her that was a bad idea. We got in an argument. She was—she was so pissed. She was pissed at everybody. She said I was a shitty friend. She said I didn't support her relationship with Jon, but that's not true. I totally supported her relationship with Jon. I kept her secret for her. Ryan could be really selfish. She said I should understand how hard it was to be with someone people disapproved of. She said I was changing, that I didn't get her the way I used to. She got really mad at Angie for some reason. She said Angie was changing me, but that's not true. Angie has nothing to do with this. Ryan was just jealous.

KG: You mean of you and Angie?

MA: Not like that. Not everything is about that. She was

jealous because we used to be best friends, and now there was someone else in the picture. But really she did it first. When Mr. Krause started writing her those love letters—oh my God, she wouldn't shut up about them. He was all she would talk about. Do you know how annoying it was to have to listen to her about it? Every day, all the time, Jon does this, Jon says that. Like I wanted to shoot myself—that's how annoying it was. Oh, I know, that sounds really bad, right? Shit. This isn't the way it was supposed to go.

DC: What happened?

MA: We got in a fight. Me and Ryan. We didn't used to fight that much. We used to be—it was different before. Before Mr. Krause. Before I came out. She was the first person I came out to. I don't know what happened. She's not my best friend anymore. She wasn't for a while. We said some really shitty things to each other that night. I think I—I was so mad. And she had my mom's gun. She was waving it around like it was—I took it away from her. I didn't think it was loaded or anything. My mom is a lot of things, but I didn't think she was actually stupid enough to leave a loaded gun lying around. I've gone shooting with her before. She thought the gun was a joke. She wanted a girly gun. She said it made her feel safe, but she left it in Marblehead in the closet. She never carried it with her.

DC: What happened when you took the gun away from Ryan?

MA: What happened? She grabbed my hair, like we were twelve or something. Oh my God. I couldn't believe her. She was—I shoved her. I didn't know the gun was loaded. I was trying to make her shut up.

KG: Are you saying that you pulled the trigger?

MA: I guess I did.

DC: Did you understand that Ryan had been shot?

MA: I—it's a little fuzzy. Maybe I was in shock? I didn't touch her. I just had to leave. I went back to Brooke. I went to my car. I still had the gun. I wrapped it in my coat and put it in my car. I think I sat there for a while. And then I decided to go to Angie's. I had to see her. I felt like if she forgave me for arguing with her, it would help or something. I know it sounds totally stupid now, but—you can ask Angie. I went to see her. It was around two in the morning. We—we made up.

DC: Did you tell Angie about what happened?

MA: No. Are you kidding? No. She didn't know.

DC: What happened after you left Angie's house?

MA: I drove back to Marblehead.

KG: What did you do with the gun?

MA: I hid it in the boathouse. Nobody goes out there in the winter. I cleaned it with bleach the next morning. I was going to put it back in the closet but I—I just didn't get around to it, and then you guys came to search the house, and it seemed—it's still in the boathouse.

KG: Okay. I have one more question, Margot. Did you take Ryan's letters?

MA: Her letters?

KG: Yes. You said they were missing that night, but we recovered them from the park. If they were taken, they were also replaced. There aren't very many people who could have done that. Did you take them?

MA: Yes. Sure, I took them. And I put them back after—after Ryan died. I—I thought maybe they would be found, and it would make people look into Mr. Krause.

DC: Margot, what you've just told us is very serious.

MA: I think I need a lawyer.

DC: Are you requesting legal representation?

MA: Yes.

DC: All right. Due to the request for legal representation, this interview is terminated at 11:31 a.m.

[End of recording]

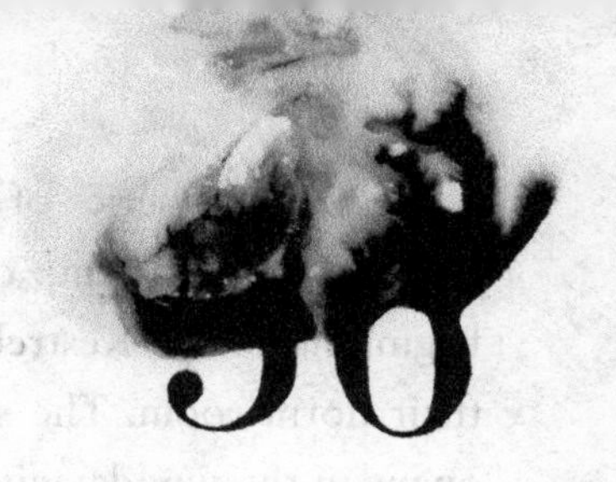

FOUR MONTHS LATER

KIM WATSON STEPS UP TO THE MICROPHONE SET UP AT one end of the Art Lounge. "Good afternoon, everyone. My name is Kim Watson, and I'm the director of the Pearson Brooke Arts Exchange Program. I'd like to welcome you to our end-of-year Pearson Brooke Arts Exchange show."

Jess applauds along with everyone else in the room, including her parents and Jamie, who is staring in fascination at a series of rainbow-colored papier-mâché elephants arranged in a ring.

"I'm so proud of all the work that these talented young artists have done this year," Kim says, beaming. "The arts exchange program has been a labor of love for me and West Bedford High's Gail Cooper-Lewis for the last few years, and we have been astounded by the work that's been produced. This year is another exceptional one, and I hope you'll enjoy viewing the wonderful art that's on display today."

Jess rocks back and forth on her feet while scanning the room. Beside her, Emily nudges her with her elbow. "Are you okay?" she whispers. "You're a little jittery."

"I'm fine," Jess responds, but she doesn't stop fidgeting.

Jess's art, a series of three color prints, has been mounted on foam board and hung on the wall nearby. The first is from the beginning of the Kestrel story, when Laney and Kestrel meet in their dorm room. The second shows the Doorway that Kestrel opens in the woods, with Kestrel outlined in gold light as magic ripples in waves from her hands. The third depicts Laney and Kestrel leaning into each other in their room, Raven's spirit superimposed over Laney.

". . . please enjoy yourselves, and be sure to help yourselves to iced tea and cupcakes outside," Kim concludes.

As the applause dies down, people begin to scatter through the Art Lounge. Jess says to Emily, "Wanna go get some cupcakes?"

"Aren't you supposed to stay and talk about your artwork?" Emily says.

Jess gives her a slightly panicked look.

"I mean, sure, let's get cupcakes," Emily says.

Plenty of people have the same idea, because there's already a crowd forming on the way to the refreshments. They get stuck in front of the circle of elephants, and Emily asks, "What is this about, anyway?"

"It's called *Circus*," Jess says. "I think it's kind of cool."

Emily gives the elephants a dubious look. "Yeah, okay. I like your comics better."

"Jess?"

She spins around to see Angie coming toward them. She's wearing a black lace baby-doll dress over black leggings and her purple Docs. She has straightened her hair and dyed it deep red, and now it cuts against her throat in a sharp bob. She smiles at Jess, but her smile falters when Jess doesn't return it.

"I'm sorry I'm late," Angie says.

"It's okay," Jess says. "You cut your hair."

Angie tucks it behind one ear a little self-consciously. "Yeah. Do you like it?"

"It's different," Jess says. "But yeah. It looks good."

Angie almost hides her disappointment by swiveling toward Emily. "You must be Emily. Hi."

"Yeah," Emily says. "You must be Angie." She and Angie look at each other for a moment as if they're sizing each other up, and then Emily says to Jess, "So I'm gonna go get those cupcakes. I'll see you?"

"Sure," Jess says. "I'll be here."

"It was nice to meet you," Angie calls after her.

Emily waves awkwardly as she leaves.

"Um, did I do something wrong?" Angie asks Jess. "I don't think she likes me."

"That's just Emily," Jess says. "So, do you want to see my comics?"

"Yes. Definitely. That's why I came."

Jess takes Angie over to the Kestrel prints. "I only mounted a few of them. Kim wanted me to show some of the black-and-white comics too, but I feel like they're not really finished."

Angie examines the three color prints with a serious expression. She points to the ghostly Raven. "What's going on here? You haven't shown me the comics in a while. I think I'm missing some of the story."

"It's kickback," Jess says.

"What do you mean?"

"It's a spoiler."

Angie gives Jess a slight smile. "Come on. Just tell me."

Jess relents. "Kestrel casts a spell to open a Doorway, but it all flies out of her control, and it ends up killing Raven. Laney's there at the same time, and because of the kickback from the spell, Raven's spirit merges with hers."

Angie looks puzzled. "So Laney and Raven are the same person now?"

"No, not really. I haven't figured it all out yet. The kickback is just way stronger than they thought it would be."

Angie steps closer to the print to get a better look. "Have you drawn all of it?"

"No. I've thumbnailed a lot of it, like I know what happens, but I only colored a few spreads. The rest is . . . it's a work in progress."

"Do you think you'll post them online as a webcomic? You wanted to do that before."

"I don't know yet. Now that I've started coloring the panels, I feel like I want to color them all. That's going to take a while."

"Well, let me know if you post them. I want to see them."

"If you really want to see them, you know you can just ask."

Angie avoids Jess's eyes. "Yeah, I . . . I know we haven't talked in a while. It's been—I've been busy."

"I heard Margot's out."

Angie crosses her arms, seeming to shrink into herself. "Yeah."

"Have you seen her?"

"Yeah. Yesterday. She's doing okay, but she has to wear an ankle bracelet. She has a good lawyer. They're probably going to suppress her confession."

Jess's eyes widen. "How?"

"She's a minor and the police didn't get her parents' permission to interview her, so her lawyer's going to argue she didn't know what she was doing when she confessed."

"Seriously, that's going to work?" Jess asks, incredulous.

"I don't know, but I hope so." Angie finally looks at Jess. Her face is drawn, and her makeup can't fully hide the bags beneath her eyes. "Don't you?"

Jess takes a breath. "I hope you're happy. That's what I hope."

"Margot makes me happy," Angie says flatly.

"I can tell," Jess says sarcastically.

Angie sighs. "I shouldn't have come."

"Then why did you?"

"Because I said I would! You're my best friend." Angie's forehead wrinkles in frustration. "Aren't you?"

Jess doesn't answer at first. "I don't know," she finally says in a low voice.

Angie blinks rapidly. She glances around the room. "How many times do I have to say this? I wish things were different. I really do. But they're not."

Jess stays quiet.

"I should go," Angie says, sounding disappointed. "I like the comics."

Jess watches her leave. She wants to run after Angie but she forces herself to stay, to smile blandly at the people who wander past her comics, to swallow the surge of anxiety that feels as if she were in a car with a driver who suddenly slammed on the brakes, and part of her is still moving forward even as the seat belt jerks her back. She shoves her hands in her pockets to hide the trembling.

She's still standing in front of her art when Emily returns with two cupcakes on two small paper plates. "Carrot or vanilla? I think the vanilla has strawberry cream filling."

Jess looks at the cupcakes. The frosting blurs in her gaze.

"Split them?" Emily suggests. "Cool, because I want both too. Hold this." She gives one of the plates to Jess, and then she pulls a plastic knife from her pocket. "Always come prepared," she quips. She slices the cupcakes in half and distributes them between both plates.

Jess stares down at her cupcake halves. The smell of buttercream almost turns her stomach.

"Here," Emily says, handing her a napkin. "I understand, the sight of them makes me want to cry too. They're absolutely delicious."

Jess takes a shallow breath. "You're not funny."

Emily makes a face as she gently touches Jess's back. "I'm so insulted."

Jess turns away from the room. She faces the panels of Kestrel and Laney's first meeting in their dorm room. The two girls smile at each other: Laney shy, Kestrel eager. They have no idea what's coming.

EPILOGUE

DECEMBER 17, 2:17 A.M.

THIS IS WHAT I REMEMBER: THE GUN GLINTING IN THE hushed, dark woods, reflecting my phone's cold light. It's a spark in Ryan's hand.

Beside me, Angie draws a sharp breath. I reach out and grab her arm, holding her back. I shouldn't have let her come with me. The snow is coming down hard, the flakes striking my face in tiny chips of ice.

Across the clearing, Margot takes a step closer to Ryan. She's holding a messenger bag with its flap open, upside down. "What the hell are you doing?" Margot demands.

"This isn't about you," Ryan says to Margot. "It's about her."

She points the gun at me. Every nerve in my body switches on. My skin feels electrified.

"Ryan, don't do that," Margot warns.

"Shut up," Ryan snaps. She takes an unsteady step toward me through the snow, the gun unwavering. "I want my letters back. Give them back, Jessica."

"Put that down," I say.

"Shut up. Give me the letters."

"What are you going to do, shoot me?" There's a roaring in my ears, and my voice sounds muffled and distant, as if someone else were speaking through me.

"You're the only one who would have taken them," Ryan says, her voice nearly a sob.

"Give me the gun," Margot says. "You can't do this."

"Shut the *fuck* up!" Ryan turns the gun on Margot, who trips in her haste to back away and lands flat on her ass in the snow. The messenger bag flies out of her hand.

"Ryan," Margot pleads. "This isn't you."

"Stop telling me who I am! You're so fucking judgmental."

"You are drunk," Margot retorts. She tries to get up, but when Ryan advances on her, she stays put. "You don't know what you're saying."

"I know exactly what I'm saying. I'm saying you're a fucking bitch and you're constantly judging me for—for everything! But you use me all the time, you know you do. You don't have the balls to do what you want. You have to make me do it for you. Are you going to make me fuck your girlfriend for you? Is that why you haven't fucked her yet?"

Angie jerks her arm out of my grasp. In three quick strides she reaches Ryan and wrenches the gun out of her hands.

"Shut up," Angie says curtly.

There's a moment of shocked silence, and then Ryan breaks into a high-pitched laugh. "Oh my God, who knew? I thought you were just a prissy little virgin."

Angie holds the gun in front of her with both hands, but I can't see it anymore; it's a void in the dark.

"Angie?" I say.

"Angie!" Margot finally scrambles to her feet.

"Angie," Ryan mocks, turning to face her. Ryan's coat falls

open; she's still wearing her silver dress. It glitters in the light of my phone as if she were covered in ice crystals. "Are you going to defend your girlfriend? Excuse me—your *girlfriends*. It's not Jess who's the idiot, it's you. You're such a selfish bitch. You think you can have Margot *and* your pathetic lackey drooling over you, as if you're—"

The gunshot cracks through the air. I flinch. The sharp smell of firecrackers stings my nostrils.

"Shit," Ryan says in surprise.

She falls to her knees. Her breathing sounds wet and wrong. She slowly slumps to the ground.

I blink against the snow. I taste the remnants of vodka in the back of my throat, a sour, bitter stain. Margot stumbles through the dark toward Ryan.

"Oh my God," Angie is saying. "Oh my God. Oh my God." She holds out the gun as if it were a dead animal.

The air between us is thick with flying snow. Moving through it feels like crawling through a doorway to another world.

I pull the gun away from her. The metal is warm.

I'm dizzy. I bend over, afraid I'm going to throw up. I carefully set the gun on the snowy ground.

"Oh my God," Angie repeats.

"It's okay," I say. "We're okay."

"What did I do?" Angie asks. "What did I do?"

I force myself to straighten up. I touch Angie's arm, but she's stiff and unyielding. "It'll be okay," I tell her.

"How is it okay?" Angie demands. She wraps her arms tight around herself.

Margot kneels down beside Ryan. I can't see what she's doing. I feel Angie shaking beneath my hand. All I want to do is make sure she's okay.

"You have to call nine-one-one," Angie says, her voice breaking. "You have to call." She suddenly grabs for my phone, and the light beam zigzags across the skeletal trees and the snowdrifts and Ryan's bare legs—she's wearing snow boots, but her legs are bent at an unnatural angle—and Angie freezes.

I take my phone back. I turn the beam down to the ground.

"You have to call," Angie says again in a small voice.

"No," Margot says. "It's too late."

"What do you mean?" I ask.

Margot stands up and comes back to us, her footsteps crunching over the snow. Her face is unreadable in the dark, but her back is straight. "Think about it."

Angie chokes back a sob.

"Where's the gun?" Margot asks.

I shine the light across the lumpy ground until I find it. It's lying a couple of feet away from the messenger bag. Margot stoops to pick up the gun and slips it into her coat pocket.

"It was an accident," Margot says. She looks at me and Angie. There is the faintest reflection of light in her eyes, a phantom glow. "It was an accident."

The weight of her words heavy as a vow.

I take a breath. The night air slides like an icicle down my throat. Angie steps into my arms and buries her head in the crook of my neck. Her entire body is quivering. The slickness of her tears is hot and cold on my skin all at once.

"I'll take Angie home," I say.

"Fine," Margot says. "I'll come to your house, Angie. Wait for me outside. I have to get my car."

"She needs to warm up and go to sleep," I object.

"She can't be alone," Margot says. "We can't leave her alone. Take her home, and I'll meet you there."

Angie trembles as I turn her away from Margot and Ryan. "Come on," I say. "Let's go home."

At the edge of the slope I pause. "Hang on." I backtrack, looking for the messenger bag. When I find it I unzip my coat and reach into the interior pocket, pulling out the stack of letters. I put them back into the bag. I shove the bag under the log.

Margot's watching me, but she says nothing.

I go back to Angie and help her down the side of the hollow. I hear her irregular sobs as we move, but eventually they stop, and she falls silent. When we reach the dark trail through the center of Ellicott Park, I reach for her hand. She's wearing gloves. I lace my fingers in hers and I don't let go.

ACKNOWLEDGMENTS

This book began on a phone call with Andrew Karre, and then it took me on a twisting journey that I truly did not expect. Thanks to Andrew for seeing it through with me. Thanks to everyone at Dutton and Penguin: Julie Strauss-Gabel, Melissa Faulner, Natalie Vielkind, Anna Booth, Rosanne Lauer, and Kristin Smith-Boyle; to copy editor Anne Heausler; and to Stina Persson for the evocative title type. Many thanks go to Jolene Altwies, Mary Carmack-Altwies, Dan Solomon, Maggie Green, Alyssa Torres, and Wendy Xu for sharing their expertise and experience in police work, law, and comics. All errors are mine! Thanks to Cindy Pon and Kate Elliott for their encouraging early reads. Thanks also to my agent, Laura Langlie. And thanks as always to Amy Lovell, who is with me every step of the way.